# THE REBOOT

## B. E. BAKER

*For my mother*
*You're as opposite Amanda's parents as they come.*
*Thanks for always doing things right.*

## DONNA

Back when I learned to drive, no one had GPS or phone apps, and even MapQuest was new and unproven. People found new places by using a big old map book, or by the simple expedient of following a long list of directions.

When someone needed you to go somewhere for them, the preparation would sound something like this:

"Make a left by that big oak tree in the center of town, then hang a right on the street named after baked goods. I think it's Pleasant Pie or something. Go past that long row of pine trees, and then turn on the road going north. You'll stay on that for a long time, like ten minutes, maybe, and then you'll see a big billboard with a baby on it. Make the next right. There's like, a bend in the road *right* before the turn off. I think the street is R street. It's a letter, anyway. Then you want the third or fourth house on the right, just after the stop sign that's hanging at a forty-five-degree angle. The house you want has a yellow door. You can't miss it."

Those were almost precisely the directions I got from my neighbor when I drove forty miles away to pick up a kitten Mom wanted for her barn, some seventeen years ago.

Is it any wonder it took me three hours and four stops at local places to place collect calls before I finally found that dumb cat? It wound up being a terrible mouser, too.

It feels like I grew up making life choices the old school way, but in the past year, I've discovered Google maps. Now, watching Abby Brooks—er, Archer—and listening to her advice? It's like I know what I need to do to find the kitten on the first try.

Or, like, instead of a kitten, true love and happiness.

A year ago, my life was a disaster.

I was lucky to have a job as a receptionist. I lived in constant fear that my son would be stolen from me by his grandparents. My husband was in jail and my worst nightmare was that he might be released. I was living with my abusive, dying father and being shouted at constantly.

Ironically, I met my Google map because I made a plan to completely shaft her. This poor woman had moved here with her kids because of a will and a bizarre twist of fate, and I wanted to make sure she got nothing because it was slightly better for me. Or, I thought it was. Turned out that wasn't even true.

Her guidance has changed everything for me.

Forever.

Now I have complete custody of my son. His father didn't go to prison like he should have (the world isn't *perfect*, even if Abby is), but I have a healthy relationship, and a job I really enjoy, and I'm living in a rental house that isn't quite perfect, but it's on its way.

Just like me.

Next up? A white picket fence, a golden lab, and riding off into the sunset.

Actually, my new place kind of already has a picket fence, and after years of being bitten, kicked, and bucked off, I'm not a huge fan of horses. But the general direction of my meandering is the same. I'm basically home free at this point, thanks to the advent of much better advice and life inspiration.

Which is why, when the expected knock on my front door comes an hour early, I don't panic. After all, my ex is notorious for being a pain in my rear end, and he's terrified of my boyfriend. I should have known he'd come early in the hopes of avoiding any run-ins with Will.

Charles is standing on my porch at seven oh three when I open the door, and he already looks antsy and annoyed.

"You're early," I say.

"You know what they say," he says. "Early to bed, early to rise, makes this man healthy, wealthy, and wise."

I arch one eyebrow and stare at his small-but-definitely-there stomach pudge. "You always sleep in, and it shows."

Charles rolls his eyes and pushes past me. It's like he's been taking lessons on how to be even ruder than he ever was before. "Aiden. Dad's here. Let's go."

"He's still asleep."

Charles' head pivots toward me slowly, his mouth dangling. "Asleep?"

"He takes ten minutes to get ready in the morning. Brush his teeth, pull on his clothes, and hand him a Pop Tart."

Charles slow claps. "Mother of the year, folks."

"You try to get him to eat something else," I say. "I'll clap for you when you succeed."

"It's all about having a firm hand," Charles says. "I'm sure it's hard as a single, working mother, but I won't have any trouble."

I grit my teeth and point at the sofa. "Sit. I'll go wake him up."

The argument he wants to start is right there, on the tip

of his tongue, but for once he doesn't start it. Miracles do happen.

A few moments later, Aiden's marching from the bathroom into the kitchen, and I'm shocked to see Charlie frying one of *my* eggs on *my* stove.

"Help yourself," I say. "What's mine is yours, clearly."

"I'm doing it for Aiden," he says. "Geez. You're so kind. Where *did* our marriage go wrong?"

"He won't eat that." I can't help one hand from popping up on my hip.

"Saying he won't do it in front of him isn't helping me," Charles hisses. "Way to cheat."

I sigh heavily and sit down. "Here, Aiden. Look. Daddy made you a delicious and nutritious breakfast." Part of me knows he's right, but what kind of person shows up early, makes themselves at home in my kitchen, and then proceeds to assume that after minimal contact with a kid, they'll know just how to make him eat something he detests?

My ex. That's who.

"Hi Dad," Aiden says. "I hate eggs."

"But this is my special *fried* egg," Charles says. "Been a favorite of the Windsor men for generations."

Aiden frowns. "I'm an Ellingson."

Charles drops his spoon. "You're also a Windsor."

"The judge did change his last name to Ellingson," I say.

"And now I can be at the beginning of the line in school." Aiden leans on the table with one elbow, his face squishing up against his hand. "Earl also starts with an E. Even if my name is Earl, I still won't be stuck at the end. Plus, the Earl men are really cool, too. For ginrations." Aiden frowns. "Does that mean a really long time?"

Charles' face flushes bright red. He bends over slowly and picks up the spatula. Then he scoops up the egg with

4

it, slides it on a plate, and shoves it in front of Aiden. "You will eat this, and you will like it."

Oh, dear. We're getting off on a very bad foot.

"I won't." Aiden presses his lips together so tightly that the entire bottom of his face goes white.

"Look, Charles, it's not like disliking fried eggs is going to make him—"

My ex throws his hands up in the air, flinging egg bits and oil from the pan across my kitchen. "The reason he doesn't like it is that he's never *exposed* to it. He's here with you all the time, indoctrinating him to—"

"Eggs are slimy," Aiden says. "And they taste like rubber." He huffs. "The only rubber I like is on tires. Mister Will let me help him change a tire last week, and I was really good at it."

Charles looks practically apoplectic.

I crouch down near Aiden and drop my voice to a whisper. "Remember how excited you are to go spend some time with Daddy this summer? You know what will make him happy? If you never, ever talk about Mister Will. Alright?"

A tap from the front door has us all looking that direction, as the man himself steps through the door.

Broad shoulders. Light grey eyes. Handsome, rugged features. An echo of his bad-boy past in the crooked spot on the bridge of his nose. He's a slender guy for this area, but he's got twenty or thirty pounds of muscle on Charles.

And no middle-squidge at all.

In fact, his trim, ripped waistline may be the very best physical feature on Will Earl.

"Mornin'," he says.

Charles frowns. "It's not a very good morning so far, actually."

Will shrugs, a half-smile tugging the corners of his mouth upward. "We farm-folk out here in the backwoods know that you reap what you sow." Will affects a pretty pronounced country accent whenever Charlie's around. I can't decide whether it's on purpose, or whether it's unconscious.

"Well, if the farm hand would kindly wait outside until we city-folk who neither reap nor sow are done, that would be great," Charles says.

"I do help out a lot around here," Will says. "But it's a pleasure to do things for your *ex*-wife and for your son."

In all the time I've known him, I can count on one hand the number of times I've seen muscles work in Charles' jaw. Generally speaking, that kind of thing looks pretty masculine. But nothing really looks hot on the devil himself. And right now, I'm worried his rage is going to short-circuit his brain and he's going to try to take a swing at Will because his masculinity has been threatened. It won't go well for him if he tries, and that will just make him nastier.

"No one needs to go outside." I hop up and grab a Pop Tart in a Ziploc bag from the windowsill. "I already have Aiden's non-manly breakfast right here."

Aiden frowns and for a split second, he looks just like his father.

It's unnerving.

"Pop Tarts are manly. I don't even need mine toasted, and I could eat it while I was doing anything." He snatches it from my hand and walks toward the door. "And they don't taste like rubber." His lip curls, and he's back to looking like my snarky little boy again.

"I'll be out to pick him up in just over a month, like we agreed," I say.

Will picks up Aiden's suitcase and gestures toward the door. "Don't let it hitcha." He must be speaking that way on purpose to bait Charles, but I doubt my ex has any idea it's not how he always talks.

It makes me smile.

6

# 2

## AMANDA

I had to wake up at three in the morning just to drive Mandy here, and now my butt has permanently molded to the crappy vinyl seat in the waiting room.

"I think my elbow may never recover," Abby says.

"Your elbow?" I turn to see what she means.

My newlywed sister-in-law has a huge red mark on her elbow from the wooden armrest.

"You'd think a *hospital* would shell out a little more money on seating for people who are worried their loved ones might *die*."

"Mandy's going to be fine. I'm more worried about you," Abby says.

"Me?" I frown and tilt my head. "Why?"

"Your super hot, and now super famous, rockstar boyfriend is back, apologetic and begging, and you shut him down."

I roll my eyes.

"He could have immediately signed another contract," Abby continues, dogged as ever. "Steve told me he turned it down because leaving you was a mistake he couldn't ever erase." She pauses, for emphasis, apparently, because she's still leaning toward me with those crazy intense eyes of hers. "He missed you, Amanda."

"Yeah, he missed me so much that he didn't tell me how he felt until his tour was over and he was back home, still single."

"Do you really think he was out there on tour, flirting and carousing?"

"Carousing? What does that even mean?"

Abby blushes, so it must be womanizing or something.

"Look, I don't know what he was doing on tour, because we *broke up*, and he didn't even try to stop it."

Abby shakes her head, but she's grinning. "I'm going to do something right now that I have never done in my entire life." Her grin disappears, and she leans closer to my ear. Her voice drops to a whisper. "I'm about to violate attorney-client privilege. I'm only doing it to help my client, but you should know that Eddy sent me his contract right after you dumped him. He said he wanted to leave the tour and follow you home. I read it and told him that he had to finish it, or he'd be subject to a draconian cancellation fee."

"I'm no lawyer, but I didn't realize he'd be subject to a fee for calling or visiting."

"He didn't call? Really?"

"He never visited."

She sighs. "It's human nature to be scared, you know."

"He's very human, then," I say. "Or he wasn't really very scared."

Her voice is soft when she says, "I meant you."

"Me?" It hits me then, what she's saying. "You think I'm not back together with him because I'm *scared*?"

"He told Steve that he proposed."

I snort. "He did. As if that makes any sense. He had some insane explanation that he only had trouble with girls hitting on him while he was on tour because we weren't

12

committed enough." My hands grip the edges of the horrible wooden armrests. "If I learned anything while being married, it's that doubling down on mistakes does not improve the situation. Ever."

"I made a mistake and wound up pregnant with Ethan," Abby says.

She's such a know-it-all.

"And marrying his father—"

"Yeah, yeah, we all know your marriage was perfect and everything was fabulous."

"It certainly wasn't perfect, but it was one of the better decisions I've ever made. All I'm saying is that sometimes people make mistakes, and sometimes they're genuinely sorry about them. The adult thing to do is to listen to their apology and give them another chance."

My saintly sister-in-law doesn't mention that I've made my share of mistakes. Bless her for that. But even her sage insight doesn't change my feelings. "I don't think I can trust him anymore."

"That's fair," Abby says. "Just make sure you're not using that as an excuse to run away. You deserve to be happy, Amanda, even if you don't think you do."

I hate this about myself, but the fact that both Mandy and Abigail are telling me to date Eddy makes me more determined to refuse him. It's stupid, but it's who I am. If they knew me a little better, they'd know that if they really were Team Eddy, they should keep their mouths shut.

"I knew that saying something would just make you dig in your heels," Abby says. "But I still thought I should do you the courtesy of telling you what I thought. It's what friends should do. And I trust you're adult enough to step away from your bad habits and make a smart decision that isn't a reaction to anyone else's words or encouragement."

Maybe she does know me—it makes me really hate

Abby sometimes. But I know she loves me, even if she's insufferable about it.

Plus, berating me totally distracted me from my angst about our wait. This procedure has taken way too long— much longer than the last time. I'm seriously starting to worry that something went wrong. I'm actively googling "how long for heart cath procedure" and scanning posts on my phone when someone calls my name.

My head snaps up, and my eyes connect with the intent face of a very beautiful man who I think must be in his mid-forties.

"Thank you so much for your patience." The doctor in the sky-blue scrubs, with the dark brown eyes that would melt butter, approaches.

I stand up, trying my best not to be distracted by the way his biceps bunch when he shifts the clipboard between his hands.

"The procedure went extremely well."

I can finally breathe. I'm not sure why I was so terrified, but I was.

"Thank goodness," Abby says. "I had the strangest sense of foreboding for some reason."

"You're kidding. You too?" I close my eyes, breathe in and out, and then force them open again. "But you're saying Amanda Saddler's fine, right? You don't have us mixed up with the wrong family?"

He frowns and looks down at the clipboard. "The chart says Amanda Saddler, and the white-haired woman who just woke up stared me right in the eye and asked, 'Am I ten years younger, now?'" The doctor can't quite help his smile. "Does that sound like the right person to you?"

For the first time in hours, my anxiety is gone. "Yes, that's definitely Mandy." She's awake and sassy as ever. "Thank goodness. When can we see her?"

"We try to monitor patients for at least a half hour

before we let visitors come back. I'll return to collect you in a bit."

"Alright."

"And hey, on a very unprofessional note, are you the lady who runs Champagne for Less?"

I blink. "Um. Yes, that's me."

"My sister's a huge fan. She's always sending me little life hacks from your reels and showing me things she bought on your recommendation. Any chance I could snap a photo for her?"

I think about my hair, pulled back into a messy bun, and my face, devoid of any makeup. "Actually—"

"Not to post anywhere. I'd be in it too, if that makes you feel any better."

Against my better judgment. . . "Oh, alright." I shuffle around until I'm standing next to him. "But don't post it."

He beams. "Thank you so much! She insisted I was lying." He swivels his phone around and lines up a selfie shot. "I won't even text her the photo. I'll just show it to her the next time I see her."

Once he's gone, Abby finally says what she's clearly been thinking since the photo. "You're less of a cynic than I expected."

Because I let him take it? "At the end of the day, a photo of me looking old and tired won't really get much attention, even if he is a big fat liar and he splashes it all over the internet."

"I guess."

"And thanks to Mandy, I don't care as much about my online persona. It's not my full-time job anymore."

I'm still thinking about that as I walk into the recovery suite to see her—specifically, how many things in my life are better because of her intervention. "Fine," I say.

"Fine?" Mandy coughs and struggles to sit up. "I don't

feel very fine, if that's what you're saying. And I'm sure I don't look very good either."

"We can call it Gold Strike," I say, "even though I think that's a terrible call. No one will remember some horse that won a race, and even if they do, they won't get the reason we named the resort that." I drop my voice. "But you've done everything for me. I owe you so much. If you want to name the resort Poo Pile, I'll do that, too."

She scrunches her nose. "I resent the fact that you're comparing my stellar name to Poo Pile."

I laugh. "So clearly the procedure went well."

Mandy blinks then, her eyes sliding sideways. "Am I hallucinating? I could swear Abby wasn't here when they took me back."

Abigail smiles. "I wasn't. I slept through my alarm and showed up late to surprise you. But I did hold Amanda's sweaty hand through the entire procedure, so you're welcome."

"My hands were not sweaty," I say.

"Wait, did she really hold your hand?" Mandy asks. "Because I would have liked to see that."

I roll my eyes. "We're both so relieved you're alright."

"Like I was going to die on some hospital table." She shakes her head. "My tomb will not read, *Died in the middle of a routine procedure.* No way."

"What will it say?" Abby asks. "I'd love to know."

"*Died saving a child from a raging fire.*" Mandy cackles. "Or maybe, *Stupidly tried to ride a horse. Again.*" She flops back to her pillow. "I have no idea what your husband sees in those creatures. I'm not even surprised that one of them wrecked your honeymoon."

"Some of the best things in my life happen when my plans are ruined," Abigail says. "Don't blame the horse for that. We love our new filly, Supernova."

"You're as ridiculous as ever," Mandy says. "Are you even human if you never complain?" She cackles again.

Her cackle might be the thing I would have missed the most if she died. I'm drowning in an ocean of gratitude, and I bend over double and hug her.

"Ouch, girl, that's my IV."

I snap back to upright, cringing a bit. "Sorry. I'm just so happy you're fine."

"Now that I am, can we focus on you?"

I grit my teeth and listen to her lecture me on letting Eddy take me on a date for the next ten minutes.

And again, when they release her, she starts in on the list of great things about Eddy. "Enough," I say. "He's not my boyfriend anymore—I don't have one."

"You don't?" A deep voice behind me has us all freezing.

I turn around slowly to see the big-bicep, dreamy brown-eyed doc jogging toward us. He's holding a manila envelope. He stops a foot away. "You forgot your discharge instructions."

"Do they usually have doctors act as gophers here?" Mandy arches one eyebrow. "Or did you do something to piss them off?"

He laughs, and it's a nice sound. Rich, full, strong. "They weren't happy when I put in my notice."

"You're quitting?" Mandy asks. "They let some idiot with one foot out the door help on my procedure?"

"I still did my strongest work," he says. "But my family up in Wyoming has been badgering me for years to move back, and I'm more afraid of my mother than I am of Dr. Hoover."

"If your mother's scarier than Doc Hoover, I never want to meet her," Mandy says. "But good luck to you."

"Where are you moving, exactly?" Abby asks. "My husband works in Wyoming."

The doc smirks. "It's not a very populous state, but I

doubt I'll run into him just because we're both living there."

"He's a doctor who works there," Abby clarifies. "I imagine the medical world is quite small."

"Oh," he says. "Of course. I'll be an internal medicine doctor at the Rock Springs Hospital."

"Still, maybe not small enough." Abby laughs. "My husband's an ER doctor in Green River."

"I had no idea you folks lived over that way."

"In Manila," I say. "So, not exactly the same."

"But dangerously close," the hot doc says. And now his eyes study me in a new way. "Close enough that we might be able to grab drinks."

"Oh," I say. "I mean, maybe." Why not?

"She has a boyfriend," Mandy says.

"Didn't she just say someone *wasn't* her boyfriend?" He tilts his head. "I'd say that means I'm cleared for take-off."

"You don't want to go out with a doctor who thinks he's a pilot," Mandy hisses. "Trust me on that."

And just for that, I give him my phone number.

Of course, while I'm doing it, I think about how Abby knew I always do whatever people tell me not to do. If I'd avoided that tendency this one time, I might not have been stuck dealing with a sulking Mandy the entire way back.

We're almost home when she says, "You're not really going to go out with that doctor, are you?"

"Why not?" I ask. "And before you say 'Eddy,' let me remind you that I'm a grown woman who can make her own decisions."

"I'm well aware, having seen you make some monumentally stupid ones lately," Mandy says. "In fact, I may petition a court to take your adult card away."

"Are you kidding me? I'm driving you home after spending all day helping you, right now. Is this really a good time to pick a fight?"

"I know a lawyer who would help me, I bet." She folds her arms and turns toward the window. "And I'm not picking a fight. You're being stupid, and I'm trying to stop you."

I actively ignore her the rest of the way home. And the second we reach the house and I get her situated in her room, I storm off to my room and slam the door.

It's not as satisfying as I thought it would be.

I'm now angry at the same person I was just over-whelmed with gratitude for. What's wrong with me? She's trying to help.

But she's also treating me like a little kid who can't make good decisions. I'm forty-three years old. I am not a kid. I may not make good decisions, but I get to keep right on making them because I am an adult.

That thought kind of takes the wind out of my sails.

She's not totally wrong. I haven't really made the best decisions on my own. I haven't had a decent relationship in years, other than Eddy, and that went down in flames. I'm still not totally sure it's not my fault.

Now that he's back, I don't know what to do.

Maybe I'm too tired to think straight. I only got four hours of sleep. I decide to take a nap in the hopes that it'll help my brain find its bliss and be calmer. I'm almost asleep when there's a knock at the front door that I can faintly hear. I wait for the girls to answer it. They're home from school. They may as well do something helpful.

"Mooom," Emery says.

Really? They can't even deal with a door-to-door sales-man? I need to have a chat with them. Because a sleep-interrupted Amanda isn't a pleasant one. I whip the door open. "Who is it, because I'm exhausted and if—" I freeze.

Eddy's standing in the doorway, a bouquet of flowers in hand. His mouth's dangling open. "Sorry. Is this a bad time?"

19

"Why are you here?" I ask.

"I've called, but you aren't answering, so I thought if I came by—"

"I was at the hospital all day with Mandy."

"Oh."

"Haven't turned my phone back on." I'd ask if everything was okay, but he's holding flowers, so he's not calling about an emergency.

He was calling to ask me out, apparently.

"Please at least let me take you to dinner." He looks so earnest, so hopeful, and so sincere that all the things Abby and Mandy said to annoy me melt away.

"Okay." I glance over at Mandy's door. "But tonight's bad. Mandy needs to be monitored. Plus, I think I have to apologize to her. I didn't get much sleep last night, worrying about today's procedure, and I've been a little crabby. Tomorrow?"

He nods readily. "Sure."

The second he leaves, my girls start whispering like preteens at a Taylor Swift concert.

"What are you two talking about?" I ask.

"Oh, just placing our bets," Maren says.

"On what?" I ask.

"How many dates it'll take for you two to get back together." Maren beams at me. "And I said one, so if you could do it tomorrow, that would be great."

# 3

# ABIGAIL

L ife's full of pivot points—places where our entire life changes direction. My decision to leave Stanford behind and go to the east coast. My breakup just before my acceptance to law school. My surprise pregnancy with Ethan. My whirlwind wedding to Nate. Izzy's birth right after we both graduated from law school. Our move to Houston. Nate's death.

That call from Mr. Swift, telling us we'd inherited a ranch.

Sometimes I wonder whether, if I knew what would happen in the end *beforehand*, I would've behaved differently in those moments that changed the course of my life. Could I have changed the outcome? Could I have saved Nate? But if that were possible, would I still have Ethan? Or would I have erased him, going back to 'fix' things?

There's no real way to know what might have happened if I'd known more in advance.

But as I've grown older, I've started to appreciate the quiet moments in my life. There are always happy times that pulse and flash in between the lows and the highs and the pivot points. They're easy to miss, easy to gloss over.

Everything's going right, so you focus on little goals or little irritations that don't matter. You don't value the fact that your husband is happy. Your kids are playful. Your garden is sprouting. The sun is shining. Your heart is at peace. You take those things for granted.

You have no idea what's lurking around that next pivot.

Probably something that will wreck you.

But without fail, once I recover from the reversal of expectations, once I round the bend, another brilliant vista appears. The pivots are painful when they happen, but without them, I'd never be here, enjoying the new views in my life.

"Can you hand me the poop scooper?" Steve asks. "I'm just going to clean up this stall now, while Farrah's out of it anyway."

Of course, not every single part of my new life is sparkly and bright. For instance, there's a *lot* more poop in my life than there was before. A lot more painfully early mornings. And our two-week honeymoon that was supposed to be full of rest and relaxation?

Yeah, it wasn't.

We didn't go anywhere at all, unless you count the day trip I made, alone, to Salt Lake City to sit with Amanda during Mandy's procedure.

"It's not like, when we drive over with that truck of your stuff, we'll never come back," I remind Steve. "You'll still be able to come over here every single day." We may have spent our honeymoon at his place, watching a horse, but we still had a lot of alone time. And now that it's ending, it feels. . .momentous.

He rolls his eyes. "Duh."

Or maybe just to me.

Steve goes right back to shoveling manure.

"Back away from the stall," I say. "And follow your *wife* to the car."

Steve's grinning from ear to ear when he turns around. "Say that again."

"Follow me to the car."

I didn't think it could, but his smile somehow widens and his eyes darken. "Not that part."

"Follow your wife," I say slowly, almost purring. Women my age should *not* purr, but it just keeps happening. Maybe it's because I have so little time left before I'm officially old —I hit the big 4-0 in another few weeks.

Steve moves faster than an old man should, scooping me up like I weigh nothing and walking toward the car. But before we hit the end of the barn, he veers to the right.

"Where are you going?" I ask, a little nervous, a little excited.

"Haven't you ever heard the phrase, 'a roll in the hay'?"

My breath catches.

"Ever wondered where it comes from?" The twinkle in his eye eliminates my nerves, and I'm laughing when he dumps me on a perfectly good pile of hay. It's pokier than I realized, but it smells nice, at least.

An hour later, when we finally reach our new home, the Birch Creek Ranch, Ethan arches one eyebrow. "Is Javier in Mexico visiting his family?"

Steve frowns. "No, he's here."

"Then why are you making Mom help with all your horse stuff?"

I blink.

"Your hair has a lot of hay in it," Ethan says. And then he pauses and pulls a face. "Please tell me that you were helping with the horses."

"I had to wrap Farrah's foot this morning," Steve says. "Abscess. Your mom was a champ and lent a hand."

"Thank gosh," Ethan says. "Because I really love you both, but. . ."

"Let's leave it at that." I comb my fingers through my hair, appalled at how much hay I managed to miss.

Steve can't seem to stop smiling, the idiot.

As soon as Ethan ducks out to check the calves, I hiss. "What about Javier? I can't believe I didn't even think about him."

"He was picking up the horse feed in Vernal—you didn't notice him returning with that huge truck as we left?"

I'm embarrassed to admit that I did *not* in fact notice that.

My last honeymoon was wrecked by morning sickness. This one was wrecked by a horse giving surprise birth and the care required for a premature newborn foal. At least we had time to get the little foal stabilized, and now we have a few days to recover before Steve has to be back at work.

When his phone rings, I don't worry about it. It's probably Javier with a question.

"What?" Steve's tone is sharp.

And now I'm worried.

"Are you sure?"

Steve's an ER doctor who trains horses. Both professions teach you never to stress. He's the calmest person I know, but with either of his jobs, I would be a basket case all the time.

The frown lines on his face worry me. "Yeah. I'll come in today, and tomorrow, too." He hangs up.

"Is everything alright?"

He sighs. "A co-worker—a friend—has Guillain-Barre Syndrome."

I have no idea what that is.

"It's really rare—where his immune system attacks his nerves. They caught it early, and hopefully he'll be fine. But Brian can't work his shifts, for sure."

"Oh."

"I'm sorry." He cringes a bit. "The good news is, extra

money." He points at my sofa. "You can buy some new furniture, or upgrade one of the rooms in the remodel you're planning at my place."

"Thank goodness. I was thinking that we needed more money." I roll my eyes up toward the ceiling, but then I force myself to be more supportive. "I'm sorry your friend is sick, and I know you have to go in. I suppose that's one of the downsides of being part of a smaller group."

Steve crosses the room and presses a kiss to my forehead. "I'll be back around midnight. I'm sorry."

"It's really fine. Not your fault at all. Just part of the job, and if anyone knows how that goes, it's me."

It gives me a chance, after the kids and I have dinner and get it cleaned up, to catch up on some of my work that's piled up during my vacation. After preparing a complaint and two motions, I'm ready to do something fun, so I pull out a book. I mean to stay up until he comes back —it seems like the right thing for a new wife to do—but I fall asleep. And the next morning, he's sleeping so peacefully that I slip out of bed so I won't wake him up. Six a.m. may be when the animals need us, but Javier's feeding Steve's, and my kids can handle ours. They told me last night to just sleep in.

Only, apparently Gabe didn't get the memo.

It sounds like he's trying to scare away a pack of wolves while working as a dishwasher.

"Gabe," I hiss. "Stop that."

He's banging on the pans so loudly that he doesn't hear me. Either that, or he's entered a new, defiant stage.

"Gabe," I shout.

He freezes. "Mom! You're awake?"

"I think everyone between here and the True Value is awake," I say. "What on earth are you doing?"

"I'm practicing," he says. "Miss Thompson says I have

25

to be loud enough to wake the dead, or they won't pick me for the parade."

"What parade?" I rub my eyes, trying to clear away the sleep so I can understand his latest nonsense.

"They need someone to play drums for the Fourth of July parade on the boats. Miss Thompson said if I'm loud enough, I can do it."

"These drums," Ethan says. "Are they made of cast iron?"

Gabe's forehead wrinkles. "What?"

"Why are you banging on an egg pan?" Ethan asks. "It's not a drum."

"I'm making my arms stronger," Gabe says. "I bang on everything I can, now. The audition's tomorrow."

"Why don't you go bang on the hay bales in the barn," Ethan says. "They'll make you way stronger, and you might live longer, too."

"Why would that make me live longer?" Gabe asks. "Is hitting hay super healthy? Like Maren's kakai berries?"

"It's acai," Ethan says. "And no. I just think that if you're out there, Mom might not kill you."

"Why would Mom kill me?" Gabe has almost no fear, ever. I think it's a youngest child thing.

"Steve's asleep," I explain. "He had to work until late, remember?"

Gabe's eyes widen into big round circles. "See ya." He ducks out the door.

But it's too late. Moments later, Steve stumbles his way through the door. "What can I do to help?" He doesn't wait for orders, in spite of his question, and starts clearing breakfast dishes from the table.

You'd think, with my kids being older, there wouldn't *be* any breakfast dishes to clear. "It's like they all suffer from the same delusion," I say.

"What are you talking about?" Ethan asks.

"It's like you think magical house fairies come and clean up all the things you leave lying around." I pick up Ethan's bowl. It's always obvious which is his. There's invariably a ring of milk on the table around the bottom of it, because he eats like some kind of water buffalo, milk sloshing everywhere as he shovels food into his mouth haphazardly.

"What was that noise?" Ethan says. "Oh!" He slaps his forehead. "I think Gabe needs me out in the barn." He ducks out even faster than his little brother did.

"Where are the girls?" Steve asks.

"Feeding the goats, chickens, and horses," I say.

"And that little heifer that was born late?"

He doesn't mention that her mother died. I already know which one he's talking about. "Ethan bottle fed her. The girls are calling her Lucy."

"Names for animals that are going to be—"

"I know," I say. "Believe me. But it's not like you can keep kids from getting attached. It's just what they do."

Steve sighs and drops onto a kitchen chair.

"Bad night last night?"

He rubs one hand across his face. "In general, if you have to cover for someone, it's going to be brutal."

"I'm sorry." I never really know what to say when he has a hard shift. It's not like my clients ever need poo dug out of their bum because of cancer treatments, or try to stab me when I won't give them pain meds. They certainly don't shove all sorts of things up their. . .nose. But the worst is when kids die. He's always a wreck after that. And it's looking like it was one of *those* kinds of nights.

"Patient came in with a persistent cough."

"Lung cancer," I say.

He nods.

I'm no medical savant, but it's always something like that, if I'm hearing about it.

"This was worse than the usual. I wasn't just telling someone they might die. She was four months pregnant."

I freeze, my hand halfway to the fridge door handle. "And?" I turn toward him slowly.

He shakes his head. "Her only chance is to terminate the pregnancy and get chemo."

"Is she going to do it?"

"I mean, she'd better. She and her husband were having it out in the exam room when a car wreck showed up. I had to run, but it didn't look good in there."

"How bad would it be if she waited?" I ask. "I mean, if she just made it to thirty-two weeks and delivered early, then she could get treatment *and* the baby could survive."

"Abby, babies take a toll on your body, and so does cancer. Believe me when I say, termination is her only smart play. I feel sorry for that husband, having to argue with his wife to try and save her life. It's his child, too."

"But if she's going to die anyway, at least she could leave him a baby to love."

Steve blinks. "It was probably stage two. She has a shot, anyway."

I shrug. "I'm just saying. It may not be as cut and dried as you're making it out to be."

He shrugs. "Maybe if I wasn't a doctor I might think that, but I am. And to me? It's very, very cut and dried. Save the person. Always nix the not-quite-a-person-yet to save the actual person."

"It must be nice to live in such a black and white place."

"I'm sorry." Steve stands up and looks around. "Did I miss the part where I started a big fight with you?" He steps toward me, one hand out tentatively. "I'd like to rewind and get a do-over."

I drop my hands on my hips. "And what would this do-over look like?"

"I'd say, 'Last night sucked.'"

"And then?"

"You'd say, 'I'm so sorry.'"

"Mhmm."

"And then I'd say, 'You're the best wife in the world.' And you'd hug me, and maybe kiss me, and no one would be mad at me, because you're always right."

"But what about the cancer mom?" I arch one eyebrow. "Would you let her try to keep her baby?"

Steve grits his teeth.

"It must be hard to be married to a lawyer."

He laughs. "Not at all. You fight all my battles for me. It's great."

"As long as you always roll over and let me have my way at home."

"A small price to pay."

"Sorry," I say.

"For?"

"For being hard to live with." I take his hand. "And for the long night and the early wake-up."

He pulls me toward him and his arms wrap around my waist. "Apology accepted."

"And I'm sorry that you have such a hard job. I didn't mean to make it worse."

He presses a kiss to my forehead. "You never make anything worse."

And after the kids are all gone, and Ethan's out distributing hay, he shows me that he means it.

No hay involved.

## ❧ 4 ❧

## DONNA

I was nine years old the first time my dear old dad hit me. He was careful with my mom. He never hit her in places that she couldn't cover up with clothes. And he only did it when she made him mad.

*She* made *him*.

It wasn't his fault.

Gaslighting at its finest.

My brother Patrick came by his anger issues honestly, and he never had anyone to show him a healthy way to act or react. As an adult, after he hit me, his wife left him.

I think that was his wake-up call.

He went to an anger management class—drove clear into Evanston to find a decent one. I went with him to two of his twenty sessions, and they really seemed to be doing a nice job. By the time he received his certificate, his wife Amelia and I both felt much better.

It's a good thing I have the information on that anger management class, because I might need it for myself.

How could my lousy brother manipulate me into giving him the ranch he had illegally mortgaged *and also* most of the life insurance proceeds that were left to me, just so he could sell up and move?

Unsurprisingly, he doesn't answer when I call.

No, the big shock is that he's waiting for me when I get home from work on Monday afternoon. Never in a million years did I expect him to actually talk to me voluntarily about it.

"I'm sorry," he says.

"Sorry?" I stalk toward him, not totally clear on exactly what I'm going to do when I reach him. "You're *selling* the family ranch? Now that I gave you the money to repay that mortgage, you're selling it?"

"Listen," he says. "Amelia's parents are upset. At me, at her, at the mess we've both made of our lives, and they want us to move back there."

"Back?" I practically choke. "You're from here. You've lived here your entire life."

"They want Amelia to move back. I'm not sure they care whether I go with her."

"To Seattle?"

He nods. "They're insisting on it, in fact."

"You're over forty. Tell them no."

"Amelia agrees with them," he says. "She never wanted to live in a small town anyway, and now she's insisting that if I don't move her back. . ."

She'll leave him again. I get it. It worked before. What dog doesn't use the same trick over and over, once it gets them that coveted piece of bacon? I know Amelia hasn't had the easiest life, but she's a bit of a female dog herself in a lot more ways than I realized. I can't help my sigh.

"I wasn't smart enough to make any stipulations on my assignment." It would have had a lot of tax implications if I had. "But I still can't believe you'd just up and leave, selling the ranch you only have because of me to a stranger. Wasn't it kind of implied that I did it because you're my brother?"

31

"I'll still be your brother when I'm living in Seattle."

"You know what I mean. I did it because I wanted my brother to be able to keep the family ranch. I wanted you to stay in the only home we've ever known."

"Technically I built the house we're in now. . ."

I'm going to strangle him with my bare hands. Would a jury convict me? I'm thinking not.

He sighs. "The thing is—"

I can't bear to hear whatever excuse he's going to make now. "Never mind." It's my own fault. I'm way too old to be thinking that he would ever change. Patrick is who Patrick is, and I'm the moron who pretended it wasn't true in a fit of optimistic sentimentality.

"None of this has been easy for me," Patrick says. "I know you're pissed, but—"

"I'm not mad," I say softly. "I'm disappointed, and I'm embarrassed at being disappointed."

"Your in-laws were bad, right?" Patrick does not know when to quit.

"They were," I say. "Yes."

"Then you should be able to relate. If I want to save my marriage, and I do, then I have to go live with mine. I'm a forty-two-year-old man, and I'll be living with my in-laws." He grimaces. "They'll spend the next few years telling me all the things I'm doing wrong, and how it's my fault that their daughter's unhappy."

"Just stay here and run the ranch instead," I say. "If Amelia wants you to deal with all that, she doesn't really love you."

His voice cracks when he says, "But I love her." I've never seen my brother so vulnerable. . .or so broken.

I had no idea he felt that deeply for his vapid wife. I'm almost impressed. "I hope it goes well for you," I say. Shockingly, in spite of my frustration with him, I actually mean it.

"I just wish she liked *me*, instead of wanting me to turn into her dad." He's looking at his shoes when he mumbles, "What if I'm no good at running an insurance company? What if I ruin this, too?"

It's hard—like, wrings-out-every-bit-of-energy-that-I-have, hard—but I put my hand on his shoulder, and I say, "You won't ruin this. You're smart, and hard-working, and most of all, you're willing. You'll make Amelia proud."

What I want to do is slap him for letting his wife push him around. For doubting himself so deeply. For selling the family farm in a terrible money grab and not even offering me back what I just gave him. The loving-sister part of me wants to tell him to put that money in a locker some place where Amelia can't spend it on shopping or pills. But that's not my job. He may be a lousy brother, but I'm not a lousy sister.

I'm just the idiot who inadvertently enabled this. How depressing.

When Will shows up half an hour after Patrick leaves, smiling broadly, I practically collapse into his arms.

He's half laughing when he asks, "Everything alright?"

I blow out the words, channeling my inner Eeyore. "Patrick came by."

Will wraps one arm around my shoulder. "My parents wanted me to ask you to dinner, but maybe we should just get takeout and veg in front of the TV."

His parents, unlike my ex-in-laws, and unlike Patrick's in-laws too, apparently, are wonderful. A home-cooked meal by two people who love us both? Yes, please.

"We should definitely go. Did your mom make rolls?"

"Does she ever *not* have fresh-baked bread?" Will's smile lifts my spirits. "I'd be at least five pounds lighter if she'd stop baking."

I jab his stomach, which is already plenty lean. "She

better keep on baking, then. I like you just the way you are."

He ducks down and brushes a kiss against my mouth. "Same."

I pull back, an inch or two from his face, and whisper, "She should stop if you like me like this. I plan to stuff my face every time she invites me over until I'm as round as the Pillsbury Doughboy."

"Heehee," Will says. "I like that cute chubby guy, so eat away." He swings me around in a circle. "Don't take this the wrong way." He bites his bottom lip and pulls me close again. "But I don't miss Aiden nearly as much as I think I *should*."

With his devilish grin and that glint in his eyes? I don't take it the wrong away at all. In fact, if I wasn't so hungry, I'd tell him to beg off with his parents. There are very few things in life as nice as making out with your very hot, very comforting boyfriend on the sofa.

But I do adore his parents, and this dough-girl needs food. So eventually I pat his chest and come up for air. "Dinner."

He blinks once. Then again. "Okay. Right. Dinner."

My stomach's still growling when I slide over into the middle seat of his truck's front bench, my side pressed to his. He holds my hand whenever he doesn't need it for driving. I've never been so happy that his truck is an automatic.

By the time I reach his parents' sprawling farmhouse, I feel much better. Yes, I stupidly gave all my money to Patrick to save a farm that didn't need saving. Again, like an idiot, some man in my life took everything that should have been mine. Father, check. Husband, check. And now brother, check mate. Ugh. I hate feeling like a moron.

But for once, I'm with a guy who doesn't just take. In

fact, as I'm sliding toward my door, he jogs around and opens it for me.

"I have hands that work," I say.

"I'm just trying to do some extra steps today. Gotta burn off those rolls," Will says. "I hear if you get your heartrate going a little bit, you burn more calories during the meal."

I swat his shoulder. "Shut up."

He leans against the door of the car, looming over me. "I will always jog around to get your door. You deserve that. I'm sorry no one else has taught you that, but I won't stop until you feel it deep in your bones."

Okay, I thought I felt better, but it must have been the same tough crust that always forms over my hurt feelings, because when he says that, the tears just bubble out. Will doesn't apologize, because he knows my feelings aren't his fault. He just pulls me against his chest and lets me sit there, sobbing against his shirt.

When his mom opens the door, waves and says, "Hey, you two. Come on inside," he just waves back.

"In a minute," he says.

And like an angel, his mother doesn't rush over to gush about what's wrong. She doesn't insert herself or try to make me sell insurance, or tell me what I'm doing wrong and lecture me.

I may have trusted the wrong people in the past, but at least Nationwide is on my side this time around. Why in the world is that dumb jingle playing in my head? My brain's a strange place.

Eventually I put all the stray thoughts and bizarre jingles out of my mind, and I straighten. "Thanks. I'm ready to go inside."

"You can lean against me and hug me any time you want, in any place." Will's smile is gentle. "Always."

That's precisely why his presence, his hug, and his

words help, because I know he won't do what all the other men in my life have done. When we walk inside, neither his father nor his mother mentions a thing about how we sat in the driveway for ten minutes.

"I hope you're okay with chicken pot pie," his mother says.

"Okay with it?" I inhale deeply. "I'd marry it, if it proposed right now."

She slams the back of her hand against Will. "Quick. Eat that pie before it gets you dumped."

"What's this now?" Will's dad's tucking his shirt in as he stands up, even though it doesn't need it. "Will's getting dumped? Again?"

"Shut up, Dad." Will hands me a plate. "I laugh at Mom's dumb jokes because she's my mom. You, on the other hand? You better watch it."

He might get a little corny around his parents, but I'll take corny Will over just about anyone else. By the time we're all done with dinner, and his mother is bringing out the peach cobbler, all my anger is just. . .gone. In fact, I may be smiling more than Will. What would my life have been like if these people were my parents?

If my dad had tucked his shirt in a dozen times a day, instead of walloping us with his belt? If my mom had made dinner with a smile and taken my dad to task over his idio-syncrasies instead of hiding and cowering? If they'd both had jobs they liked, or if they had liked each other? If they'd been equally yoked? Would I have been bright and cheery instead of sharp and edgy? Would I have married a small-town boy right off the bat instead of heading out to California to spend a lot of money on a fancy degree that I never even got?

The one thing I'm pretty sure of is that I wouldn't have had Aiden. So I suppose it's a waste of time wondering, because I wouldn't trade all those things for my sweet son.

But I'm determined to appreciate what I have now that I have it and not let my parental baggage ruin my future anymore. The entire way home, I don't have to force myself to smile or remind myself to breathe. It's nice.

When Will talks about the new heifers, I listen. When I tell him about the plumbing nightmare at work, he offers suggestions and laughs at appropriate times. And when we pull up in front of my house, I don't even want to go inside. I just want to stay here, talking to him all night long.

Until I notice the old white car parked in the driveway.

"What's Beth doing here?"

But it hits me then what a terrible aunt I am. I thought about Patrick. I thought about Amelia. I thought about myself. Not once did I consider how Beth, who has lived in Manila for her entire life, would feel about being uprooted to Seattle.

From a tiny town to the big city.

I made that transition between high school and college and it was rough enough. I can't imagine being forced into it, at the end of high school, no less. At a time when I'm supposed to be wide-eyed and excited, full of hope for the future. Considering she's the one who approached me about her parents' issues, she's already way too involved parenting them. She's getting no instruction or teaching directed her way.

I hate that I forgot about her in this whole mess, but at least she trusts me enough to show up.

"Hey, I better go." I toss my head.

Beth's leaning against her car door.

"Yeah, of course." Before I can stop him, he hops out and zooms around the truck again, opening my door.

"You're going to give me whiplash one of these days," I say.

"Oh, I hope I do," he says. "And then I would take you to the ER, and jump out, and run around, and get your door there, too." He leans in for a kiss, but in a surprise move, presses it on the top of my head. "Go and be amazing. You're the only amazing person in her life, I imagine."

Will waves as he drives away, and I wave back. Then I force myself to walk toward Beth's car. I'm not sure what to say to her. I'm a little angry she manipulated me into giving her family the money, just so they could sell and leave. I'm also nervous about what she may be feeling and how I might comfort her.

But mostly, I'm sad she's leaving.

With Patrick, my feelings are mixed and confused and complicated. With his wife, they're downright frosty.

But I was in the hospital when Beth was born. She's the person who made me an aunt. She's always listened to me, always looked up to me, and I thought, always been honest with me. And now that she's almost fully baked, she's leaving. She has always said she couldn't wait to leave Manila, but it still bums me out.

"Hey," I say lamely.

"Hi, Aunt Donna." She circles the car toward me slowly.

"I saw the sign in the yard."

She winces. "I had no idea." She swallows. "I swear."

As she says the words, I know it's true. Her parents probably had a plan when they sent her to beg me for money—winding her up and turning her toward me, her big, wide eyes full of hope and faith—it sounds just like Amelia. But there's no way she could have feigned the doe eyes she's turning on me now. She looks almost as upset as I feel.

"I don't even want to go." Her hands grab the material of her pants and tighten, bunching it up until her knuckles are white. "I've never lived anywhere but here."

"You graduated already," I say. "You always said you wanted to get out of here the second you could, and now you can live at home while doing it." I force a smile. "Maybe it'll be for the best."

"I didn't get into Whitman, Washington University, WSU, or the U."

"Out of state is hard."

"The only place I got in was UVU." Her nose scrunches. "Mom and Dad want me to just go to community college in Seattle."

"A lot of people start at a community college. It's harder to get in when you're at such a tiny school for high school."

"Says my aunt who went to Stanford." She sighs.

"But didn't graduate," I say.

She swallows, her eyes trained on her sneakers. "The thing is, I always said I wanted to leave, but that was just talk."

"Oh?"

"I like it here. And you're here. And you have this big house now, and I thought I might take my first year or two online, like Ethan's doing. I was wondering. . ." She digs at a pile of rocks on the ground with the toe of her blue and white sneaker.

She's wondering. . . whether she could live with me? I'm almost ashamed that my first thought was whether there was anything for my brother to gain from this. But it's a valid question. Is there any angle he could approach to somehow steal *more* from me?

I spend a little too much time wondering, apparently.

Because Beth nods and says, "I get it. It's fine. I mean, there's no way my parents would take care of Aiden, and there's only one of you to do all the stuff."

Before I have another second to think things through, I reach out with both hands and pull Beth, the gangly teenager who's a full two inches taller than I am, toward my chest. "Yes."

She freezes at first, her entire body stiffening.

39

"Of course you can live with me," I whisper against her hair. "For as long as you want. Always." Could she have been feeling as unloved and unsafe and unvalued as I did at her age?

Could she be just as broken?

The last thing I'm going to do is set her up for someone like Charles to destroy. My brother may be a mess, and my dad may have caused it, but I won't allow it to continue into another generation if there's a single thing I can do to stop it.

Beth finally pulls away, but she still looks nervous. "Thanks."

"When did you want to move in?" I imagine it won't be right away, since the ranch was *just* listed for sale. Those kinds of things take a while, I think.

"Is tomorrow too soon?"

I choke and swallow my gum.

Beth races over to pat me on my back. "Are you alright?"

I cough a few times. "Totally fine. I'm way too old to be chewing gum."

"So I guess tomorrow's not great," she says.

"Won't your parents be around for a while longer?"

She shakes her head. "They're packing the house so that it'll show better, and they said we may as well just leave now."

Geez. I guess Patrick was just waiting for the ink to dry on the deed transfer. "Alright, well. Sure. Tomorrow's fine."

"They aren't moving for two more weeks, but as soon as they find out I'm not going. . ."

It's going to get really uncomfortable for her to be there, duh. Patrick's always such a peach when I get in his way. I guess we'll find out how helpful all that anger management stuff really was. I hope it was worth the million dollars I lost on it.

I try, for the next half hour, to relocate the zen place I found about two or three rolls into dinner at the Earls. I've brushed my teeth, and I've put on my pajamas, and I'm nearly ready for bed when my phone bings.

It's a text from Will. EVERYTHING OKAY?

How do I respond to that? Will he be upset? Annoyed? Angry? Frustrated I made the decision on my own? I run through all the reactions I imagine he might have, and none of them are good.

Another kid relying on you always means more trouble.

And in this case, more expense, too. I really doubt that Patrick's going to start sending me money to help care for his daughter, but she'll eat more food, use more toiletries, and need more, well. More everything.

What was I thinking, just saying yes?

Before I can second guess everything about my life and who I am, I chomp down on the bullet and text him back. SHE WANTED TO LIVE WITH ME.

I wince as I hit send. I can't help it. I should've told him I said yes, but I couldn't do it. Baby steps, Donna. Maybe I can ease him in slowly to the idea before telling him I agreed to it. I could make him feel like he has a voice.

Which helps me realize that this is probably something that I should've checked with him about before answering. I've never been in a healthy relationship, and now I'm worried I've wrecked this one by being a complete relationship moron. My utter panic totally wrecks any progress I was making toward finding that calm place again.

When my phone bings again, my heart races. I can't bring myself to look at it. What if he says, NO WAY. Or if he tells me this is just another play by Patrick? What if he absolutely and positively forbids me to have Beth live with me? My hands begin to shake. I'm starting to sweat. The food I just ate is churning, churning, and I'm worried that peach cobbler is going to come right back up.

But finally, I remind myself that I'm an adult. The only way to know how bad it is. . .is to read the text.

TELL HER YES. SHE'S FAMILY, AND YOU'RE THE ONLY GOOD ROLE MODEL SHE'S GOT.

Before I even fully process the words, I'm crying.

There was not a single part of me that thought he might be happy about it, or that he might agree with what I did. I'm so scarred from Charles and Patrick and my dad that I assume the worst in everyone.

My phone bings again, and this time I rush to read it.

I CAN'T TELL YOU WHAT TO DO, BUT THAT'S MY VOTE. IF WE'RE VOTING. BUT WHATEVER YOU DO, I'M HAPPY TO PUNCH PATRICK. JUST SAY THE WORD.

WHAT WORD IS THAT? I ask. I'LL SAY IT. Laughing emoji.

PUNCH, he texts. OF COURSE.

WHAT IF I SAID I WANTED FRUIT PUNCH? WOULD YOU GO SLUG SOMEONE?

MAYBE. AND I'D HAVE PLAUSIBLE DENIA-BILITY FOR IT.

I'm laughing when I go to bed. With Will in my corner, how bad can it really be to have a teenager in the house?

# AMANDA

You'd think, once you had worked with someone for a long time, things would get easier. Some things do, of course, but Mandy's just as bull-headed today as she was on our very first renovation.

"Once those two deals close," Mandy says, "we'll have the money to cover everything from design through inspections. I think we should keep the duplex for now—not list it. With the housing crunch that moron over in Dutch John is creating around here—"

"To be fair, it's not all David's fault," I say. "Derek's leather processing and beef manufacturing plants didn't help either."

Mandy waves her hand through the air without looking up. "With each of those duplexes having two bedrooms, we could house eight men there easily if we need to bring in more labor."

"Men," I say. "Or women."

Mandy looks up this time. "Don't be all PC with me, young lady."

I point at the blueprints. "If we sold the duplex and just brought in trailer rentals, we'd have enough capital from the sale to cover building the staff housing on site immediately."

"But we need the well dug, so we'll need to get started on that right away. Approvals for water are notoriously slow around here. If Haversham gets his knickers in a knot over something, we'll be sitting on our hands for two or three months, sometimes."

"Taxes on the duplex alone—"

"Mom," Emery says hesitantly.

"Yeah?" I don't look back at her. I can't give Mandy an inch, or she walks all over me.

"You said to tell you when it was five o'clock."

"Yeah, thanks." I wave at her. "Taxes on the duplex will cost enough, now that it'll be reassessed, that within a year, or maybe eighteen months—"

"Because of your date." Mandy's eyes light up. "That's why the time matters." Her grin is maniacal. "Fine. Let's list the duplex. It's solved."

Is she kidding right now? "Are you really going to just give me my way whenever I have a date? Do you think I'm more likely to forgive Eddy if I'm in a good mood?"

Mandy shakes her head slowly, her eyes totally serious. "Not at all. I would *never* think you were capricious in any way."

I hate when she uses words I don't know. "Well, you better not be kidding right now. My date with Eddy has nothing to do with our business stuff." I stand up and straighten my shoulders. "But I'll call and get that duplex listed, because I'm too smart to ever ignore a chance to do the smart thing."

"Atta girl," Mandy says. "Or better yet, I'll do it for you, and you go get ready."

I don't need her to manage me. "I'll call *and* I'll get ready. I'm great at multitasking." I press talk on my phone and head for my room.

As I explain the listing timelines and set up an appointment for photos of the duplex now that it's done, I rifle through outfits in my closet. None of them look quite right.

"Nothing too fancy." Maren's tone is bored from where she's lounging on my bed.

I startle. "I didn't even realize you were in here."

"You need help, Mom," she says. "I could hardly let you get dressed alone."

That annoys me even more. "I'm an *influencer*. No one around here is better than I am at choosing what to wear—not even my snooty teenage daughter."

Maren sits up. "For a photo shoot? Sure. For a meet and greet with possible sponsors? You're still right. But you're going to see an ex in a tiny town, and having been through three relationships here in Manila already, I can tell you. It's a whole new football game."

"I think the phrase is a whole new *ball* game." I'm correcting inane things because I'm busy trying to process the other thing she said. She's been through *three relationships?* With who?? How have I heard nothing about them? Knowing Maren, the more I ask, the less information she'll offer.

Maren waves her hand. "Whatever."

She can't even get a sports idiom right, but she thinks I need her help? My fingers close around a hanger with a sky blue sundress on it. It really makes my eyes pop—and I know that for a fact. At least two hundred followers said so.

Although, the filter did help.

"No way," Maren says.

"Oh, come on. This dress is great, and the weather outside is finally decent for once."

She shakes her head. "Wearing something like that means you're trying too hard."

My mouth dangles open.

"You've been really *easy, breezy, whatever* since Eddy came back and started begging. But if you want to keep that momentum, you need to show him that he's way more interested than you are."

My daughter's a total brat, acting like I'm playing a game with Eddy. "I'm not trying to keep momentum." I drop my hands to my hips, not realizing I was still holding the dress. I whip it back up off the floor. "Look, thanks for wanting to help, but get out." I point at the door.

She ignores me.

"I'm wearing this," I say. "Because it's the perfect choice." In actuality, I doubt it matters much what I wear. Eddy has never cared much about clothing. He compliments me when it's something really obvious, but usually doesn't seem to be able to tell the difference between casual elegance and just casual.

By the time I finally get Maren to march out, I've only got ten minutes before Eddy's supposed to pick me up. I throw the dress on and swipe some mascara on my lashes. . .when I get a text from him.

ANY CHANCE YOU CAN MEET ME AT MY OFFICE?

I can't help remembering what he said to me the first time he called to ask me out. "Um, if it's a date, I think I ought to pick you up." But today, on our do-over, he's not even picking me up? He did walk to my door to ask me out, flowers in hand. I squelch my irritation.

No matter what Maren says, I'm trying to be fair and even-handed.

SURE.

There's not much of a reason for me to be annoyed. I mean, we're supposed to be 'starting over,' but can you really start over when you've been so involved in someone else's life for so long?

Probably not.

46

Still, when I march out to the front yard, climb into my car, and slam the door, no one even seems to take notice. Mandy didn't comment on my beautiful blue dress. Maren didn't say she was wrong or wish me luck. And Emery wasn't anywhere to be seen.

But it's fine.

I don't need anyone pulling for me. In fact, it annoyed me when they were. So I put the car in drive, and I head on down the road to Eddy's vet practice. The same wooden sign out front that's always been there swings in the wind a bit.

Dutton Animals.

It's strikingly dark against the light reddish brick.

Walking toward his practice reminds me of the day I drove out here, intent on asking him a question—asking for a favor, really. His dad's a park ranger, and our ranch had lost its permit to have cows out there.

"Morning," a female voice says.

It's Krystal, Eddy's little sister. She's lugging a box to her car, presumably, but it looks heavy.

I rush over. "Here, let me help."

"Not a chance," she says. "Eddy would kill me."

She drops the box on the top of her trunk and presses a button, releasing the latch. Of course, the weight of the box keeps the trunk from opening.

I stifle a chuckle and grab the box.

"Hey," she says, her green eyes sparkling just like Eddy's. "I'd have gotten it figured out."

"Now you don't have to," I say.

"Eddy did me a big favor," she says.

"And now he's got you sorting his files for him, doesn't he?"

"Scanning them in. He does pay me," she says, "but we both hate this kind of thing."

"Dragging the business into the twentieth century isn't

47

easy, is it?"

"It's the twenty-first century," Krystal says.

"I know." I can't help my smirk as I drop the box into her finally-open trunk.

"Ah, now I get the joke."

"Is Eddy still inside?"

Krystal nods. "And listen, even if his idea is kind of dumb, he really does mean well. Try to remember that."

His idea? What is she talking about?

I'm a little nervous as I circle to the front of the building and approach the door. I really hope he's not going to propose again or anything. He wouldn't be that stupid, would he?

But when I open the door, he's on one knee.

My heart stops, dead.

If I turn him down twice, are we just done? Trying to dig our way out of one failed proposal would be hard enough. I'm not sure anyone could propose twice, be refused twice, and somehow just keep pursuing.

But I can't say yes. I just can't. So I'm going to have to refuse him again, and it breaks my heart to even contemplate it.

Eddy looks up into my face, and then he stands back up, brushing off his pants as he does. "That dumb machine. I swear, all it has to do is heat up water and drip it through a filter into a pot. How hard is that?"

I look down and realize he was kneeling on one knee. . .looking at the innards of his ancient coffee machine.

"Oh."

"Oh?" Eddy turns toward me. "I know. This is going all wrong. First I make you drive here yourself, which is practically a crime already, but that first day, the only way I got you here was to let you drive. Like a skittish filly, you were all kinds of spooky."

Is he trying to recreate the day I came to ask him for a favor?

"Remember? I met you outside with two cups of coffee. It wasn't really smooth? But it was *kind of* smooth." He points at the edge of the very vintage, battered wooden desk where there's a stack of sugar packets, some creamer containers, and a single peppermint.

He must consider that to be our first date. Now that I'm thinking about it, I think he did call it a 'walking coffee date.' My heart flipped over in my chest when he said he'd have done me the favor just for our walking coffee date, or whatever it was.

And those are exactly the kinds of feelings he's trying to remind me of. . . Not very smoothly, though. He's swearing under his breath as he presses buttons, unplugs the coffeemaker and jostles the back, and plugs it back in. I can't help but notice, as his hair falls down over his eyes, that he's every bit as handsome as when we first met a year ago.

Actually, now that I know him? He might even be hotter.

Dark hair. Bright green eyes. A lanky build with well-defined muscles. A square jaw. Dark, slashing brows.

And a perfectly shaped mouth with sinfully full lips.

He sighs. "Can you just wait here? I'll run across the street and grab some coffee and we can start over—"

I put my hand on his arm. "Eddy."

He becomes as still as a statue in Central Park.

"When I agreed to start over, I didn't literally mean we needed to start over." I can't help my small smile. "You don't have to stress out."

His head finally turns, his eyes meeting mine. "I do, though. You aren't sure about us, and I want you to remember how good it was. How perfect things were."

"Were?"

"Before I screwed everything up." He starts moving toward the door.

I catch his hand. "Wait."

My fingers are so small compared to his rough, much darker hands. Sun, wind, animals. All of those things have taken their toll, and I can see it on his hands, but it's not off-putting. It's manly. It's impressive.

His aren't the hands of a rock star, though he does have callouses from guitar strings as well. I realize that I'm stroking his hand, my fingertips touching each of his fingers lightly, and I look up at his face.

He's watching me, half nervous, half hopeful.

I swallow and force myself to drop his hand. But he shifts then, sliding his hand against mine again, and then twining our fingers together. "I'm sorry," he says. His voice is raw. Vulnerable. Desperate. "So sorry."

I can't look at his eyes. Not when they're pleading with me like that.

"This was supposed to be fun," I say. "Light. Easy."

He drops my hand immediately, like it's burning him. "It will be. Just let me run grab some coffee, and—"

"You don't have to recreate anything," I say. "The best way forward isn't to try and redo. We need to make our own new beginnings."

"I don't know where to start," he says. "Our start was *so* good last time."

"I'm not expecting something that would be in a book or on a television show," I say. "This is the real world. I'm not an idiot."

"You're the brightest woman I know," he says.

I scowl. "Don't lie. You've met Abby."

Eddy rolls his eyes. "I don't just mean book-smart. You're business savvy. You're able to pivot when things go wrong. You're resilient in the face of problems that would cripple anyone else."

"This isn't feeling very light and airy," I say.

He inhales slowly. "Right. Happy. Easy. Like cotton candy."

"I like cotton candy."

"No carnivals close, so that's a dead end." His brow draws together and I realize that he's not kidding. He's literally casting around desperately for ideas on how to win me back. . .breezy edition.

"How about I walk over with you to get some coffee?"

I can tell by the way the muscle in his jaw works that I'm ruining his plans for a perfect second first date.

"Let's not worry so much about making plans and focus more on just *being* together." I offer him my hand.

He takes it.

Like always, energy practically dances between that connection. I may be annoyed with him. I may not trust him anymore. But my body still screams *YES* whenever he's near. That's not a bad thing. And when we walk across the street, the movement seems to burn off some of our nervous energy.

One thing I didn't consider when I suggested we try to restart was how many, many people would be watching us. Every person in Brownings turns and stares when we walk through the door. Their eyes widen and mouths drop open. Their gazes dart down to our joined hands, zip back up to our faces, and then they turn toward each other and the whispers start.

"No, we're not together again," Eddy says. "We're just on a date. Just a regular couple, on a date."

"Maybe in Hollywood you're a regular couple." Jason, who runs the local gas station, stands up. "But here in Manila, you stand out a mite bit."

I can't help smiling. "We'd like two black coffees, to go."

While we wait, Eddy points out all the things that have

changed while he was gone. "Another letter burned out in the sign out front."

"Good eye," I say. "They're debating just replacing the whole thing with a wooden one, or trying to figure out how to replace the one letter. Apparently the sign wasn't made well, and as each letter goes out, they have to order a new one."

"There's also a new bell." He points at the front table. "The old bell wasn't good enough?"

"The Harper boy knocked it over and it broke." Greta Davis hands us two cups of coffee. "It's great to have you back."

"Thanks." Eddy takes the cups and hands me one. "It's nice to be back." He tries to pay Greta, but she waves him off.

"It's on the house this time, and it's not that I'm not happy you're back." Greta's eyes crinkle when she smiles. She smooths a few flyaway red hairs back into place. "But it's nice to see the *two of you* in here together." She winks and walks back toward the kitchen.

Everyone's still murmuring as we walk back through the door and into the beautiful sunshine.

"Small town—not many coffee options," Eddy says. "Should've expected that."

"I guess, but don't they have their own stuff to worry about?" I sigh.

"Not really," he says. "A New York City influencer who's developing a retreat in town and who was recently a bachelorette on social media does stand out, just like Jason said."

"And the town rock star?" I shake my head. "He doesn't add anything."

"Retired rock star," Eddy says.

I blow on my coffee, which is so hot it's practically burning my hand through the paper cup. "Really?"

He shrugs. "I may still release a few singles here and

there, but I signed the termination agreement yesterday, so it's official. I no longer have an active agreement with the label requiring me to come out with new projects."

I know he said he was doing that, but I'm still surprised he went through with it.

He's peeking sideways at me. "Does that make you happy?"

"Don't do it for me, one way or another," I say. "Do what *you* want to do."

He stops then and turns toward me. "I made that mistake before. I never should have considered only what I wanted. But you have to believe me, Amanda. I'll always put you first in the future."

"It wasn't a mistake," I say. "If you'd stayed here for me, you'd be the one who was frustrated. You'd resent me for ruining your dreams."

"But my dream was stupid," he says. "Being famous just caused problems, and it's not like I really needed more money to do the things I want in life."

"You wouldn't have known any of that," I say, "if you hadn't gone and tried to fulfill that dream."

He nods, and starts moving along again, slower this time. But eventually we do reach his office, and he offers me the same things as he did on that first walking-coffee-date, including the peppermint. "Still three sugars and one cream?"

I nod.

He makes a big production of dumping one packet of sugar at a time in my coffee and then using a tiny wooden stick to stir it. Finally, he cracks the creamer lid and starts to pour it, lifting it dramatically high for the last few drops. "Your drink, milady."

"You don't have to try so hard," I say.

"Apparently, I do." Eddy jams his hands in his pockets

and sits on the edge of the desk. "Since you're still so angry."

This date was clearly a mistake. "I'm not angry." He doesn't understand, and I can't tell whether he's really obtuse or I'm truly an enigma.

"What, then? What's wrong? Stuff you found charming before makes you scowl. Do you just not like me anymore?"

I feel. . .too much. That's the problem. I'm angry he left, and that makes me feel guilty. I'm delighted he's back, but that makes me feel pathetic. And I yearn for him to touch me, but when he does, I crave more, and that makes me angry with myself.

"I think I just need some time," I say. "I need to figure out what I want without feeling like everyone in this teeny tiny microcosm of the world is pressuring me."

"I'm not trying to pressure—"

There's a knock at the door.

It's a business, not a home. Why would someone knock?

Eddy straightens and strides toward the glass door. I can make out the shape of a woman on the other side. My mind races wildly. Who could it be? Is it some girl from his tour, come to tell him she's pregnant? A local girl bringing him baked goods and asking him out, now that we've broken up?

Why are those my top two options? What's wrong with me?

The woman standing outside when he opens the glass door is neither young nor beautiful. She looks. . .sturdy. Her hair's grey, swept back into a neat bun. Her eyes are almost flinty, but for some reason, she's beaming at Eddy.

And she's holding a potted plant of some kind.

"You brought her back."

"Excuse me?" Eddy asks. "Mrs. Jenkins, what are you—"

"Call me Dolores." She shoves the pot toward him. "I

54

was just so happy when I heard her voice." Her eyes shift to me, and her smile cranks up another notch. "Amanda Brooks, I'm a huge fan."

A fan?

Of what? It seems strange to think of people out here hunting down tips or discounts on extravagant luxuries and designer brands. Maybe she started to follow me after I moved out here?

"Do you follow me on Insta?" I ask.

She shakes her head. "I'm not sure what that means, but my John Cabot roses have *never* been as happy as they were last year, when you started coming around. I swear, they love the sound of your voice, and they'll climb higher than ever now that you're back."

I have no idea what to say to this woman. I glance back at Eddy and realize the pot he's holding has. . .roses in it. Bright pink roses.

"I thought you might like to have this one." She points at me, and then she points at Eddy, and then she backs out. "I won't bore you two youngsters, but please do spend some time outside. Alright?"

"Thanks," Eddy says.

"Not you." Dolores narrows her eyes. "Your voice ticks them off. Just your girlfriend there, that's who they like." She smiles at me one more time, and then she spins on her heel and darts across the street.

This seems as good a time as any to end this bizarre not-date. "I should go."

"Wait." Eddy reaches for me, but I dodge his hand.

"I need to think about all this," I say. "It all just feels. . .so complicated."

"How's it complicated?" Eddy puts the rose pot down. "Look, a lot of people seem to be getting involved, and I get that's not ideal, but you and I love each other. Don't we?"

"I loved my husband at first," I say. "But we made each other miserable."

"I'm nothing like him."

I think about that, really think about it. Paul was brilliant, handsome, and hard-working. He and Eddy have those things in common. Paul could command a room and often did. Eddy does the same. After we first met, Paul decided that he wanted me, and he stopped at nothing until I was his.

Once he succeeded, he didn't care at all.

At the end of the day, once Eddy had me, he had no concerns about traveling away on tour. It wasn't until after I dumped him that he cared to win me back. And even then, it wasn't until it was convenient for him to try.

"I think the two of you have more in common than I realized."

"I treasure you," Eddy says. "I'll show you that."

The trouble is, I'm not sure he *can* show me that, not in the ways I need him to.

"Sure," I say. "Maybe."

It's hard to drive away, but it also feels safer. It feels like something I *have* to do. I'm almost home when my phone rings. It's not a number I know, and usually I don't answer those, but our agent did just tell me that a new photographer would be touching base to set up photos on the duplex.

"Hello?"

"Amanda?" It's a man's voice, and it sounds vaguely familiar, but I can't place why.

"Yes."

"You know, I had to go in and talk to HR before I could call you, and even then, I only got approval because you weren't a patient."

Huh? "Who is this?"

My phone bings. "I sent a little reminder to your phone."

I pull over, significantly annoyed, and pull up the photo. "Since I live in the boonies, it's taking about twelve minutes for this photo to upload."

"I didn't even think of that," he says. "So much for being cute."

But in that moment, the photo does load, and I remember just how cute he actually *is* in person. "Doctor Harkey," I say. "From Salt Lake."

"Formerly from Salt Lake," he says. "I just moved to Green River."

Right.

"I was hoping you might let me take you to dinner."

"I thought you mentioned drinks." I pull into my own driveway, put my car in park, and kill the engine.

"The thing is, drinks is pretty non-committal. I've given it a little more thought, and I've also been encouraged by my sister. She said I should swing for the fences."

"The fences being. . ." I climb out of the car and head for the front door, remembering his sister follows me. The whole thing makes me laugh a little. I'm a perfectly normal person, and anyone who met me in real life might think I'm a mess. But if someone follows me on insta, they get a distorted view of my value.

And then I look up. Emery, Maren, and Mandy are all standing on the porch.

Staring at me.

I freeze.

"A full-fledged date. I mean, sure, you're a famous Instagram influencer, and you're beautiful, and you're probably way out my league, but how will I know if I don't try?"

"Fine," I say. "Let's do lunch one day." That seems less committal than a dinner.

"Depending on my case load, I might have time tomorrow."

"My schedule's pretty flexible right now. You can just text me tomorrow and let me know."

"I can pick you up—"

"Don't bother." The last thing I want is Dr. Brown Eyes being interrogated by the insane people who are glaring at me right now. "Since it's for lunch, I can drive out there, run some errands, and meet you whenever you have time."

"Great," he says. "But for the record, I really don't mind picking you up."

"Noted." I hang up.

"It didn't sound like you were talking to Eddy," Mandy says. "And you've only been gone for an hour and twenty-four minutes."

"That's not promising," Maren says. "What went wrong?"

I push past them and open the door. "Nothing."

Mandy hops up and follows me so fast that she practically tramples me. "Something did. Spill."

"I'm fine. Eddy's fine. We're all fine."

Mandy snatches my phone. "Then why's some other guy asking you on a date? And more importantly, why are you saying yes?"

"You're not my mother," I say. "And even if you were, I'm a grown woman. I don't have to answer any of those questions." I grab my phone back and plow past her toward my room.

"Amanda Brooks." Mandy's tone is not playful. She sounds downright angry.

I spin on the ball of my foot. "What?"

"What happened on your date tonight?"

"He tried to recreate our first. . .well, sort-of date," I say. "But it was just awkward and it made me sad."

Mandy's face falls. "He's trying so hard."

"He left!" I hate the wobble in my voice. "He didn't try when it mattered."

"He couldn't come home any faster than he did, and the second his plane landed, he came to that wedding and proposed." Mandy steps closer, her eyes flashing. "What more did you want? China with your initials on it? Sky writing with an airplane?"

"I can't trust him."

"Admit the truth," Mandy says. "You just *won't* forgive him, no matter what he did, and no matter what he does."

"I'm not you, and he's not Jedediah," I say.

Mandy flinches like I slapped her. "I think you're the one being like Jed here."

"Excuse me?"

"I went out with his brother, and he could never forgive me for it."

"You—that's the reason you're so angry? You really think this is like that? Mandy, that was more than fifty years ago."

"And you're the same bull-headed moron that Jedediah was. I sat here, waiting for him, for years. Only, Eddy's doing way more than I did. He's begging. He's apologizing. He's doing everything he can think to do to gain forgiveness, and you're ruining it."

I understand a little more why she's getting *so* involved. "My first husband married me and set me on a shelf, expecting me and the girls to be lovely and make him look better." I sigh. "I can't even risk being stuck in a relationship like that again. I have to feel safe *and* free. Do you understand that?"

"Eddy went after a dream," Mandy says. "He didn't set you on a shelf."

"What if he has another dream?" I ask. "What then? I should just wait around here forever, hoping he'll always come back to me? Hoping he'll put me first. . .one day? When it's convenient?"

"He's putting you first now, you ninny. And you think that he'll have some other hidden occupation that was ended early by someone making him take a fall as a murderer? Really?"

"Shut up," I say. "If you're not even going to try to understand me, then just stop talking."

I storm off to my room, and I'm a little disappointed when she really does leave me alone to stew.

# 6

## ABIGAIL

For years, I spent all my work hours in an office. The only sounds I heard were other people talking quietly or laughing in the break room, sometimes. The only things I ever smelled were takeout around lunch time or body odor from the most obnoxious partner.

The office my sweet husband made for me, with Mandy's help and guidance, is perfectly quiet.

Until Wednesday and Thursday afternoons, when it's full of the sounds of laughter and permeated by the scent of fresh-baked cookies.

It's a Wednesday, so Maren has cheer, but Izzy, Emery, and Whitney are all here, baking cowboy cookies. The nutty scent of baking pecans, the exotic smell of coconut, and the undercurrent of cinnamon brighten even an afternoon filled with tax talk.

"No," I say. "I told you, we sent the support for that number. I won't agree to the figure you just sent, because it doesn't take into account the charitable donations, and they are one hundred percent valid and documented."

IRS agents can be really, really obtuse sometimes.

"Sure. If I have to, I'll file a motion." I hang up.

"Mom?" Izzy pokes her head around the corner. "Wanna give your stamp of approval before we open the doors to customers?"

Which really just means flipping the OPEN light on underneath the Double or Nothing sign. My door's always unlocked while I'm here. "Always."

Izzy sets a small plate with a large, chewy cookie on it at the edge of my desk, and then she hands me a glass of milk. I trained her well. Cowboy cookies without milk? Blasphemous.

I take a bite and close my eyes. "I've taught you well."

She beams before ducking out. A short moment later, I hear the jingle of the bell over the door. Being the only bakery in town has its perks. Even though it's a business run by children, they almost always sell out.

I finish up a complaint I was drafting when the agent called, and then I type up a very strongly worded email reiterating the things I told him over the phone. I reattach the documents we had couriered over for good measure.

And I copy his boss.

No harm in escalating when someone's being obtuse.

I reach for the rest of my cookie as a reward now that I'm done, and a wave of nausea rolls over me. It's bad enough that I drop the cookie. I glance at the clock.

Four p.m.

It could be a stomach bug.

I mean, that's always possible.

But when I pull out my calendar, and I glance at the big red circle around last Tuesday, more than a week past, I somehow feel certain it's *not* a stomach bug.

My period is literally never eight days late.

Which means it's probably time for a pregnancy test. I was on birth control. The voice in my head sounds like a whiny teenage girl, asking me, *How could this have happened? You* just *got married. Are you an idiot? Did you miss a day?*

I tell it to shut up.

And then I head out to buy a pregnancy test. One of the worst things about small towns is that they have *nothing* that you need unless it's your routine milk, eggs, bread, etc. I'm stuck driving an hour to Rock Springs for the closest Walgreens.

Which is why I've put it off so long.

I suppose I could've gone to the clinic in town, but only if I wanted everyone to know my business the second I do. It's like they've never heard of HIPAA or confidentiality or *common decency*. I can practically hear Doc Oliver, who drives up from Vernal, saying, "It's not like people wouldn't notice when you started to show in a few months."

I groan.

"Mom?" Izzy hands a bag of cookies to Linda and frowns. "Are you leaving?"

"I have to go meet a client," I say. "They need to show me something."

"Oh." She nods. "Alright, well, I'll see you at home, then?"

"I'll pick up dinner," I say. "I have to pass through Rock Springs."

"Wow, that's far," she says. "Can you get Broadway Burgers? We haven't had those in forever."

The thought of sitting in the car with that smell for an hour makes my stomach turn. "Not today," I say. "They're no good if they sit."

"Plus, the shakes would totally melt," Emery says. "And that's the best part."

There aren't many fast food options, even in Rock Springs. It's funny that my girls and their cousins already know them all. "Let's go next week," I say.

Hopefully I'll feel up to it.

I have to stop for gas before I get on my way, but I'm almost done filling up when I hear my name.

"Mrs. Brooks."

Well, almost my name. "It's Mrs. Archer, now," I say. "Or it will be, once I file the right forms with the recorder's office."

"Right." David Park slaps his hand against his forehead.

"What are you in town for?" I ask.

He glances left, and then he glances right. "Actually. I wanted to come by and see you while I was here."

My eyes widen. "Me?"

"I know Amanda and Mrs. Saddler weren't pleased at first, when I started building my resort, but surely now that they're planning their own over here, there are no hard feelings, right?"

I open my mouth, but I'm not sure what to say.

"I want to hire you." He beams, and egads, he's pretty when he smiles.

"Hire me?"

"Your legal services?" He frowns. "You did hang up a shingle, did you not?"

I glance over my shoulder, where you can see my little combination cookie and legal shop. "I suppose I did."

"I have been paying some overpriced lawyers out in California to dig through things, but I think it's high time I found someone local."

"Oh." His business would be huge. But it's strange talking about it over a gasoline pump. "Well, maybe you can come in and talk to me—"

"Now?"

I almost groan. "I can't right now, but first thing tomorrow would be fine."

"Is there a conflict of interest?" he asks. "Between representing me and Amanda Saddler?"

My shoulders fall. "I certainly hope not. Do you plan to do anything that might injure them or their interests?"

"Good heavens, no," he says. "But I just wanted to make sure no one's upset."

"I can ask them if you'd like," I say. "I don't foresee any trouble."

"If I told you something as a sort of new client consult, would it be confidential?"

"Of course," I say.

"I want to make an offer on a ranch over here that just went up for sale. A lot of our early clients are asking for a dude ranch experience. Instead of trying to carve out a ranch from scratch, I'd rather buy one, complete with cows and bulls, and find people to run it."

"The Ellingson ranch, you mean?" I blink. "Wow, okay."

"Do you think you could help me with that?"

"Of course," I say. "I imagine you'd need to be over here more often."

David shrugs. "Probably."

I think about Amanda and the ranting phone call she made to me last night about how everyone in town wants her to just marry Eddy. I suppose there's at least one person who's about to be around more who doesn't want that at all. "Let's talk more in the morning," I say. "But I'd be happy to represent you with that."

"Great. I'm so glad I ran into you!" David waves as he heads inside to pay for his gasoline. The credit card swiper never works at the pump he's on, but he apparently already knows that. He may not be a local, but he catches on quickly, clearly. Having him buy a ranch over here will definitely make things more interesting.

Assuming he doesn't get into some kind of fist fight with Eddy and end up having to wake Steve in the middle of the night to sew the two of them up.

Eventually, I do reach the faraway pharmacy. They have an entire rack of pregnancy tests. There are cheap, or sort-of cheap, pee-on-the-stick/check the color tests. That's all

I've ever taken before. There are also digital ones that will display the word "pregnant" or "not pregnant." And there are even some that sync to your phone and send you an email with all sorts of information included.

Of course, those cost as much as my first live birth.

Alright, not quite that much, but they aren't even close to cheap.

I suppose the people standing right where I am aren't always very worried about cost. In the end, I buy three tests. One cheap one. One digital one. And a double pack that says it's the earliest detection possible.

I pick up sandwiches from Jimmy Johns, because the smell won't kill me, and head straight home. I consider taking the tests inside and telling Steve what's going on. But then I remember that he's not even home. He's working yet another shift to cover for that poor, sick doctor friend of his.

It's probably for the best.

If it comes up negative, he'd probably be really bummed. Since I'm hoping it comes up negative, it might be better for me to find out the answer when he's not around. Then he never even has to know. He won't get his hopes up or his heart broken.

The tests say they can tell up to two days before my period was due, and that morning urine is best. Should I wait for that? Or should I take the test now? I've never been much for waiting, but since I have three, one of which has *two* tests, I decide to just take one now.

I start with the cheapest one.

Waiting for the read on the test is always the longest three minutes of my life. I stare, and I stare, and I stare.

And I realize I should have saved my money.

These tests sucked back when I was young, and they still suck now. There's a bright pink line. . .and a very, very, very faint pink line. So what does that mean? Is it some kind of reverb in the paper? The package says pregnant should be shown by two bright pink lines.

I chuck it in the trash.

And I eat dinner with my kids. There's no way I could even try to pee again this soon. I make sure to drink my entire glass of water. And then I help the girls and Ethan feed all the horses.

By this point, I'm all kinds of nervous.

Steve gets home soon, and I feel like I need to know the answer before he's staring me in the face. Will he be delighted? Or will I be relieved? Which is it? Which? Which?

I finish up with the animals and rush into the house. This time, I'm smart enough to take a plastic disposable cup with me and pee into that. Now I can take as many tests as I need to take to be totally sure. I won't waste all my pee on one stupid test that malfunctions. Of course, I managed to pee all over my hand in the collection process, but since I have four kids and numerous animals now, I know there are way worse things than a little pee on my hand. If it washes off—it's not too bad.

I pop all three tests out of their packaging, and I use a dropper from one package to put the right amount of urine on each test.

And then I wait.

As if the tests know each other, as if they're old friends carpooling to a barbecue, they all display their results within seconds of one another.

Pregnant.

Pregnant.

Positive.

My hands tremble as I wash them off. Thoughts zip around inside my brain at a hundred miles per hour. And my heart swells inside my body. Steve and I almost broke up because he wanted to have a child, whereas I didn't.

At least, I thought I didn't.

But now that the test results are right in front of me, I feel nothing but a sense of complete elation. A life milestone I thought was way, way behind me is now coming up again fast.

Newborn baby smell, and diapers, and bottles, and swaddling. It all comes at me in a whoosh—in a flurry of memories. The feeling of having a baby nestled in my arms. The swelling sensation of love and protectiveness that only a mother can truly understand. And the joy that comes from watching that child grow, one day at a time, into a miraculous little person and knowing that *you made that*.

Suddenly, I'm desperate to destroy all the evidence of this amazing miracle. Steve shouldn't find out he's going to be a father again like this. His first time around, he was lied to. He was told it wasn't even his. And he believed that lie for years and years, only to be broadsided in the worst way.

This news should be celebrated. It should be special. I chuck all the tests and boxes and instructions into a bag and I double tie it and rush it out to the trash. To my shock, the kids don't even seem to notice what I'm doing.

"Can you believe that?" Ethan's raucous laughter floods the entire house. "They're playing the Harry Potter theme song on their washer and dryer!"

The other three kids are all hunched over his phone.

I've never been more grateful for stupid Instagram reels than I am right now.

I'm closing the lid on the trash can when a car pulls up. Steve's home almost thirty minutes early! My heart races, but as I walk back toward the house, I realize it's not Steve.

Amanda Saddler's climbing out of her car.

"Mandy?"

"Help me out, would you?"

I jog over and help her stand. "Are you supposed to be out and about?"

She pshaws. It's not a sound I was very familiar with before meeting her. "Girl, please. I coulda walked here, but driving's easier. It's a block."

I've learned not to argue with her. It's pointless. "What was so urgent that you had to rush over?"

She arches one eyebrow. "Amanda has lost her mind."

I can't argue with her about that. "She's certainly hot under the collar about everyone telling her to date Eddy."

"That girl is a total idiot, is what she is. She's sore we're all telling her what to do, and that's making her do the opposite."

"You're right," I say. "Which is why I told her to dump him."

Mandy's eyes bug out and her mouth dangles.

"She now has no idea what to do. No matter what decision she makes, she'll be going along with someone's advice. I'm hoping her pride will let her back down and make her own decision."

Mandy slowly smiles and slaps her knee. "You're a genius."

"I hope it helps. She's not going to get anywhere until she realizes that she loves him, wholly and completely, but to do that—"

"She has to love herself first," Mandy says. "And she has to realize that time is all we got in this world, and it ain't unlimited."

"Exactly," I say. "Yes, you're totally right."

"I knew you'd get me," Mandy says. "So you'll understand when I say I need to revoke that will you made for me."

"You what?"

"I need to undo it. Revoke ain't the right word?"

"Oh, no, it is." But I'm confused. "Are you that upset with her?"

"I need her to think I am," she says. "And to think that—"

"Are you sure you want to trick her?" I sigh.

She huffs. "I can't get through to her with talking."

"Well, all you have to do to revoke a will is tear it up and mean it."

"You're sure all I have to do is tear it up?"

I nod.

"First easy legal advice, ever." She starts to shuffle back to her car, and turns back to say, "Probably because tearing up a will means more work for that lawyer later." She cackles.

I love her cackle.

I'm overcome with a burning desire to tell her about the baby, but I can't very well tell someone else when the father doesn't even know. It's hard, but I keep my mouth shut as she gets in, closes the door, and drives away.

It has been a really strange day.

First the nausea.

Then David Park's news about buying the Ellingson property.

And now Mandy, revoking her will that leaves everything to Amanda.

As I think about the bombshells being dropped all day, I decide today is *not* the day to tell Steve. I want it to be a happy day. I don't want to just spring it on him the second he walks in the door from a miserable shift of slogging his way from patient to patient.

It should be special.

Maybe I could make some sugar cookies, frost them pink and blue, and ask him which he prefers. . .until he understands what I'm asking. That would be funny.

And totally different than his last experience. Happy. Light. It would also show him that I'm excited about this.

Yes. That's what I'll do. I've just decided, when more head-lights turn down our drive.

I can't help my smile—I'm sure it's a knowing smile. I hope it doesn't give me away. But when it gets closer, I realize this isn't my husband either. It's a shiny, sleek sports car. The door opens.

And Helen slides out, obviously.

Good grief. Did some strange magical dates converge? Summer solstice and some kind of bizarre constellation? It's not the middle of June yet, so it can't be that. But *something* weird is going on today. No normal day should be full of this much upheaval.

"What's wrong with you?" Helen asks, studying my face.

"Other than the fact that my pain-in-the-rear sister just showed up, unannounced? Again?"

"Your strange lack of reaction to my arrival is what feels weird," she says. "Something's up."

"Nothing is up," I say. "So why don't you tell me why you're here."

"Maybe say hello, first, neighbor," Helen says.

"Neighbor?"

Her smile practically lights up my dark front porch. "I just put an offer down on the ranch down the road. The Ellingsons own it for now, but soon I will."

Yeah, there's definitely some kind of weirdness at play.

I'm pregnant.

Mandy's breaking up with Amanda.

And now David Park and my sister Helen—who hate each other—are about to start a bidding war for the ranch down the road. They don't even know it, yet. Whatever's going on, I only know that I want as far away from it as I can get.

So, of course, I'm right here in the center of the storm.

# 7

## DONNA

Usually I like cowboy boots on hot men, probably because I grew up in a place where most of the good-looking men I met wore boots. That, and the only concerts I went to in my formative years were country singers—Tim McGraw in a tank top, pair of faded jeans, and some cowboy boots? YES, please.

But they look *so* wrong on David Park.

"Um, did a little shopping, did you?"

My boss is standing in front of the webcam on his computer, using it like a mirror, and he's turning back and forth, staring at the small image of himself—or more particularly, of his feet.

"I can't decide whether I can pull these off."

I'm smart enough not to just blurt out that he can't, but my face must be a little too transparent.

"I take it that you vote no."

My forced smile doesn't seem to help, so I scramble to get away from being the villain. "I mean, I wouldn't say that."

"Because I'm your boss, but pretend I'm your boyfriend asking. What would you say then?"

My heart accelerates a little bit when he says boyfriend. I'm really happy with Will, but I spent a lot of months crushing on this ridiculously handsome billionaire. "If you were my boyfriend, I'd say that cowboy boots don't really fit with your overall image."

"So basically, I'm not at all rugged." He laughs, and then he sighs. "Disappointing, but probably accurate."

I shrug. "You're handsome enough and confident enough to pull off most anything, but I wouldn't say this dovetails with your natural style."

"Too bad," he says. "Because I'm about to buy a dude ranch over in your hometown, and I'll need something to wear that will keep my toes safe when I'm riding a horse or, like, moving cattle around."

I can't think of a single thing more ridiculous than the idea of David Park, corporate mogul, *moving* cattle around. Actually, I don't think I've ever heard anyone say they are 'moving cattle around.' The whole thing is as ridiculous as imagining Will, addressing a boardroom full of investors in a suit and tie.

"I doubt sneakers will really be appropriate, so what else could I wear?"

Something he said finally sinks in. "Wait. A *dude* ranch?" What even is that, exactly? I've never been quite sure.

His eyes widen. "Wait. You didn't know?"

I blink.

"I assumed your brother would have told you."

There must be neurons loose in my brain, because it feels like a moment right out of a movie. How many ranches could there really be for sale in my hometown? He must be talking about buying my family ranch, from *Patrick*. I shake my head a bit, as if to clear out the cobwebs. "It's been a long weekend. My niece is moving in, and that has been nonstop drama. Did you say you're putting in an offer on my brother's ranch—my family home?"

David Park beams. "You were so upset he was selling. That's what gave me the idea. At least this way, you'll be able to have a say in what's done with it." He's beaming at me, like this is exactly what I wanted.

I have no idea how to respond.

"And, it's the perfect time. Now that we're winding up a lot of the details here, I'll be hiring a property manager who'll take over most of what you've been doing in the interim."

A property manager, who will know how to run a retreat properly, something about which I know nothing.

I'm about to be out of a job.

"But don't worry," he says. "Who better to run the ranch operation out there than you?"

"What exactly are you thinking we'll do with it?" I ask.

"You know a lot of the guests here have been asking about the local economy, and when we tell them how many ranchers live around here, they all want to see a cattle ranch up close."

"Yeah, that's true," I say. "But—"

"We'll be able to offer them an authentic cattle ranch experience. Or, you know, as much of one as they want. There may be a bit of a learning curve, showing the cute stuff and not the manure and mud and whatnot."

"Whatnot?"

"You know, like slaughtering the cows and stuff would probably not be very fascinating to them. Those things would definitely not be part of the tour."

"We don't kill them," I say. "We take them to a sale yard and people like that Derek guy come and buy them."

"Right," David says. "Of course."

"So you're thinking we'll get rid of most of the cattle and—"

He stands up, shaking his head vehemently. "Not at all. You'll be in charge of supervising the people who run the actual ranch, and then we'll have a little bunkhouse built and guests can go stay there. They'll have a chance to learn as much or as little as they want to know from the ranch hands, when time permits, and from the guides we'll be paying to stay there."

I can pretty much guarantee that every single resident of Manila will hate this. It might even be more wrong than those shiny black boots David's wearing. Plus, what kind of person is going to be willing to run a ranch with *tourists* traipsing all over the place? Forget the liability and the hassle—there would be no privacy at all. It sounds absolutely awful.

And I need to figure out how to make it work, because if I don't, I'm out of a job. "Well, that's pretty exciting." But I have to ask. "What happens if Patrick doesn't sell to you?"

David waves his hand through the air. "He will, I'm sure. The only other people to offer were some locals— Kevin something and his brother. Their offer was a mess, or so my agent says. Small towns are strange, but everyone knows everyone's business and that can be helpful in situations like this."

Oh, no. Poor Kevin and Jeff. If my family's ranch has to go to someone else, at least I know they'll do a nice job running it. "But if they *did* happen to beat your offer, what would happen to me? Would I get two weeks' severance, at least?"

David sits down abruptly and wheels his desk chair over until he's less than a foot away. "Donna Ellingson. What kind of boss do you think I am?"

I'm not quite sure, honestly. He's smart as a whip. He's hard-working. He's kind and polite and respectful. He seems to value people and sustainable business. He saved me by offering me a good job when I had no skills to recommend me other than my familiarity with the area.

But none of that means he'll do any more than the legal minimum for someone who didn't have a job with his company before six months ago and will soon be superfluous.

"You'll have a job with our corporate office in California whenever you want one, and if for some reason this dude ranch plan doesn't happen, I'd do my best to find you something else you could do here. Barring all else, a very comfortable six-week severance package with benefits and a strong recommendation would be the absolute minimum I'd offer."

I should have known he'd do at least that much, but the possibility that everything will work out being contingent on my *brother* makes me ridiculously nervous. As if my day needed to get worse, when I call Aiden on my way home, he doesn't answer his phone.

He's always supposed to answer on my drive home, per our mutual agreement. It's the time window I was promised. So far, he's answered less than a third of the time. When I call Charles, he always has some kind of self-righteous, indignant excuse. They were eating dinner. Aiden was busy with friends. He was at a ball game.

He's being a great father, and I'm not necessary—that's the message. Aiden's having way more fun out there with his father and grandparents than he does here with me. The sad part is that it might actually be true. When you're able to parent for just a week here or there, or even a few weeks over the summer, it's easy to make every day into a party.

But kids don't flourish from partying all the time. They have to buckle down and learn. They need a routine. They need to eat their broccoli. It's just that no one thanks you for making them a model human being. No, what they want is another KitKat bar—never mind the stomachache coming around the bend.

I force myself not to worry about Aiden not answering yet again. I'm sure it's fine—totally fine. After all, he comes home in less than three weeks. Then it's back to normal for all of us. There'll probably be a bit of a bumpy transition, but then things will level out, I'm sure. Aiden will get used to going to bed on time again, to limited screen time, and to reading books instead of watching television. He'll stop complaining every time he can't have fast food for dinner, and he'll start eating his vegetables without twenty minutes of negotiations and pouting first.

This is what happens every time he visits his dad—only it'll be worse this time because of how long he's there. Five weeks is an eternity for young kids.

When I pull up in front of my house, Will's waiting for me. And my rancher boyfriend looks *just right* in cowboy boots. They're well-worn, they look great with his Wranglers, and he walks in them like he's been wearing them for his entire life.

"Hey," I say.

"Hope you don't mind that I was waiting on you," he says. "I finished up early today and didn't want to miss out on even a minute of our time."

*Our time.* My heart does a little flip-flop at that. He's always saying things that make me a little weak-kneed, and he doesn't even seem to realize it. I think that's why it works, instead of triggering my corny reflex. He really would rather sit around bored for half an hour than miss out on fifteen minutes with me. How adorable is that? And why did it take me so long to fall for him?

When my stomach growls, I stifle a groan. Dinner just keeps coming around every single day, like a sneaky assassin that wants me to look unprepared and dimwitted. "What did you want to do for dinner?"

"Beth's moving in tonight?" Will asks. "Is that right?"

"She brought her three suitcases over last night," I say. "I think that's all she's got."

Will frowns. "Are you kidding?"

I shrug. "She said they packed the rest to take with them. Patrick apparently told her she's not going to last two weeks, and she'll thank them for taking her other stuff to Washington."

"Well." His nostrils flare. "I'd be lying if I said I'll miss that guy. Hope that doesn't offend you."

I laugh.

"Dinner with Beth, then?" he asks.

"Sure."

He takes my bag that doubles as a briefcase for any files I bring home, and we head for the door. His phone bings three times before we reach it.

"Just Mom," he says. "Inviting us to dinner. I'll tell her we've got plans."

I think about her rolls and start to salivate. I grab his arm and yank before he can make that huge mistake. "Why would you do that?"

He meets my eyes. "You want to go back? We went like three days ago."

I shrug. "Will there be bread?"

He laughs. "Probably, but lemme ask."

Another bing, and he swivels his screen around. His mother responded with a photo. Be still my greedy little heart. Beautiful, shamrock-shaped rolls, all golden and soft.

"Italian food," he says. "She made lasagna, apparently."

"Yes," I say. "But make sure Beth can come, if she wants to." It would really suck for me if we can't get those rolls, but I need to stay loyal. I mean, I *really should* stay loyal on her first official night eating dinner, right?

But the rolls. I can't help sighing at my own goodness.

"Mom knows she's moving in. I'm sure she's more than welcome."

Will knows his mother, and I know Beth. The second she sets eyes on the image of the rolls, she's nodding her head vigorously. "Oh, yes, let's go there for dinner."

"She's as good a cook as Abby," I say. "Only, we get invited a lot more often."

"Suh-weet," Beth says, as though the word has two syllables. Teenagers are a little obnoxious, but their exuberance is also charming. I'm trying to focus on the good things.

"Did you get your room set up?" I ask. She's taking the room that was supposed to double as both a guest room and my office. Since I've been doing most of my after-hours work while sitting on my bed, and I haven't had any guests, I'm guessing I'll survive just fine without it. Thankfully Will set up the bed last night, and then he dragged the chest of drawers out of the storage closet and into her room.

"Those drawers are all full of table cloths and stuff." Beth shrugs. "I wasn't sure what to do with them."

Moths and dust bunnies are probably keeping them company. I'd toss the lot of them, but they're from my mom. "I forgot about that. I'll clean those out tomorrow."

"No rush by me. I got the sheets you left on the bed, so I have somewhere to sleep."

So far, parenting someone else's teen has been a breeze, but that feels a little bit too much like famous last words, so I retract them in my head before they can come back to bite me.

I've also been expecting some kind of fallout from Patrick and Amelia, but they just kind of shrugged it off. Clearly my brother doesn't think Beth will stay. Or, the scarier thought is that he doesn't care whether she does. Could he be relieved? Surely he's not that selfish.

I'm choosing not to think that badly of my brother.

When we arrive at Will's parents', the smell of garlic and onions hits me like an olfactory wall. I pause for a moment to enjoy it. My mom used to cook, when she was feeling up to it, but it was never really very good. She made spaghetti in a crock pot, for instance. It turned into a gelatinous mass of goo we ladled out with a big spoon, and it was made with the cheapest can of spaghetti sauce we could buy at the store, and the cheapest noodles. She'd just dump it into the crock pot with a few cups of water and let it run.

I had no idea how gross it was until I left home. The first time I tried to make spaghetti that way, my roommates were horrified.

I'm loving the idea of having a mother and father who are both happy to see me, and who actively make meals and invite me to come over and eat them. It's inspiring to see someone being the kind of mother I hope I'll be to Aiden one day. Although, if I want to do that, I'll need to take lessons on cooking from Abby or Will's mom.

The kinds of meals Charlie demanded were not practical: braised Cornish game hens with a cherry sauce, crab-meat-garnished eggs benedict with a fresh hollandaise sauce, or paté-crusted quail on a bed of mushroom risotto.

I can make those, thanks to terrifying grilling by a chef at the Culinary Lab Cooking school who taught private classes—that was my Christmas present one year, so I could make presentable dinners and pretend I made them all the time—but I hated making and eating that kind of pretentious junk. When no one was coming over, I usually ate whatever I made for Aiden, so a lot of mac and cheese, peanut butter sandwiches, and hotdogs.

"Welcome, Beth," Mrs. Earl says. "I'm so happy you could come, too."

"Actually," Mr. Earl says, "that's why we invited these two goofballs back. We heard there was a new family member who would be around and wanted to say hello."

Beth's a little shy at first, but by the time Mrs. Earl

passes around the rolls and salad, she's smiling and chatting comfortably. They have a natural way of connecting with people that I love.

"I can't believe that ranch is going to be sold," Mrs. Earl says as she's collecting the empty plates after dinner. "It has belonged to the Ellingsons for as long as I can remember."

"But with Patrick leaving, there's no one from our family to run it," I say. "It really is the end of an era."

"You don't think Aiden might want it?" Mr. Earl asks.

I snort. "He's a kid. He wants everything. That doesn't mean he gets everything."

"But later on, when he's an adult, do you think he'll be disappointed?"

I can't imagine my nerdy little guy running a ranch, even as an adult. Although, he did get his hands pretty dirty helping Will with that car. Who knows? I shrug. "It's happening when he's so young, I think he'll just accept it."

"Would you consider buying it yourself?" Mr. Earl asks. "Will could help you run it—"

I can't help it. I start laughing. "I'm utterly unfit to run a ranch," I say. "And beyond that, I have no interest in it."

"Leave her alone, Bob," Mrs. Earl says. "I had no interest either in being involved with yours, and I've done just fine with my hotel."

"And now we have two businesses with no one to take over running them," Mr. Earl says.

"It's a good problem to have," Will says. "And you know I'll take over the ranch when you're truly ready to be done."

It's good for Will to have a plan in place.

"Won't your sister take over the hotel?" I ask. "She's off at college, but—"

Will sighs. "She's positive she won't. She's fallen in love with stage design and wants to work on plays and movies. Not much of that around here."

"How's your job going?" Beth asks me. "It must be cool working for a billionaire."

"Mr. Park's demanding," I say. "And I don't like driving all the way over to Dutch John every day, but the job's challenging in the best way and I've learned a lot."

"It's neat you were able to find it just as your brother cut you out of the school gig," Will says. "Sometimes the timing in life works out perfectly." He takes my hand under the table. He could totally do it out in the open, but it feels more fun this way, somehow. Like it's our secret. It makes me feel like giggling.

"How's the retreat going over there?" Mr. Earl asks. "Lots of guests starting to arrive?"

"So far, so good," I say. "We're not far from most everything being done. Or at least, all the big stuff. The soft launch has gone well, and we have a hard and fast launch in about six weeks." I stand up, reluctantly, and start helping Mrs. Earl gather up the dishes. I feel like I need to be doing *something*, now that I'm thinking about my impending unemployment.

"You're the assistant project manager?" Mrs. Earl asks. "Is that what Will tells me?"

I nod. "Yep."

"What happens when it's all finished?" she asks.

My future mother-in-law's smarter than I am, apparently. For some reason, I didn't see the obvious. "Um, well." I drop the fork I was holding.

"I'm sure they'll have something for her to do over there," Will says. "She's been indispensable to Mr. Park."

I wince. "He did say he could find me a job—in California."

Will stiffens.

"But also, he's made an offer on your dad's ranch, or so he says." I look at Beth. "If he buys it, he wants me to kind of start a new project there." I hope I'm not telling her

82

something I shouldn't disclose. Patrick would *hate* the idea of people poking around on his ranch, learning about cows and the country life.

"A project?" Will still looks stunned.

"He thought I could run it," I say. "Since I know a little about ranches and cowboys and whatnot."

Will laughs.

Beth shifts in her chair.

"Wait," Will says. "Are you serious? You're going to give tours to city people who come into town? Like, get paid so they can laugh at us?"

"It won't be like that," I say. "A lot of people are curious, and that doesn't mean they'll be laughing—"

"Like we're zoo animals?" Mr. Earl asks.

"No," I say. "Nothing like that."

"If your work is ending, you should come work for me," Mrs. Earl says. "I'm always short-staffed—"

"I don't want to make beds and mop floors," I snap. "I may not have a college degree, but I almost do. I want to use my brain."

Mrs. Earl frowns. It may be the first time she's ever frowned at me. "Are you saying I *don't* use my brain, running a hotel?"

"No," I say. "I'm not saying that at all, but your position is filled. You already run it. What would I do? I'd have to clean rooms, right? I mean, it's either that, or do what you're already doing."

"You could take over for me, so that I could work part time."

But splitting one job between two people. . .means we'd both be part time. Plus, I'd essentially be taking over her life, just like Will's essentially been stuck taking over for his father. Patrick's words come back to me then, as if he's standing right here, mocking me.

*I just wish she liked me, instead of wanting me to turn into her dad.*

Does Will want me to turn into his mother? Does his father want Will to become just like he is? They're happy, it's true, and I like them a lot, but I need to live my own life, and so does Will.

"Thank you so much for dinner," I say abruptly. "But I have a long way to drive in the morning, and I better get to bed so I'm not too tired to do it. After all. I may only have a few weeks left. I should do my best work while I still have a job."

## ❧ 8 ❧

## AMANDA

**M**andy isn't talking to me, other than terse answers to work things, but it might have been worth it. So far, this date with the hot doctor is really panning out.

I might end up with someone just as smart as Abigail. Who knows?

"So, I had them draw four vials of blood, right?" His eyes are practically sparkling.

"Okay," I say.

"And then it turns out, we didn't need all four tests. We only needed three."

"Okay," I say again like a dope.

"But when I go back into the room, the patient's looking at the last vial. It's still sitting on the counter."

"Yeah." Look at me. Spicing my side of this convo up with a *yeah*. So maybe the date isn't going as well from my end. I bite my lip so at least he might think about wanting to kiss me.

"Anyhow, the patient points at the blood we didn't use. 'What about that one?' she asks. And then I explain that we don't need it. It's extra. And she looks horrified. Like, stands up, throws up an index finger and starts berating me."

"People are pretty crazy," I say.

"Oh, that's not even the good part yet."

I blink.

"The second I go to leave the room, she hops up and runs to the counter. Before I can stop her, she pops the top off that vial and *drinks* it. I say, 'Whoa, what are you doing?' and she says, 'I didn't want to waste it.'" He laughs then, and it's carefree, unselfconscious, and contagious.

His story was weirdly funny, in a medical way, but it's his manner and the way he tells it that really makes me laugh.

"And people think those werewolf movies are harmless." He shakes his head. "Some people can't tell reality from fiction."

"Vampire," I say.

"Huh?"

"They're vampire movies, the ones where people drink blood." I smile a little bit, enjoying correcting him just a bit too much. But then, it's nice when the super smart person you're talking to screws up a few little things. Makes them seem more human. That's actually my biggest problem with Abby. Girlfriend never makes a single mistake. Not ever. Or at least, not one I'm smart enough to catch. It's exhausting, always feeling less-than around her.

"You'd think a doctor would know that," someone at the table next to us says.

And then, almost in slow motion, like I'm on a romantic comedy set in Hollywood, filming a movie or something, I turn toward the sound.

A gorgeous face, a famous face, a face I know quite well is smirking at me. "Fancy seeing you here," Eddy says.

I'm going to kill Mandy. It's the only way he could possibly have known that I'm here. Green River may not be huge, but there's no way Eddy *coincidentally* ended up at the taqueria closest to the hospital where Dr. Travis Harkey works.

No. Way.

"Don't let me interrupt," Eddy says. "Just overheard part of your conversation and found it funny that the physician didn't know it was vampires who suck blood, not werewolves."

"Maybe work a little harder not to interrupt other people," I say. "It's rude."

"Isn't that—" My date cuts off and turns to face me. "Is he your boyfriend. . . or not?"

"Yes," Eddy says.

At the same time as I say, "Not."

"A stalker, then?" Travis asks. "Because I may have taken an oath to do no harm, but I don't count keeping women safe as doing harm." He flexes his pecs, and I wonder whether it was on purpose or some kind of masculine reflex.

Eddy starts laughing. "I'm real scared, doc. Let me tell you how terrified I am."

"You should be," Travis says. "Because in school, they taught me where all the organs in your body are, and I'm pretty sure I could rupture most of them using just this fork."

"Okay." I stand up. "I think we were essentially done, and I know you said you only had half an hour." Which is the only reason I agreed to meet him for lunch. "You'd better head back in, doc."

"Are you sure I should?" He glares at Eddy.

"Move along, eager beaver." Eddy waves. "Lives to save and all that do-gooderly stuff. Meanwhile, I can take any day off for lunch, because we vets mostly put the broken things down." He arches one eyebrow and glares full-on.

Travis stands up, throws a handful of bills on the table, glances at me for confirmation, and walks away, not taking

Eddy's juvenile bait at all. It makes me like him more, to be honest.

Meanwhile, Eddy's muttering to himself like a mental patient. "Yeah, that's right. Walk away, loser. You've got blood pressure medicine to prescribe and *werewolves* to deal with."

I roll my eyes, but I walk the three feet over to his table and sit down. "What do you think you're doing here?"

"You know, Steve drove all the way out here under the pretense of buying zip ties, and then he and Abby started dating after that."

"Eddy."

"Why are you dating that loser?"

"By loser, do you mean the physician who just saved a patient's life, moments before buying me lunch?"

Eddy's eye roll would make any sorority girl at UCLA jealous.

"How in the world did you think that crashing my date was going to help us?"

"Help? You think I thought I was helping something?" Eddy stands up, and even though as far as I can tell he's only had chips and salsa, he tosses a big wad of cash on the table. "When I went by your place, and Mandy told me you were here, on a date with one of her doctors, I stopped thinking. I just started driving. It was that, or start drinking."

"That's really great." I stand up, too. "You're definitely winning me over with this 'I'm an inch away from losing it' spiel."

"I don't want to win you over." His eyes are haunted. "I just want you to want me like I want you again."

"Well, I don't." My words are hasty, cruel, and apparently effective.

Eddy's shoulders droop. His eyes flutter. And then he turns and starts to walk away.

I should let him go. I clearly can't handle anything he makes me feel. But in that moment, my heart feels shredded and flambéed. I know I did the damage, but it feels like I was also the victim.

"Wait," I say.

But he doesn't.

I have to rush after him, the only sound in my world the pounding of my flats on the pavement and the beating of my heart in my ears.

"Eddy!" I catch his arm just as he reaches his truck.

"What do you want?" He yanks free of my grasp, and when he turns to face me, he looks angry. "I love you, Amanda. I love you more than I love drinking and drugs. I love you more than I love rock and roll. More than I love my guitar. More than I love healing broken things, and that's my whole job. It's my passion. It's the only thing that got me through the darkest part of my entire life."

I have no idea what to say to him.

"Did I ever tell you how I knew I was going to be a vet?"

I shake my head.

"I had been sober for over a year. A very hard, very dark year. But I had made it, and then I got my college admittance letters, and I didn't get in to a single school."

He pauses, his eyes not focused. "I knew why. It was my own fault, but it still hurt. And suddenly the only thing I wanted was a drink. I'd never wanted a drink so badly in my entire life. I knew where my parents kept their alcohol locked up—because of me. But I knew where their key was, too."

I can't make a simple "uh huh," or "sure," while listening to him talk. It's not that kind of story. So I don't say anything at all.

"I went outside to get the key. They kept it underneath

a bird house. But when I went out there, do you know what I heard?"

I shake my head.

"A tiny squeaking sound. I almost ignored it and just went inside, but I hadn't heard it before. It sounded like a baby chick."

What was it? I want to ask, but I don't want to push. It feels like a story he has to tell at his own pace.

"It was a squirrel. Two, actually. They had hair on them, but not too much. They were skinny—emaciated looking, really. And those two little guys were squeaking every thirty seconds or so." He finally meets my eyes. "You can't bottle feed a squirrel. Not at that age. And no place we called would take them. I had to dropper feed them, or they would choke—asphyxiate. I dropper fed those squirrels around the clock until they got big enough to release. They loved me like I was their dad."

"You didn't keep them?"

"They hated everyone else," he says. "And they were destroying things all over the house. Mom said it was them or her."

"That must have been hard."

"It made me think that if I could save them, maybe I could save other animals. It gave me a purpose. I became a vet tech, and then eventually went to community college, applied for a university transfer, and then went to vet school."

"I didn't know."

"But Amanda, I love you more than that, more than healing animals. More than everything. And you don't care. I blew it, and now it's too late."

I can't tell him what he wants to hear. It may not be too late, but it may be. I just don't know yet.

"Why did you tell me to wait?" His eyes are angry, sad, upset, hurt, and hopeful all at the same time.

"I meant to wait for me, but really I meant that I wanted you to wait a little longer," I say. "I didn't go on a date to hurt you. I went to see what it made me feel."

He swallows.

"When David Park took me to the wedding, I just didn't want to be alone. I was numb—nothing he said or did had any effect on me. But this felt different. I liked the look of the handsome doctor. I liked how it made me feel when he asked me out."

And now I'm just hurting him more.

"But on that date?"

Eddy inhales.

I shrug. "Nothing. I felt nothing for him, about him, or with him."

"What does that mean?"

"I don't know," I say. "Look. You have your past, and I have mine. My husband married me, and then proceeded to forget all about me. I know you're not like him, but you are in some ways, too. I need to. . .I don't know. I need to decide whether I can trust you. I need faith that you won't leave me again."

He keeps staring at me.

"That will take time. I need you to wait, even if I'm not waiting. That's what I need. Patience and faith from you, even if it may be imbalanced, because that's how I felt while you were gone. Imbalanced. Abandoned. Unimportant."

"Are you punishing me? Or trying to work things out?"

I shrug. "I don't know. Maybe both." I stare at him for a moment. Why do we want to hurt the people we love the most? "Can you handle it?"

He steps toward me. He's much taller, but he doesn't get so close that I have to crane my neck. "I can do anything, if you're there at the end of it."

"I can't promise I will be," I say.

"The chance is enough for me."

The whole drive home, I keep seeing his earnest, intent eyes as he says, "The chance is enough for me."

Would it be enough for me, if our roles were reversed? I'm not sure. But his calm willingness to do whatever I asked means something. It soothed something inside of me.

It sticks with me all day.

My interactions with Mandy are smoother. My ability to deal with Maren's drama when she comes home from school is improved, too. And when Emery starts to bawl like she's at her father's funeral again because Maren shot her a sideways look for a clearly exaggerated story about a friend of hers from school, I'm remarkably zen about it.

"Must've been a great date," Mandy mutters after dinner.

"It went well." I can't help my secret smile. She would be pleased if she knew the best part of the date was having Eddy crash it.

"I thought maybe it would be horrible," Mandy says.

"Nope." My smile widens.

"Well, I'm going to toss some things on that burn pile," Mandy says. "I went through all those old files and pulled everything more than five years old, just like Abigail said I could. May as well get rid of them."

I don't argue with her. I just nod and watch her duck out the door.

She's doing really well with her physical therapy, looking more spry every day. I have no idea why she got a bug in her head today about clearing things out, but I'm not going to stop her. The amount of clutter in this house is pretty horrifying. I suppose that comes with more than eighty years of life, but still.

A shriek, followed by a yip outside, has me darting out the

front door. Did she fall? Is she short of breath? As I make it outside, there's a giant crash and then an explosion. Something in that burn pile caught something in Mandy's old barn on fire.

And now I have a sinking feeling that it's all going to burn.

I whip out my phone and call 911.

"Daggett County Emergency Services." The person who picks up sounds utterly calm.

"I need to report a fire," I practically shout. "I need someone here right away."

"What's the address of the affected property?"

"It's Amanda Saddler's place," I shout.

"I'll need the property address, ma'am."

I'm rattling it off, when I hear Mandy shouting.

"What's wrong?" I look around.

"Roscoe," Mandy says. "He went into the barn."

"Why would he do that?" My voice sounds hysterical. "Why? He never goes in there."

"He shot into the corner, there," Mandy says. "Maybe he saw something? Maybe he tucked a toy in there?"

I ball my hands into fists.

"What's going to happen, Mom?" Emery asks, her eyes huge beside me. "Is Roscoe going to burn up?"

I wrap an arm around her. "No, baby. Roscoe's sensible. He's going to be fine."

I call for him, over and over, until my voice is ragged, but he never shows up.

Neither does the fire department.

"Can you go inside and get my phone?" Amanda Saddler asks. "I want to record some of this." Her eyes look so sad. Almost desperate.

"Sure," I say. I drag the girls inside with me. They don't need to watch as Mandy's barn burns to the ground with Roscoe inside.

I'm sure Mandy's trying to distract me, too. But when I come back out, Mandy's also gone.

And Roscoe's wagging his tail at me, covered in soot and ash.

I glance around frantically. Where did Mandy go? How did Roscoe get back? And then I see a chunk of her sweater, caught on the side of the broken barn window. She must have gone inside to get Roscoe out.

"Mandy!" I race for the window, desperate to see where she is now, but the fire department's finally here, and someone's holding me back.

"MANDY!" I beat on the man's arms and chest. "Let me go. She went inside. Let me go."

They're putting on suits to prepare to go into the barn to search for her when there's another huge explosion.

And the barn roof collapses.

The man closest to me meets my eyes.

And I know.

If she's in there, there's no way she's alive. Not anymore.

# 9

# ABIGAIL

When someone dies, it always feels a little surreal. I remember staring at Nate's body in the casket and thinking, "It doesn't even look like him. Maybe it's not. Maybe he's still alive and this isn't happening."

Although, Nate was a little different.

From the day his eyes turned yellow, until the day he died, it was like a new thing happened to him every day to change him from the Nate I knew, to the bizarre, unknowable Nate that passed away. His body betrayed him, and no matter what we did, it just kept on letting us down in new ways.

But this funeral is even more . . .abnormal.

All they could find was Amanda Saddler's necklace, a scrap of her sweater, one shoe, and her dentures, half melted. It's wrong—losing someone so completely in that way. It's hard for those left behind to truly mourn. If I'm being honest, I'm half in denial, so I shouldn't be surprised that poor Amanda, who has never been the best at acceptance and peace, is really, really struggling.

A lot of people have shown up to pay their respects, but

she's not letting any of them walk by the memorial area. I push past the line of people and insert myself next to her.

"This whole thing is a joke," she's muttering. "Who wades into a burning building for a *dog*?" Amanda's got dark grey runnels down her face where tears have streaked her cheeks nonstop. Her eyes are puffy. Her hair, usually picture perfect, looks like a swallow made a nest in it.

"Amanda," I say.

"No," she says. "Don't tell me people are waiting. Don't tell me I have to move. Don't tell me that they want to walk by." She turns to face the line of people. "She burned up in a building. Did you hear? There's not even anything *in* this casket. You don't even need to walk by here."

I don't bother pointing out that, by that logic, she doesn't need to stand there either. Instead, I wrap an arm around her shoulders and forcibly drag her away from the casket, while trying my best to look like I'm consoling her. "Listen, the point of a funeral is—"

"Yes," she nearly shouts. "*What is the point?* Please, tell me." She looks from side to side, seeing the people, but also not really seeing them. "Who *are* all these people? I barely know any of them. They didn't come over to see her. They didn't go to lunch with her. They never called. She was basically alone up there, on the top of that hill, and until we showed up, she was constantly lonely. But here they are, pretending they were close, pretending they cared about her, *now that she's gone.*" More tears are streaming down her face.

It's a really good thing no one is videotaping this. Steve's standing about ten feet away, monitoring to make sure. Something like this going viral about Champagne for Less would be *very, very* bad.

Amanda's about two feet past the mental break I was worried was coming, so I hug her, right here, in the middle of the funeral parlor. My arms wrap around her as tightly as they can, in the same way I wanted to at her husband's funeral, but I couldn't.

I didn't know her well enough then, but I do now.

That sad day, I was just one of the droves of people who walked by awkwardly, feeling compelled to show my sorrow at his passing, but not really understanding what it meant to the very near and the very dear.

But not this time.

This time, I know Amanda, and I knew Mandy. I can be here for her in a way I wasn't then.

Plus, I've lost my own person and I know how it feels.

Funerals bring out the strangest responses from people.

There are those of us who have lost someone too early, someone who was *everything* to us. Those of us who have been wrecked by death, and who (eventually) kept soldiering on afterward. I've never served in combat or gone to war, but I suspect it's a bit like that connection. I've heard veterans can see each other across the room and feel a link to other vets. A tiny head bob. A knowing look. They *get* it.

Those people walk by and say something like, "I'm so sorry. I'm still reeling from the loss of my sister." Or my brother. Or my husband. My child. My mother.

They *understand.*

And then there are the fresh, the shiny, and the new souls of the world. They may not actually be young, but they're young in spirit and in heart, because they've never endured a traumatic loss. They may have seen death from afar, and they may know in general terms what it's like, but they don't *really get it*. They invariably say things like, "I'm so sorry for your loss. When my cat died. . ." Or they pat your arm and say, "I totally get it. My grandfather passed when I was seven." Or even worse, they tell you how wrecked they are at *your* loss. "Your husband meant the world to me. If you have time, I'd love to get together and chat. I think it might help me process."

If I'm ever at a funeral for someone I wasn't close to, my main goal is to make no part of that funeral about me. It's not about me. It's about the immediate family and close friends of the bereaved. It just is.

Because what Amanda needs to learn is that the funeral today isn't actually for Amanda Saddler at all. It's about Amanda Saddler, but it's *for* Amanda Brooks. It's for the ones who are left behind, so they can come to grips with their loss and process it. So they can accept that the person they shaped their life around is gone and now their life shape will forever be changed.

Because shapes are always changing. That's what happens when life moves on, and although we have a hole in our hearts, those hearts have to keep on pumping for the other people we love. For the people who have shaped their lives around ours. Kids. Friends. Lovers. Siblings.

At least instead of blocking the line, instead of shouting at everyone here, Amanda's now quietly fuming in the corner. She might look a little lost and homeless, but she's not accosting anyone.

Finally, though, the time for the formal funeral service comes. We all migrate into the largest room the funeral home has to offer. It's crammed entirely full.

Amanda's supposed to be giving the eulogy.

There's no one better to do it. She insisted, and I knew she was right so I didn't argue, but now I feel like I should have. After Nate died, I knew I should get up and speak, but the hole in my heart was just too big, too raw, and too deep. The loss was so profound that I couldn't make any sense of it. And that's your job when you're up there, talking about the person who's gone. You're supposed to make sense of their life for all the people their death has terrified.

Amanda's clearly not going to do it. She's looking at her hands and whispering something.

So, when the time comes, I hate it. I'm grieving too. But I stand up.

Because there's no one else.

My heart races. My mind shrinks from the task. I should have known this would happen, but I didn't, and I've prepared nothing. I have no idea what to say. But it's been my job for years to speak for those who can't speak for themselves, like Mandy. I defend people when they can't do a task themselves, like Amanda Brooks. So I pick up the mantle today, and I walk to the microphone.

So many people are gathered.

Some of them are familiar. Some of them are utterly new. It's a brisk morning, and plenty of people are wearing black shawls. One person in the back is even wearing a dark hoodie with their face covered. They almost look like an executioner or something. Like the grim reaper is here, waiting for me to finish so he can retrieve Mandy's melted dentures.

It's a solemn group.

"We're gathered here today for a bad reason. Someone we all dearly love has died in an unexpected way." I wipe a tear from my cheek.

"When I came for the summer, Amanda Saddler welcomed me brightly. She'd been in this community longer than I'd been alive, longer than my mother had been alive, and yet, while plenty of people were less than friendly, she was delighted to have me move in next door."

I look the people who are gathered in the eye, one at a time, scanning the audience. "I'm sure you all had similar experiences with her. For a woman in her eighties, she had seemingly limitless energy. She bounded. She conquered. She never shrank back. And when I left to go back to Houston. . .and then returned with no notice and even less of a plan? She showed up to help me clean and unpack. She didn't rest on the excuse of her age. She didn't stand back and let others do things that needed to be done. She plowed ahead and did them herself, always."

"One of the most surprising things I discovered about her is how deeply she loved the people who mattered to her. She never wavered. She never faltered. When my children and I lost the ranch, she took it upon herself to right what she perceived as a wrong. When our dear friend Donna needed a place to stay, she sprang into the breach."

I wish I knew more about her early years. I wish I could say something about the younger Mandy. "When it came to gift giving, no one can match her. She thought about what we needed, and she gave that. As a mother, I can say that she was one of the best mothers I knew, even without having children of her own. She made the hard choices her adopted daughters needed without flinching, up to and including being willing to change her name, to a nickname she disliked, so we would all be less confused."

A few people chuckle at that one.

"Mandy Saddler spoke the hard truths that we didn't want to hear, much less say, and then she stood by and patted our backs while we came to grips with the revelations in her words. On the day she died, she went into that building to save someone else we cared for, a beloved dog, who had saved Amanda Brooks' life in the past. But really, she did it because she didn't want to watch the pain his loss would cause her darling adopted daughter, Amanda. Roscoe's alive today, because Mandy took Amanda under her wing, and when she did that, she never backed down. If that stupid roof hadn't collapsed. . ."

I take a moment, because now I can't speak at all. Emery described it for me, or I would have no idea what happened. Amanda won't talk about it at all.

This is far from the eulogy she deserves, but at least

Amanda's now listening, not bawling or muttering or yelling. I think that's progress. Now I just need to make some kind of sense of it all. "In the end, I'm so grateful for what Amanda Saddler has taught me and my children about loving fiercely, about apologizing when she's wrong, and about standing up for what's right, no matter the stakes. She's a beautiful person we will never forget. She's a soul that deserves to be remembered and revered for many years to come. I'm so grateful she came into our lives when she did." Tears are threatening again, and my brain feels mushy. I can't even seem to flog it into something better, no matter how hard I try. I finish lamely, with, "She will forever be missed." And then I rush back to my seat.

The rest of the funeral passes in a blur—from the moment I sit down, it's like my mind goes blank. I greet people. I murmur my condolences and my gratitude they came, and then I move to the next person.

It's strange to me that Amanda and I are hosting a funeral for a woman we didn't even know fifteen months ago. Amanda Saddler lived a very long life, but perhaps her most charming quality was her willingness to change things up, and that enabled her to make important attachments at a time when most people are in a nursing home or living with family.

That thought somehow makes me even more profoundly sad. There are so many things about her I hadn't learned. So many things I didn't know, and now I don't have a chance to learn them.

One of the great things about Steve is that our relationship is fresh and new. But I can't help drawing the parallels at today's funeral between my first marriage and my current marriage. Nate knew everything about me. Nate could practically finish my sentences on his own. Steve is exciting, but like Amanda Saddler, there are so many things I don't yet know about him that it's a little frightening that we're married.

It feels like I'm a usurper today, in some ways, pretending to have been important to Amanda, when so many people knew her better than I did. There were surely many people who had a bigger role in her story, but I'm the only one here to do a miserable job trying to tell it.

I regret not telling Mandy about my new baby when I had the chance. Now she'll never know, other than seeing it while looking down from heaven, which I firmly believe exists, and where I'm sure she went. One hand goes to my stomach as I think about how my life story is about to shift in a dramatic way. Babies are the ultimate plot twist. They change everything, forever.

And I still haven't told Steve.

The day I was going to. . .Amanda Saddler passed. And now it's the funeral. It feels too macabre, somehow, to spring this on him while everyone is reeling from her sudden and unexpected death. He would still be excited, but it feels *wrong* to be excited in this somber moment in time. I don't want that for our baby, for his or her new life to be overshadowed by a very distressing, very harrowing death.

So I wait. And I wait. And I wait some more. And as life trudges along, I decide that three days after the funeral is enough. It's no longer the only thing we think about. It's no longer the only thing we talk about. As sobering as that thought is, that we're only afforded a few *days* after our death, to have it coloring everything for everyone, I decide that Steve could use some happy news.

We all could.

I spend two hours in the middle of the day with my sign outdoors flipped to CLOSED, baking in the kitchen at my law office. It still feels weird, thinking of working in a place where I can also be *baking*. My life has certainly changed a lot in one year.

By the time I'm done, I'm staring at two perfect cookies. One is a pink frosted heart. The other is a blue one.

Each of them has another heart made of the opposite color of frosting nestled inside. It's just frosting, but I think the sentiment comes through loud and clear. We're going to have another little heart join our lives—in fact, it's already inside of me, beating by now. The joy I feel when I think about that eclipses everything else in my life.

I imagine a little boy with Steve's mischievous smile.

Or a little girl, with Steve's dancing eyes.

Either one would be a tremendous blessing that I never even considered. So what if I feel super sick and want to puke at the thought of eating one of the adorable cookies? Even when I have to race for the bathroom because *I thought about* thinking about eating one. . .it's alright. This is only temporary.

A baby will be in our lives forever.

It will change everything.

I carefully wrap the cookies in a little white box and then I stick the box in a bag, and I place it in the bottom of my bag. Steve won't be off work until seven, and he won't be home until after eight, and the rest of the day *crawls* by like an inchworm. No, like an inchworm in a pan of drying Elmer's glue.

Clients come by. Meetings are had. Research is done. Minutes tick and tock and tick some more. But finally, it's time to go home. And then it's time to make dinner. I help kids with homework. I review some paperwork for Ethan, and we plan the dates we'll go up and check on the cows.

I'm sliding leftover enchiladas into Tupperware when I break the bad news to him. "I don't think I'll be able to go up with you to check on the cows this year." I shouldn't really have done the cattle drive, probably, but I hadn't found out yet when we went.

"What?" Ethan's brow furrows. "But—"

"Don't worry," I say. "I have so many client meetings that I'm kind of worn out, but Jeff and Kevin can each go every other week. And of course, Steve can fill in when they can't."

"I thought Kevin and Jeff weren't doing part time for us anymore?"

They don't really want to, but I pushed pretty hard. And of course, I'm paying them. No one really understands why I can't rearrange my client things and go, especially since I usually like going up to check on the cattle—it's a long ride, but it's peaceful and the weather is gorgeous. I can't tell them my real reason, so I try to keep it vague. I'm sure that riding's probably still fine this early in pregnancy, but with my age, I'm not taking any chances. Leo will just have to miss me for a bit.

I'm sliding the last enchilada that will fit into the container when Ethan reaches for it. "Here, let me—"

But I didn't realize what he was doing. I went to set the container on the counter right as Ethan went to grab it, sending it flying backward, where it splatters all over my arms, shirt, and pants.

"Oh, no," Ethan says. "I'm sorry."

Steve will be home in less than an hour, and now I look like a kid who was fingerpainting with tomato sauce and melted cheese. "It's no big deal." Nothing in the world makes more messes than a baby. Maybe it's a good reminder of my impending future.

"I'll clean this up. Why don't you go shower?" Ethan looks sick. "I really am sorry. I was trying to help. Who knew I'd still be such a clumsy mess? I'm almost twenty."

"I don't think almost nineteen counts as almost twenty."

Or, I hope it doesn't. "I'm not ready to have a twenty-year-old son."

"You better get ready." Ethan grabs a rag and grins at me. "The alternative isn't good."

Of course, then we both think about death, which makes us think about Amanda Saddler, and then I burst into tears.

"Oh, man," Ethan says. "I am so sorry. It's not a good day for me. Just go shower. I'll clean up, and we can pretend none of this happened."

I start to hug him, remember I'm covered with goo, and pause. "I love you, honey. You did nothing wrong. It's good that we still miss her, and I'll try and brace myself for the impending doom of a twenty-year-old son."

We're both smiling as I head for the shower. Once I'm undressing in front of the mirror, I realize that I managed, somehow, to get sauce in my hair. No wonder he suggested I shower and not just change my clothes.

I'm nearly done, shaving my armpits, when I feel it. I wish what I felt was the baby moving. It's way too early for that, but that would have been a good surprise. This is definitely not good.

It's a lump.

It's not very big. The size of a grape, maybe. But it stops my heart dead in my chest. It should *not* be there, on the side of my breast.

It should not be there at all.

Twenty minutes until Steve comes home and I give him cookies and tell him he's going to be a dad again. But all I keep hearing on repeat in my head is what he said, not that long ago, about a patient.

*Save the person. Always nix the not-quite-a-person-yet to save the existing person.*

Nix the 'not-quite-a-person-yet.'

It's just a tiny lump. Maybe it's nothing. But I can't help thinking about how we discovered Nate was sick. He had been complaining of heartburn for weeks. *Weeks.* I bought him Tums and told him to stop eating blueberries and tacos and anything spicy or acidic. I ignored his first symptom, basically.

It wasn't until his eyes turned yellow that we realized something was wrong.

And by then, it was far too late.

Steve might hear that story and tell me the moral is how important it is to act quickly in situations like this. But to me, the moral of the story is that it's very, very hard to live with yourself if you knowingly delay treatment on someone you love.

Which means, if this *is* a tumor, and if the tumor *is* cancerous, Steve is not going to find out until I'm about to have this baby. First I need to find out what's going on with this stupid lump, and then I'll decide when to tell him about the baby, and not a minute sooner.

Because there's no way I'm terminating this pregnancy.

If I've learned anything from Nate, it's that dying is the easy part. Living with yourself after someone you love has died? That's the hard part, and I don't think I could do it if I had to kill my own child. That thought propels me out of the shower and into my clothes.

My hair's still dripping on my shoulders when I reach the kitchen, and none of the kids are around when I chuck the cookies into the garbage disposal. I'm grinding them up when Steve walks in the door.

"Hey honey." He smiles.

I force a smile in return, but inside, I'm crying.

And maybe even dying.

# 10

# DONNA

Old people die.

It happens.

I know firsthand. I've lost my mother and my father, too.

A year ago, Amanda Saddler's passing barely would have registered with me. I mean, I've known her all my life, and she died in a rather unexpected way, leaping into a fire to save a dog, but it's not like her death is a huge shock.

We all knew it was coming sooner or later. But probably sooner, given her age and her heart complications.

So I'm surprised by how much it rocks me.

I can barely speak during her funeral, because I can't stop crying. Thanks to Amanda and Abigail, I've gotten quite close to her over the past months. When my mother and father shafted me, when my brother abandoned me, and when no one else in the world seemed to care, she did.

I'm living in a great rental house right now, much more than I should have been able to afford, and it's all because of her. Who knows what crap Charles might have pulled with Aiden's custody if she hadn't helped me out when she did?

Even so, I've mostly only spent a few girls' nights with her. I know Abby and Amanda are suffering much more than I am. I try to keep my chin up about it, and for me, that means doing something. I haven't done much scrapbooking in the last five or six years—hard to want to document a life you don't even like living—but after combing through my photo reel from the past year, I found a lot of great ones of her.

I'm arranging them carefully, page by page, when my phone rings.

"Hello?" I answer without thinking when I'm preoccupied. I really shouldn't do that, because it always leads to conversations like this.

"Dee," Patrick says. "I'm so glad you answered. I was worried you might screen me."

I suppress my automatic groan reflex. "Why would I screen you? Your daughter's *living* with me. You may have something critical to share."

"This isn't about Beth."

I knew it wouldn't be. He hasn't mentioned her living with me one single time since she moved in. You'd think that, just by watching an ostrich at a zoo, he'd have learned that sticking your head in the ground fixes nothing. But no, Patrick insists on doing it figuratively with most anything distasteful in his life.

"To what do I owe this pleasure, then?" I ask.

"Pleasure." He snorts. At least he's self-aware enough to know that I don't like to talk to him. "Believe it or not, this is a courtesy call from a caring brother."

This should be rich. I don't give him the pleasure of asking again why he's calling. This time, I just wait.

"Ahem. Well, yes. So, I'm calling to tell you that, even though I've had offers literally *pouring* in for the ranch, I will do the right thing and choose yours."

"Excuse me?"

"What? You don't believe me? I've had five offers already—it's true."

How can that be? Is he lying? What would he stand to gain, and what on earth does he mean that he'll accept *mine*?

He clears his throat again. "Fine. I'll admit that I was a little shocked myself there's so much interest."

"Patrick, *what are you talking about?*"

"First I got an offer above asking price from that Park fellow who's bought all that land over in Dutch John."

Okay, that's the one I know about. Still no new information.

"Okay." Does he remember I work for David? "I know about that."

"Oh, so you *do* know about some of the offers."

I grit my teeth.

"I've also had an offer from some investment capital guru named Helen Fisher. I looked her up, and she's legit. She owns, like, billions of dollars in stuff. Real estate all over. Companies. Stock. I can't figure out why she'd want my ranch, but maybe she knows David Park."

"She's Abigail's sister," I say.

My brother swears under his breath, using the kind of language Dad would've whipped him for using. Finally, he stops and says, "That stupid lawyer's sister is that rich? What are they doing here, really?"

"Focus, Patrick. Who else?"

"As if those two weren't enough, those local boys also scraped together a rather decent proposal."

Local boys? "You mean. . .wait, who?"

"Kevin and Jeff—they were working over at the Jones ranch for a while, then for Jed. I figured you knew about that one, too."

"I'm far less connected than you think."

"Your boss made an offer. Your best friend's tycoon

sister made an offer. Your friends' former employees made an offer."

"My boss wants it so that he can have tour groups see what a ranch looks like, and I'm sure you hate the idea of any working ranch being a tourist attraction, but—"

"I wasn't going to pick that guy, anyway—"

"But David Park plans to have me step in and help out. So I promise that the things you despise—"

"Wait." Patrick ruffles some papers. "You—are you saying you want me to take the offer from Mr. Park?"

"Who else's offer would I want you to accept?" I'm so confused now. Only, it hits me then what words he used earlier. He didn't say my *boss's* offer. He said he would choose *my offer*. "I didn't make an offer, Patrick."

"But your new boyfriend did."

There must've been some kind of misunderstanding. "I'm not dating David Park," I say. "I did sort of have a crush on him for a little while, but I'm dating—"

"Will Earl," Patrick says. "Do you really think I don't even know who you're dating? Although, this paperwork doesn't say whether it's an offer from him or his dad, I suppose. Is he a junior? His dad's named Will, too, right?"

I feel as though someone struck me in the face. My fingers go numb. My brain's sluggish. "You're saying the Earls made an offer on your ranch?"

"It's for right at the asking price," Patrick says. "I thought you'd want me to take it, since it's fair, even though it's not the highest amount."

"I had no idea they were offering any sort of money for the property," I say. "And I don't want you to give them special treatment."

Patrick starts to laugh. "Oh, Donna."

The patronizing undertone of his laughter puts my hackles up. "Why is this funny?"

"You looked so smug up there on your high horse. I

wonder how it feels, to know that your future in-laws want to control you, too." He hangs up.

I mean, it's Patrick. I don't care what he thinks. He's the pig who stole money from Mom and Dad's ranch to deal with his personal crap. Then he lied about it. He hit me. He left me to care for Dad, all the while intending to rob me blind. Once I figured him out, he manipulated me into giving him all the money anyway. . .and now he's selling the ranch he swore meant so much to him.

I really have no reason to care what he thinks.

So when Will shows up with burgers, I am perfectly calm. I'm not going to let Patrick rattle me. My in-laws are nothing like his. They're not even my in-laws, for heaven's sake. I'm just dating Will. None of the things Patrick's insinuating are even close to true. It's probably all a big misunderstanding.

But Will has barely stepped through the door when I ask, "Why did your parents put an offer on my brother's ranch without even asking me about it?"

Will's eyes widen and he drops the bag he's holding.

Fries spill out all over the floor, and the ketchup container spins round and round and round, finally stopping against my toe. Luckily, the lid stayed on. These are the details I'm focused on, because Will still hasn't answered my very pointed, very clear question.

"Do you have bronchitis?" I ask. "Did you lose your voice?"

"No," Will says. "It feels like we're in the middle of a fight, but I'm just getting here." He blinks. "I'm sorry, I'm trying really hard to catch up."

He's right, of course. I'm being monstrously unfair. It's like I've convicted him without a judge, a jury, or a trial. My tone sounded totally nuts. "I thought I wasn't upset, but I guess I am."

"My parents?" He bends over and rights the bag. Then

he starts to collect fries in his hands. "You're saying they're buying your family's ranch?"

"Not likely," I say. "Their offer was for asking price, and apparently my dad's mismanaged ranch has bizarrely become some kind of hot commodity out here in nowheres-ville."

Will's brow furrows. "It's a hot commodity? Why?"

"I had no idea either, but my boss wants it, as you know."

"Right. His authentic tourist trap."

"Apparently Kevin and Jeff do, but that's not really a surprise. They've wanted their own place for years. But also, Abby's sister inexplicably offered on it. . . and your parents. Patrick's insufferably giddy."

"I might have mentioned to my parents that your brother kind of tricked you into giving all the money from your dad's estate to him, and how crappy it was that he's now selling it and moving." Will sighs as he stands up, his hands full of floor-fries. "I'm going to. . ." He gestures at the kitchen.

"Right." I grab the bag and follow him. I set the bag on the counter and grab a paper towel, get it wet, and squeeze it out as he throws the fries out.

By the time I get back into the entryway to wipe the floor down, he's done washing his hands and he joins me. The sight of Will, crouching down next to me on the floor, nothing to do, but hands all jittery with concern, realigns my brain.

"I'm sorry." I stand up slowly. "I know you didn't do anything wrong."

"But your brother called and told you all this, and he always gets you all twisted up in a pretzel."

I snort. "Something like that, yes."

"Right, well, here's the thing. I certainly didn't offer on the ranch, and no one ran the idea past me. My guess is that my sentimental dad is more upset than we knew about your brother stealing from you and then selling up. And he and my mother probably figured I could work it until Aiden's old enough to take up the task himself." He's chuckling softly and shaking his head. "Dad's like that— gets really weird and nostalgic about family land."

"What if Aiden doesn't want to be a rancher?"

"That would never even occur to my dad." Will laughs. "He thinks that it's everyone's dream like it was his. You should hear him go off about how you can ranch *and* do whatever else you want to do. As if it's a side gig. Did they even consider what might happen if you dumped me? And assuming we stay together, why couldn't Aiden just take over *my* ranch?"

That's when it hits me. It feels like an assault, almost. Like his parents are buying the ranch because Will's ranch couldn't possibly go to a child who isn't Will's.

Am I being totally nuts?

Yes.

Does that mean I'm wrong?

"Do you think your parents would be okay with Aiden taking over your ranch?"

Will blinks. "I don't see why not."

"He's not your son."

Will shrugs. "I mean, not technically, no, but if we get married one day, and I'm not trying to say you have to marry me, but if we do, he'd be as good as my son."

"But not to your parents," I say.

"I don't think that's a fair assumption to make." Will frowns. "But even if they didn't want him to take over my ranch one day, which is a big stretch, they're the ones trying to buy him another one. Isn't that kind of the same thing?"

"Not if they're doing it to keep him away from yours."

"You're sounding. . . a little bit tin-foil hat right now," Will says. "I say that out of a good place."

I laugh. He's totally right. "Okay, look, I told my brother to just take whatever offer he wants, and not to give your parents priority."

"Thank goodness," Will says. "The last thing I need is another ranch I don't really want."

"Wait, you don't want your dad's?"

He shrugs. "I mean, I guess I do? I don't *not* want it, but I'd rather make money in other ways."

"Like with cars?"

Will shrugs. "I'm good at it. It's a side business, but I've been making the same profit Dad and I make on the ranch by fixing up and selling high end cars and resto-mods for the past five years. If I could do it full time. . ." He shrugs. "But the ranch is fine. I don't hate it."

But if he was suddenly running two ranches? "How do you even find time to work on cars when you're running just the one ranch?"

He shrugs again, and this time, he tosses his head toward the kitchen. "Can you interrogate me about my hopes and dreams while we're eating? Because I'm starving."

I laugh. "Yes." I follow him into the kitchen and he pulls what's left of the fries out of the bag. Two hamburgers follow. "Nothing for Beth, huh?"

"I messaged her," he says. "She told me she was eating dinner at her friend Kate's house."

"Look at you, being all polite to my sponger niece."

"She's family."

My family never paid much attention to whether I had dinner, at least, not anyone other than Mom. And once she died. . .

He takes a giant bite of his burger and then chews a few times before he swallows. With as fast as men wolf down their food, it's a wonder there aren't more people in the ER for choking. "To answer your question, ranch work's pretty intense during some seasons. Spring, for instance. Early fall. Winter has a lot of hay spreading, and so on, but there's a lot of down time, too. I spend that downtime working on cars, because it's a hobby that I love. I've been lucky that it also makes me money, most of the time."

"Kind of the best of both worlds."

"I guess." Will's phone rings.

When I glance at the screen, it says *Dad*. I grit my teeth.

He ignores the call.

"Just pick up," I say. "I want to hear what they say when you ask about the ranch."

Will purses his lips, but he listens to my request, swiping the bottom of his phone to answer the call. "Hello?"

"Hey." His dad's voice is tinny and small, but I can hear it. "How are all the cows doing?"

"Fine," Will says. "I refilled the salt. They're gaining weight on schedule. I accounted for all the calves."

"Great," he says. "That's great."

"I'm in the middle of dinner, though," Will says.

"Oh, I'll let you go, then. Sorry to interrupt."

I clear my throat.

"Wait, Dad." Will frowns.

"Yeah?"

"So, Donna's brother called her today." Will winces a little, which makes me even more nervous. "She said you guys put an offer on his ranch?" He's full-on grimacing, now. My sweet boyfriend has always been conflict averse in his personal life, unless it's to protect me from someone like Charlie or Patrick, and this looks painful.

"Oh, well, that."

"That?" Will looks like he's being waterboarded.

His dad coughs. "We thought it might be a nice

wedding present, you know. Later on. It was your mom's idea."

"Dad, we aren't even engaged, and—"

"This ain't the kind of thing you can wait on, son. Once it's sold, it's gone. Do you know how often ranches are up for sale around here? Almost never. Plus we know how much you love Donna."

Now I'm the one cringing. Will hasn't said *I love you* yet, but I've had the distinct impression it's because he doesn't want to pressure me.

"Dad, you didn't even ask me about it."

"That's not how surprises work, you know. And if we do buy it and you don't want it, we'd clearly have no trouble selling it."

"We can barely handle the ranch we have," Will says.

"Look, you may end up with more than one son," his dad says. "And if you do, there won't be nothing wrong with having one ranch that's underutilized or run by some ranch hands until you need the second one."

"Alright, Dad. It's fine. I get it."

"So you ain't mad, right?"

"Why would I be mad that you're trying to do something nice?" Will chuckles. "But maybe the next time you want to spend millions of my inheritance, check with me first."

"I'll make a note of it." His dad hangs up.

"See?" Will says. "No big deal."

I wonder if we listened to the same conversation. "Your parents think we need a wedding gift?"

"No," Will says.

"No?"

"I mean, he said that, but he didn't mean it."

"What if you have more than one son?" My voice is getting shrill.

"There's nothing for you to be angry about," Will says. "Calm down."

I hate when people tell me to calm down. They don't get to tell me that my feelings aren't valid. Charlie used to do that all the time—insisting that any reaction on my part was irrational and all my fault. I stand up, my hands flying to my hips. "If I'm not calm, I have a reason for it."

Will sets the last two bites of his hamburger down, which for him is a pretty significant move. "What's going on with you?"

"What's going on with *me*?" Fury rises up inside of me. "Your parents put an offer down on my family's ranch, and when they confirm they did it for *me*, without even asking whether I want it, you're just like, 'oh, that's fine. Carry on'?"

Will blinks.

"You know what? If you really can't see why I'm upset, I think you should leave."

Will's brow furrows. He opens his mouth and then closes it again.

His parents are trying to mold us into little clones of themselves, from buying the ranch to badgering me to work for his mother, and they want to preserve their land for Will's *real* children, but they're disguising it as some kind of charitable act—how can he not even see any of that?

Will's shoulders droop, and he sucks air through his teeth.

"Get out." Somehow, having him sit there, pretending none of them have done anything wrong, only infuriates me more. He's letting me spin out; all the while, he's acting like he's baffled.

"Are you serious?" His eyes are wide when they meet mine.

"As a barn fire," I say. "Now get out."

He doesn't even pick up his hamburger. He just stands

up, slides his phone into his pocket and walks to the front door. No less than three times, he pauses, looks over his shoulder at me with stupidly forlorn puppy dog eyes, and then finally ducks out the front door.

I'm so spitting mad when he leaves that for a moment, I just pace. But I need to tell someone what's going on, so I pick up my phone. When I was going through this kind of crap with Charlie, I had no one to talk to. He wouldn't *let* me talk to my friends about anything that was going on. If he ever found out, there would have been literal heck to pay. But now I have real friends who care.

I call Amanda first. With the way things are with Eddy, she'll probably be the most understanding. Unfortunately, her phone just rings and rings and then goes to voicemail. I heave a heavy sigh into the phone. "It's Donna. Call me when you get this."

I'm apparently desperate enough to call God herself, so I dial Abigail.

"Hello?" Of course she answers on the second ring.

"Abby," I say. "I need to talk."

"You need to talk to Abigail the lawyer? Or Abby the friend?"

She differentiates between the two? What a strange person. "Um, I guess Abby." Then I burst into tears.

It takes me a few moments to get coherent, but she's patient and kind while I get the gist of the story out. And then I sit back, inhale deeply, and wait for her rage. She's so articulate that whatever she says will surely rip Will and his parents to shreds.

"Let me make sure I understand everything," Abby says. "You're upset with Will."

"Exactly," I say.

"Because his parents put an offer on your family's ranch that your brother's selling."

"Right."

118

"But his parents did that, not him."

She must not have heard this part. I'm probably too upset to be very clear. "But he talked to his dad on the phone, and he wasn't even angry that they did it."

"And. . .and what they *did* that's so egregious," Abby says, "is offer to purchase the Ellingson ranch as a wedding gift for you and Will, if things do work out, so that your future children would have more than one ranch, if any of them want to work one."

"Right." She's finally getting it.

"I'm sorry," she says. "I must not understand."

She's so smart. How is this hard? "What doesn't make sense?"

"At the risk of ticking you off at me too, I'm not sure why you're mad at his parents, much less at Will. It sounds like they tried to do something really nice, and if Will got mad at them for that, even if their offer on the land was a little misguided, wouldn't he be a terrible son?"

"Did you hear the part where they don't want to leave their ranch to Aiden?"

"Did *you* hear that part?" Abby asks. "Because I'm not at *all* sure that's what they are saying. But even if they are, buying him another ranch that's of equal value feels pretty. . .equitable. Especially since you and Will aren't even engaged."

"Abigail."

"Donna," she says. "You listen for just a second. Sometimes it's hard to see the forest for the trees, and I think that may be where you are. You spent so long with someone who was always out to get you that you're seeing weapons and assassination plots where there are really proposals and flower bouquets."

"Are you saying I'm the crazy one?"

Silence.

Oh shoot. That is what she's saying.

Am I the crazy one?

"Your ex is a taker," Abby says. "He took and took and took, and he's taking still. His parents taught him to do that—to beg, borrow, steal, and manipulate anything he possibly could from every situation. But Will isn't like that. Will and his parents are givers. Don't project your stuff onto them when all they're trying to do is love you."

"Project?" I'm laughing now, and even to myself, I sound a little unhinged. "Abby, I kicked Will out."

"Oh, no." She starts laughing too.

I wipe away the tears my nervous laughter has created. "None of this is funny." I hiccup once. "It's sad." My laughter evaporates as the reality sinks in. "You're saying I'm the one who was wrong, and I think you might be right. I kicked my perfect, generous, calm, long-suffering boyfriend out of my house. What am I supposed to do now?" I'm practically supersonic by the end.

"Will knows you're dealing with baggage from Charlie, because you always have been."

"Are you saying I've always been crazy and he won't be surprised?" My voice is far, far too shrill. I need to bring it back down to planet Calm.

"Donna, I think you need to watch an episode of your favorite TV show. Knit a hat. Go for a walk. Do something that usually makes you feel happy. And then, call Will and apologize. He loves you, and he'll forgive you."

There's the love word again. It's like everyone I know is pushing me toward telling Will I love him. And I should, I guess, but don't I need to feel it in my bones? You don't say you love someone because everyone says you should.

And how do I know whether I do or not? Even if I do love him, it means nothing. It's no guarantee. I learned that the long, hard, depression way.

"Believe me," Abby continues, as if my long silence was because I'm nervous about Will forgiving me. "If that boy was willing to wait for months while you turned him down over and over, he'll be fine when you apologize."

Was she right? Is that my fear?

I think about telling him I'm sorry. . .and I realize she's right. How does she always know every stupid thing? "What if this is the last straw?" I can barely whisper. "What if he's just done waiting on me to stop being nuts?"

"He's not done," Abby says. "You're more amazing than you personally will believe, but he knows it."

"On that note, you're sure I'm *totally* wrong?" Is there some way I can get out of this without having to grovel? There must be some way.

"I mean, I wasn't there, but if you told me the worst of what he said and did, then yeah. You owe him a big 'I'm sorry.'"

After I hang up, I mull it over. Just the facts of what happened—trying to extricate my feelings about my family and my ex.

Will's family saw my ranch was for sale. I told them I felt betrayed by my brother, and they know that I gave up my inheritance that he tried to steal. They probably feel pretty incensed on my behalf.

And now that land's being sold to the highest bidder.

So they generously make a full price offer, hoping to spare me the pain of losing the ranch I've now lost twice. Their son tried to talk me down, but when that didn't work, he picked up the phone call and asked his dad like I wanted. They confirmed they were trying to surprise us. . .and then I got angrier.

Because a kind man and his kind family want to take care of me.

It's not like I could afford to buy it myself.

They don't know that my disappointment and sadness about Patrick selling is more about the pain of being betrayed than the loss of the land I never wanted. They're trying to do the right thing, and that's not common these days.

And I ordered Will to get out.

He went without a fuss.

I just hope he'll come back again as calmly. I whip out my phone and start to bang out a text message.

I'M SORRY. I OVERREACTED. FORGIVE ME?

But instead of pressing send. . . I delete it. Because sending a text is the cowardly thing to do. He deserves to hear from me directly. He should hear it in my voice. In person would be better, but I don't know where he is.

So I dial.

He picks up before the first ring has even finished. "Hello?"

"Oh. That was fast. Wow."

"Donna?"

"I'm sorry." The words tumble out in a rush. I must be afraid I'll freeze up. "I overreacted, and I was a little crazy, and I want to see you. Are you far?"

He chuckles, and it's low and sexy, and now I really want to see him.

"I'll drive to you. I'll grovel. Whatever."

The front door opens, and Will walks through. He's smiling and it's one of the most beautiful things I've ever seen.

I drop my phone on the table. "How are you—"

He shrugs again. "I never left. I wasn't sure where to go or what to do."

"I'm so sorry," I say. "I called Abby—"

"God bless her." Will laughs.

I laugh too, but then somewhere between one breath and the next it turns into a sob.

Will clears the space between us in a heartbeat and pulls me against his chest. "I'd beat that miserable excuse for a man to a pulp if I could."

"Wait." I hiccup and drag in a breath. "Patrick? Or Charlie?"

"Yes," Will says. "And your dad, if he wasn't already dead."

I collapse against him then, and his arms tighten around me. "I'm sorry," I whisper.

"You never have to be sorry with me."

I've always thought the phrase, "Loving someone means never having to say sorry," was the dumbest thing I'd ever heard. But with a tiny adjustment, it makes sense to me. When you love someone, you're always sorry for hurting them, even when it's inadvertent, even when the damage is coming from a past wound.

But you never want them to *feel sorry* when you love them. Love lifts you up when things are hard, just like Will lifts me. Just like he's holding me right now.

Just like I hope he'll keep holding me forever.

# AMANDA

In movies and books, after someone dies, they always leave behind beautifully written letters. Sometimes they also leave valuable or sentimental mementos, things that comfort and change the lives of those around them.

After my husband Paul died, all he left was a pile of debt and a stack of expired options. I couldn't pay our monthly credit card bill, much less funeral expenses. I remember being pretty disappointed not to find. . .well, anything else at all. No letters. No diaries showing his deepfelt but far-buried tender feelings for me.

Nothing.

It was like there really was a ledger where his heart should have been, and our marriage was just as broken as I'd always thought.

When Mandy died. . .it took me a while to even accept that she *had* died. They never found a body, first of all. The barn burned to the ground, burning far hotter than usual thanks to some kind of barrels of chemicals she had stored in there. We didn't press them to extricate whatever remains were left because. . .just. Ugh. It's disconcerting to look at someone's corpse at the funeral after they've died, but I don't think I realized how much it helps people to process that they're actually gone.

I keep expecting Mandy to pop up around every corner. "Surprise," I imagine her saying. "I'm not really dead!"

But she's not there, not around any corner at all.

It's been weeks now, and in quiet moments sometimes, I realize that she really *is* gone. Those moments are the worst. They hit me like an unexpected sledgehammer to the gut.

The only thing that showed up after her death was this thing I can't stop staring at—a Toilet Timer, patent pending. It should be called a Tacky Toilet Timer, really, if they're going for apropos alliteration. That would give them three Ts instead of just two. It's large, eight or ten inches tall, sand-filled, and it's shaped like a standard hour glass. It runs for just under five minutes. For some reason, even though it's tacky, even though it's garish, and even though I know that it's fairly morose of me to do it, I just keep flipping it over and watching the sand grains run out. Every time I miss her, I reach for her last stupid purchase on Amazon.

The idiotic toilet timer.

I almost never needed to use her bathroom. Only when both Maren *and* Emery were using the other two bathrooms at the same time and I really had to go did I duck into hers. But apparently it bothered Mandy. It bugged her enough that she bought a timer so she could tell me when I was in there too long.

It should tick me off.

Instead, I just feel numb, watching those sand molecules drain through. Pitter pitter pitter, they just drain away. And then I flip it over, and it starts all over again.

No last words. No letters. No sentimental mementos.

Just a timer telling me I spent too much time pooping.

Notably lacking? A last will and testament.

Last night, I finally cornered Abby. She's been frustratingly hard to reach lately. I badgered her with voicemails, and I refocused her about it twice via text, and then I caught her in town, and she finally confessed: Mandy *had* come to see her. . .to ask how to revoke her will. The very same will Mandy told me left everything to me.

Which is why *I've* been avoiding the phone.

Contractors are calling.

They gave us a few weeks' grace, in light of Mandy's passing, but they need to get started on the construction of the main resort building. . . or they need to move on to other projects.

It was so hard for us to line them all up. It was irritating to get all the approvals. And now, like that stupid sand, it's all about to run out and disappear, and it will be like the project we planned had never existed at all.

On top of the retreat we were planning, Mandy and I never put anything down on paper about how we ran our business. She and I both worked on the homes and commercial buildings she owned, renovating them together, and then listing them for sale. Then she'd receive the proceeds into escrow, and the real estate agency would cut us each a check for half.

Each time, Mandy filled out a form, designating or assigning or some legal thing, half her profits to me. I didn't care how she did it—it seemed like the easiest method to both of us. But now the places that are being sold in the next three months. . .are going into her estate. She's not here to assign the profits to me. And there's no will saying what she had is now mine, or paper that defines half the profits as going to me.

I'm about to be stiffed on the last few months' work. Also not insignificant: I'm about to be homeless. For the second time in a year. Just this morning, I got a letter in the mail. It was a letter I've been expecting, frankly. A letter I've been dreading. And now it's here, and I still feel very, very numb.

It announced that Mandy's second cousin once removed, some lady named Lacey Lease, is coming to meet with me later this afternoon. She's Amanda Saddler's only living relative. In the absence of a will, she inherits everything. She told me over the phone last night that she plans to sell it all off, as is.

"I'm from California," she said. "There's no way I'm going to live in some podunk little backwater town. I'm going to sell up and get out of Dodge."

I flip the Toilet Timer over again, absentmindedly, and keep on waiting. She should be here any minute. I expect we'll be evicted sometime during her visit.

I'm not even dreading it.

When my surroundings change, when I'm not living in the house we shared, when my feet are to the proverbial fire, maybe then everything will feel *real* again.

When I hear the knock at the door, I force myself to stand up. I'm wearing pajama pants, I realize belatedly. I run my hands down the sides of my head, smoothing the tangled mess of my hair. Only then do I glance down and see the big orange stain on the front of my white t-shirt. I'm positive it wasn't there yesterday morning, but I can't even remember eating anything orange since then.

Never mind.

It's not going to make a difference to this lady. Even if I looked insta-ready, she'd kick me out just the same.

Roscoe's going insane at the door, barking and snarling. He didn't do this before, but ever since Mandy died, it's like he thinks every person who comes over is a threat to me.

Or maybe he blames them for my condition. By the second week, he stopped even asking me to throw the ball for him. Now he kind of curls up under my feet, or sits with his head tucked under my hand, no matter where I go.

Unless someone knocks on the door.

I shuffle to the door and order Roscoe to his place. He stops barking abruptly and goes, his eyes casting pathetic looks my way, but listening. I don't even bother to holler at the kids that they've left the house a mess. After all, I'm pretty sure they're at school. I kick Maren's pom poms toward the corner, nearly breaking my toe on the pair of metal spurs that were hiding underneath them. If Emery were here, I'd. . .eh. Probably do nothing.

It all feels like too much work.

Paul's death energized me. Suddenly, if I didn't figure something out, my two small children and I would be out on our ears. But for some reason, Mandy's death has done the opposite. In some ways, it's freeing. I refuse to worry about what happens tomorrow.

We have no idea whether tomorrow will even come.

So what if I have to move us into a hotel and live on whatever weird endorsements I still have coming in from Champagne for Less? I can do that. The backwoods hotels around here would probably even let me bring Roscoe and Mandy's dumb pig, who mopes around the garden outside eating anything he wants. I can have Abby do my hair to save money—if I really even need to get it done. I can wear the clothes I've had for years. I can paint my own nails.

No biggie.

It's not like we'll starve.

Especially since, no matter how many times I tell him not to, Eddy keeps bringing us food. He cleans the kitchen. He washes and folds laundry. He makes me shower and then insists on blow drying my hair. It's annoying, really. But it's also a bit comforting that someone else is, like, talking to the girls, and you know, buying them boxes of tampons, or whatever.

I finally reach the door and swing it open with a forced smile on my face, Roscoe back to bristling and snarling at my side.

"Roscoe," I snap. "Place. Now."

Except it's not the chipper, irritating, forceful woman I spoke to on the phone last night. It's someone far, far worse.

"Amanda," Helen says. "Don't you just look like a pile of burning garbage."

"Roscoe, get her," I mumble. My poor dog shoots off his place. . .and stops in front of Helen to growl and bark. I make a note to myself to teach him what 'get her' means so he can do better next time.

Helen's eyes widen and she glares at Roscoe. "Knock it off, mutt."

Roscoe cuts off and sits, his whole head ducking down.

"How'd you do that?" I arch one eyebrow at the traitor. "Some guard dog you are."

"Amanda." Helen crosses her arms.

I forgot she was still here for a second. "What are you doing here?"

Her lip curls. Her eyes scan me head to toe. "Does Abby know?"

"Does she know her sister's a horrible witch?" I shrug. "Probably."

Helen laughs. It sounds eerily similar to how I imagine it would sound if Abby turned into granite and tried to laugh. Then, without another word, she shoves past me and walks into the house. "Did your housekeeper die, too?"

"I don't have one," I say. "And you're not supposed to say 'die' around bereaved people. Don't you know that? It's like, Loss 101."

Helen arches one eyebrow. "I'm not the kind of person who tiptoes around things. You didn't used to be, either."

Ha. That's an understatement. She's more like a sniper

who takes people out with one shot to the head. No, no, she's like the crazed terrorist who lobs bombs at things and walks away cackling.

"I have a proposal to make," Helen says. "And I thought you might be interested."

"A proposal?"

She practically sneers. "Some rabid bunch of idiots have created some kind of feeding frenzy over that ramshackle little ranch that just went up for sale."

I'm so lost.

"You look like I'm speaking to you in another language," she says. "Entiende las palabras que estoy deciendo?" She snaps twice right in front of my face.

I roll my eyes. "Your scorn comes through in every tongue, I promise."

"Good. I'm glad to hear that some things are penetrating." She folds her arms, eyeing the sofa as if she doesn't trust it to be clean enough to sit on. It's her own fault really. Who wears a white suit? "I'm here on business, believe it or not."

"I don't own this ranch," I say, and something about saying the words out loud pains me. For the first time in days, I feel something, and it's not good. "Mandy didn't leave me anything. Apparently she destroyed the will she'd made."

Helen perches on the arm of the sofa. "I know. Abby might have mentioned it."

"Oh?"

"More like ranted about it." She waves her hand through the air. "I know you're probably all emotional about it, but try to let that go for just a moment."

"Okay."

"In business, you learn to cut your losses quickly for things that are outside of your control."

"Okay."

"I did happen to take a peek at your business plan," she says.

"My what?" I stand up this time. "That's confidential."

"Sure, sure," Helen says. "I shouldn't have logged into my sister's laptop and looked over it. Sue me." She smirks as if that's the most ludicrous idea ever. "But it's actually quite good."

"It's also quite useless at this point." Like a sailboat on a calm day, my outrage goes limp. "I don't own the land. I don't own anything, actually." I start to laugh, and I can't seem to stop. Suddenly, I'm bent over double, laughing so hard that tears are leaking from my eyes.

"Amanda Brooks."

I can't seem to stop laughing. I wonder what that means.

Helen pushes me into a chair, and then she slaps me. "Amanda Brooks, stop that right now."

I should be furious with her, but I'm not. Every single person in my life has been walking around me like I'm made of glass that's about to shatter from the slightest breeze. It's almost refreshing to have someone talk to me. . .well, like Amanda Saddler would have done. Mandy would have slapped me, too, if she thought I needed it.

And I clearly did.

"What?"

"I'm willing to front the capital on this deal, and I'm willing to let you keep the main details essentially the same as they were before," Helen says. "You may not have been left with the land, but it will be within your control, anyway."

I've been waiting my entire life for my fairy godmother to show up, but I never really thought she'd sound like a drill sergeant and wear designer pumps. I definitely didn't envision that she'd make me feel like a worthless idiot with every sentence she uttered. If it were anyone else in the world saying this, I might consider it. As it is, the only thing worse than losing this house and land and the future I had planned. . .is having Helen Fisher crush it under her ten thousand dollar shoe.

"Tempting," I say. "Very tempting, but. . . not if my life depended on it."

Helen doesn't rage. She doesn't scrape. She doesn't even try to convince me to change my mind. She simply looks at me, and then purses her lips. "Alright."

"Alright?" I start to walk toward the door. "You don't sound too upset, so I think that means we can go ahead and conclude this business meeting that I never set up." I gesture for the door. "Give your sister my love, if you can figure out how to do that with your tin heart."

Helen laughs again, and this time, it sounds *exactly* like Abby. "Believe it or not, Abby's been even pricklier than you lately." She glances down at the pronounced orange stain over my left boob. "Although, she is keeping much cleaner, and I hear her call you at regular intervals to check in." She scrunches her nose. "Maybe, if you ever get your head above the surface of the water, you could call her and see how *she's* handling things." She reaches for the door. "On second thought, don't bother. Worrying about other people has never been *your thing*, has it?"

And with that, she's gone. Even more quickly than she arrived.

What did she mean, it's not my thing to worry about other people? It's kind of all I do, as a mom.

I mean, not *lately*, because Mandy died. And before that, I was busy trying to earn enough money to take care of Emery and Maren's future. And before that, my business was struggling. . . and before that Paul died.

I fall to the sofa, like a string of dominoes when just one gets flicked. Or maybe more like the twin towers just. . .collapsed when their center melted.

Because apparently I'm a selfish narcissist who didn't even realize she was one.

I've never been the kind of person to worry about other people. Not my friends. Not my sister-in-law. Not my own girls. I've justified it by saying it makes them stronger. I've told myself I'll lend a hand when I get back on my feet. But I always have another excuse as to why that hasn't happened.

I spend all my time worrying about myself.

Has everyone in my entire life known this all along? Do my girls know? Does Donna know? Did Mandy know? Does Abby know now?

If they do, why do they love me? Why do they keep helping me? Why haven't they left me like Mandy did, revoked their love, and cut me off?

When there's another knock on the door this time, I don't even bother answering it. I'm sobbing too hard. I'm sure my face is now puffy and red, in addition to my hair being tangled, my shirt being stained, and my pants being fleecy men's pajama bottoms.

When the door cracks open, the last face I expect to see is Eddy's gorgeous one.

The two of us together are like a Botticelli. . .and a Picasso.

Plus, I'm terribly worried now, that he's a giver, and I'm a taker. Does that mean I broke up with him. . .because for one single moment in time he picked himself instead of me? That was all it took? I couldn't handle one moment of selfishness from him, because it's my constant?

"Amanda?"

"It's been a really lousy day, Eddy," I say. "I should prob-ably go shower." That usually gets rid of him.

He glances behind him. "There's a lady here. She said you agreed to meet with her?"

I swear under my breath. That stupid woman who's

coming to take everything. I force myself to my feet and swipe at my cheeks. The great thing about losing someone you love is that, even if you're crying bitter tears because you've realized that you're a particularly foul, hairy-backed monster, people will mostly assume you're crying from sorrow at your recent loss.

And, wow! I'm even worse than I thought. I'm *glad* that I can use Mandy to hide my misery over being a horrible person. Ugh.

"Amanda Brooks?" The woman who steps around the corner doesn't look anything like I expected her to after our conversation this morning. "Hey there, girl. It's me, Lacey Lease." She waves, like we're co-cheerleaders who have bumped into one another at the mall. So she still *sounds* like she did on the phone, and that wave is right in line. I just thought, because of that vibe, that she'd be thin and posh and stylish.

Instead, she's like a pig that's been dressed up in designer clothing.

Her lips are overfull of some kind of injectable. Her makeup's about three levels too thick. Her hair is dark, judging by the very visible roots, but bleached to a level one blonde all over. It's also fuzzy from the strain, and clearly blow-dried within an inch of its ability to survive.

She's quite heavyset, and yet she's wearing very, very tight clothing. I can't tell whether she gained a lot and is in denial, or whether she's like I recently realized I am—completely clueless about her actual self.

"I'm Amanda Brooks," I say. "It's been a rough few weeks."

She glances around the room, and her lips don't curl up at all. When she turns to face me, her eyes skim right over me, and I understand. She isn't judging me. She's checking out the bones of her new house. "This is nicer than I expected. She must've remodeled it."

"Um, yes," I say. "She did."

"That'll make it much easier to sell, I'd say."

"Oh."

"Sorry." She giggles. "Is that rude? I mean, it *is* all mine now."

Eddy clenches his hands into fists beside her.

"Not that I'll have it long." Her jaw drops. "Oh." She turns to face me. "I didn't even think to ask you this when we spoke, but would you want to buy it? I should probably give you first dibs."

Buy it? Myself? As in, stay here in Manila, living next door to Abby, even without Mandy around? Without a job?

In nearly as disconcerting a moment as I had when Helen told me I only care about myself, it hits me then. I've had *weeks* of lying around and mourning and lamenting, and I haven't thought at all about what I'm going to do now.

This house is not mine.

This ranch is not mine.

None of her properties are mine.

And I have no job.

That means I have zero reasons to stay here.

In light of all of that, what am I going to do?

The heavy woman in the skintight clothing and bright pink lipstick reaches into her oversized Prada bag and rummages around. "Also, the court said I should give you this."

She extends her hand toward me, a wide manila folder with my name scrawled across the front clasped in her breakfast sausage fingers.

"What is it?" I know I should take it. I should move my hand and make my fingers curl around it. But I can't bring myself to do it.

"It's a copy of the will," she says. "Just in case you were thinking of, I don't know, contesting it, or whatever."

It can't be.

I thought she was inheriting under the intestacy laws. Is she really saying that. . .not only did Mandy revoke the will leaving things to me. . .she wrote a new one? Giving things to *this woman* instead? My brain revolts against the idea.

We were arguing, yes. But we were arguing because she loved me. She wanted what was best for me. We didn't agree on what that was, but she hadn't given up on me.

Right?

She dove into a *fire* to save my *dog*. How could she have done this and then done that?

"Thanks," I say. "But I think what I really need to know is, how long can my girls and I stay here?"

Lacey's brow furrows. She fakes a smile, and I notice her bright pink lipstick is smeared across the front of her big, probably capped, teeth. "I mean, I'm not like the wicked witch of the west, or anything. I never minded that Aunt Amanda took on *projects* or whatever, but you can't just stay here forever, either."

"Projects?" Eddy has largely said nothing over the past few moments, letting me handle things however I'd like. I'd almost forgotten he was here. "Projects?" His eyes are bulging, and so are the veins in his arms, probably from clenching his hands too hard at his side. "Mandy *begged* Amanda Brooks to move in, threw a fit when she tried to leave, and benefitted greatly from Amanda Brooks' stellar work and killer eye at remodeling all the places they've worked on together and sold."

"Be that as it may," Lacey says, "that collaboration is now complete." She shrugs and tilts her head in a faux-condolence way. "So how about we say one week? I mean, it *has* been several weeks already."

"It's fine," I say. I also put one hand on his wrist, because Eddy looks like he's going to strangle the woman.

"And when you leave, if you could clear out all this. . .stuff?" Now she looks around like I expected her to do earlier, clearly eying the mess my children and I have made condescendingly. "I expect it to be clean in a week when I have my realtor come over for photos."

That's when it hits me.

Helen has seen my business model.

I own nothing.

I'm about to be evicted.

In exactly one week, she can buy it from this horrible Medusa and do whatever she wants. Helen may be the devil, but she was actually doing me a solid today, offering to work with me.

And I kicked her out on her rear.

I'm not only a huge narcissist. I'm also an utter moron. The second Lacey leaves, I begin to cry. Again.

Eddy's arms don't immediately wrap around my waist to comfort me, and I wonder why. When I look to see where he went, I notice that he's crouched down at the coffee table, pulling the will out of the envelope. "How could she leave everything to this *awful*—"

He freezes.

"What?"

"It's old," he says. "Like, really, really old. She made this will twenty years ago, and she left everything to someone named Adeline Lease."

"I'm assuming that's Lacey's mother," I say.

"But if we could find the newer will," Eddy says, "maybe the court would—"

"But Abigail would have to take the stand," I say. "She's the one who drew it up, and she said Mandy came by and told her she wanted to revoke it." I sink into the oversized chair Mandy loved. "Even without this stupid will, she's her only relative. She'll inherit everything, because Mandy was so mad at me for not taking you back that she was cutting me off."

Eddy looks almost pleased.

"Could you not smirk about that?"

Eddy shuffles toward me on his knees, his eyes intent on mine. He's so tall that even with me sitting down and him on his knees, he's still looking down. "Amanda Brooks," he says quietly. "You are a brilliant, talented, amazing woman, and bad things keep happening to you."

"I'm a selfish narcissist," I say. "I realized that today." What started as kind of a confession-adjacent joke turns fast, and I choke on a sob. "I don't know why you even like me."

"Would you fault a butterfly for knowing it's lovely?" He leans closer until our foreheads are touching. "You're a little selfish. You've had to be, because the people who were supposed to take care of you never did. The only person who would keep you safe was you, but that's not true anymore."

Is he right? Is it really not entirely my fault that I'm so awful?

"It's hard when you're constantly told how great you are, especially when you're working hard to achieve success, to remember to think about other people. The world turns us inward, toward ourselves, first and foremost."

"I've been a terrible friend, a terrible mother, and a terrible girlfriend," I say. "I'm sorry."

"I will argue about that later. For now, I'll just say that you don't need this ranch," he says. "You don't need the job Mandy gave you. And you certainly don't need to stay in a hotel." He grins, and it practically bowls me over. Sometimes I forget, for a nanosecond, just how devastatingly handsome he is. And then he grins that sideways grin, and my mind goes blank.

"I am about to be evicted," I say. "And a devil came by to make a deal earlier, and I turned her away."

"What are you talking about?" he asks.

I explain what Helen offered.

"Are you considering it now?" His eyebrows rise. "Truly? Abby's sister?"

I flop backward and slump down so I can lean my head against the back of the chair. "Maybe."

He stands up and sits on the sofa arm next to me, not unlike Helen was doing earlier. "I was worried you might move back to New York."

I snort. "I considered it for the first time, today."

"Don't." He takes my hand. "I know life sucks right now. I know everything feels bleak."

His hand on mine is firm, warm, and strong. For the first time since he came back, I don't feel like a fool around him. I don't have any desire to slap him. In fact, I wish I was clean and poised and. . .

I want him to kiss me.

As if he can sense it, as if the atmosphere around us itself has shifted, Eddy's shoulders square. His hand, where it's touching mine, stills. And tightens.

He drops back to his knees, never releasing my hand, and he yanks me up to an upright position again, closer to him. "Amanda." His eyes are intent on mine. His mouth isn't smiling, but it is pleased. His full lips curve.

Eddy wraps his free hand around the back of my neck and pulls me closer until our lips meet.

Every cell in my body comes alive. My heart pounds in my ears. My hands tremble. My breath comes faster and faster and faster.

"You said you needed a shower?" Eddy's breathing is shallow against my mouth. "Are you sure your faucet's working? You don't need me to take a look at it?"

"Actually," I say—

The front door opens then, and Emery breezes through, Maren on her heels.

"—until Mom can get herself together." Maren freezes

when she sees us, Eddy practically melted against me, our faces still touching.

We spring apart then, like two teenagers in the back of an old station wagon at a drive-in movie. "I was—your mom had something stuck in her teeth." Eddy swallows, and his Adam's apple shifts.

I burst out laughing.

"So are you two back together, then?" Emery asks.

I hate how hopeful she sounds. Did I not hear that before, my baby's fear about the future, or did I just not care? "Yes," I say carefully. "Eddy and I are back together."

Eddy leaps to his feet and starts whooping, and to my surprise and borderline horror, Emery and Maren join him. It's not how I would have played this scene out in my head, but it is the first happy thing that's happened in my life in a very long time.

I guess I'll take it.

# 12

# ABIGAIL

Once, when I was thirteen, I called and lied to my sister Helen. I told her I spilled something on my pants, because I didn't want to confess to her —to anyone—that I'd started my period. I asked her to bring me a new pair of jeans during lunch. As an upperclassman, she had off-campus lunch.

She brought them to me, but when I tried to take them out of her hands, she snatched them back. "Tell me why you really need these."

I swallowed and looked down at my feet. I still recall staring intently at my snowy-white Keds.

"Abigail."

I snapped my eyes up and met hers. "I spilled chocolate milk on my other ones."

"You hate chocolate milk."

I tilted my chin upward. "That's why I spilled it."

She laughed. "You're a horrible liar." She handed me the jeans, and then she dropped her voice to a whisper. "I also put some pads inside there, so be careful where you open them. Congrats on starting your period, you little punk."

Then she walked away, cool as could be. She literally

figured out that I had lied, realized *why*, and then gave me what I needed in the circumstance. She may be awful sometimes, and most people may be terrified of her, but she was pretty amazing back in the day. She also taught me something about myself.

I suck at lying.

In spite of being a lawyer, I never really improved.

Which is why I waited until the kids were in school to set this appointment up. I only had to lie to Ethan this morning, because Steve's at work. I kept it simple, too. I told him I have a hearing for a client in Salt Lake City, because that's where I'm going. It would have been easier to go to a local clinic or hospital, but I figured Steve would probably find out. I picked an OB who didn't go to the same school as Steve, and who wasn't in residency at the same place or even around the same time. I'm also paying in cash, because there's no way I want Steve to see this appointment on his insurance. Or our credit card.

Why did I insist that we should have joint everything?

Apparently on top of being a bad liar, I'm also dumb.

Because I'm a new patient, and because I'm not in an emergency room, I'm not a top priority. Or maybe it's simply the nature of healthcare. Either way, I've been waiting for an hour when they finally call my name. I'm led back so that. . .I can wait in the exam room, in a weird paper gown, for half an hour more before a gruff woman walks into the room.

She's tall—like, close to six feet—and she has a face that would probably curdle milk. "What's the problem?"

"Oh." I sit up. "I had to write it down on a lot of forms already." So why is she asking me now?

She waves her hand through the air as she plonks down on a sliding round stool and zooms toward my knees. "I don't read all that. Just tell me why you're here."

"Um. Okay. Well." I'm not sure why, but blurting out

that I have a lump in my breast seems. . . too hard. I can't force the words out.

"You had a long period? More discharge than you expected?" She eyes me up and down. "No, wait." She points at me. "I know. You found a lump."

My eyes widen, and I inhale sharply.

"Bingo. Alright. When'd you notice it?"

"Wait." I splutter. "How did you know what it was?"

She tilts her head sideways, her salt and pepper hair barely moving when she does. "Pale face, nervous affect, relatively young." She shrugs. "I've been doing this for a long time. You learn to spot 'em."

"I noticed it in the shower."

"A month ago."

How is she doing this? "Yeah," I say. "About three weeks ago."

She nods and wheels a little closer. "I'm going to have to do an exam."

Scrubbing toilets is smelly, and tiring, and you have to bend over to do it. The exam's less fun than that, but it's not as bad as trimming cow hooves, so it could be worse.

"Alright, the good news is that you found it pretty early. It's not too large."

"And the bad news?"

"You're going to need a biopsy to confirm."

"To confirm. . . what exactly?"

"Whether it's malignant or benign."

This woman does not have a very good bedside manner. "So it could be cancer?" That word just slides out. Maybe it's Nate that makes it easy to say. Maybe it's the month I've sat on this fear. Or maybe it's the frank manner this doctor has, just spitting things out, unvarnished, without any judgment.

On second thought, maybe her bedside manner's fine.

"It could be," she says. "You seem like someone who

spends less time clutching her pearls and more time evaluating facts, so I'll tell you that it's quite likely. But until you have a biopsy, there's no way to know for sure."

"Can you do one of those today?"

"There are two types of biopsy that we could perform," the doctor says. "One of them's called a fine needle biopsy, and it can be done in the office. Not today, but right here, as an outpatient procedure."

"But not today?" My hopes of walking out of here with a clean bill of health wilt.

She shakes her head. "I wouldn't recommend that biopsy in any case."

"Why not?" I like the word 'fine' before the needle. It makes it sound small. Minor. Inconsequential.

"The other option's a core-needle biopsy, and frankly, I strongly prefer that option in cases like this. The FNA is an easier procedure, but it's not as conclusive."

"Meaning?"

"Whether it comes back positive or negative, there's a lot more doubt with that one."

"The test results could be wrong?"

"Let's say you get a great result, and it comes up benign. Will you sleep better at night, knowing there's a decent chance it wasn't right?"

I swallow.

"Or if it comes up as cancerous, and then you go home and tell everyone you're going to fight this. . .only to discover there's nothing to fight." She shrugs. "I try not to tell anyone they need to look the abyss in the eye until it's required."

"When can I set that one up?"

"It can be done here as well, but I prefer doing an MRI-guided biopsy. When the mass is palpable, as it is here, false negatives happen less than four percent of the time when there's an image-guided core biopsy. That kind of test must be performed in the hospital—for the imaging."

Which means I'd have to come back another day. And it's unlikely I can come alone. "Would someone need to be with me?"

"You should have a caretaker with you," she says. "Surely there's someone who—"

"I live quite far away," I say. "In a very small town." I sigh.

"I'm going to discharge you with instructions to set up a biopsy in the next ten days." She glares at me. "I can't make you do it, but time is of the essence in matters like this."

"If it was cancerous." I inhale and exhale slowly. "What kind of timeline would I be looking at?"

"That depends on the stage of cancer," she says. "But you should know that it must divide thirty times before you can even feel it. By the time you could detect it, it's *already* been there for two to five years."

That's a horrifying thought. It means that, if this *is* cancer, it was already there, lurking, when Nate was sick.

"I'm not trying to scare you, but most breast cancer happens in women over fifty." She drums her fingers on the edge of the counter. "Since you appear to be in your early forties, the likelihood that the cancer is aggressive, if it is cancer, goes up. That tumor will likely double in size every six or so months."

Six months. That's what I needed to hear. Six months isn't that long, and by my calculations, I'm already close to fifteen weeks along on this pregnancy. Six months would take me to the end.

Surely twice the size it is now isn't so bad, right? It's small.

The nurse is talking to her, saying something about the next patient. The doctor stands and spins on her heel to leave.

"One more thing," I say. "What if I were to get pregnant?"

She snorts. "Oh, I'd advise strongly against that."

"Why?"

"There have been some studies lately linking the pregnancy hormones and the growth rate of cancer, for one," she says. "But beyond that, there are plenty of cancer treatments that aren't conducive to a viable pregnancy. Why limit your options like that when you don't know what you might need?"

"Right." I nod. "Thanks."

I must have gotten better at lying, because she seems to have no idea that I'm already pregnant. Or maybe it's just Helen who's good at spotting my lies. I leave without setting up any appointments, but I promise the office staff I'll call once I have my calendar in front of me. They hassle me a bit, but eventually they let it go. After all, they don't know me. My life isn't a priority to them.

On the drive home, I run through all the scenarios. I did the same thing when Nate was diagnosed, so I already have the neural pathways set.

If I have cancer and I fail to treat it, my tumor may grow a bit, but not that fast. It's already been growing for two to five years without my knowledge. That thought sends a shiver up my spine, but I shake it off. It's actually sort of encouraging. Six months won't make much of a difference.

If I have it and tell Steve, he'll make me terminate the pregnancy to get every single treatment under the sun. I'm absolutely not alright with that scenario, nor do I want to take something he'd be excited about and ruin it with this cancer scare.

If I don't have cancer and I tell Steve about the lump, it'll color the entire thing. We'll argue. We'll fight, and it will have been for nothing.

And if the worst happens and I die, I might have died either way. But if I do, at least my kids have Steve now. There's no doubt in my mind that no matter what happens to me, he'll keep taking care of them. He'll be there for their performances, he'll drive them to practices, he'll teach them horseback lessons, and he'll walk them down the aisle for their weddings.

Ethan's practically done. Izzy's mostly baked. Whitney and Gabe still need a lot of guidance, but Steve can handle it, I'm sure. So when I get back, instead of fretting or wallowing or bawling, I get to work, drafting a new will that leaves everything to Steve, as a trustee and guardian for the kids.

All five of them.

When I finally drive home, I'm exhausted. The whole day has been draining, and I know basically nothing more than I did this morning. I really thought that when I got home tonight, I'd at least know what I was dealing with. But maybe it's for the best. Maybe I'm not supposed to know right now.

The second I walk in the door, Steve hops to his feet. "I had Javier bring Leo in, and I'll text him now and tell him to tack him up." He lifts a basket up in the air, his face bursting into a smile. "We're going on a picnic date."

Like the day he gave me Leo. Like our wedding. A ride out into the woods, just the two of us.

"I haven't seen the kids much," I say feebly. "They've been asking to talk to me about things, and—"

"It's fine, Mom." Gabe saunters out of his room. "I just started a new book, and I'll probably just read all night anyway."

"And we're going to be riding tonight too," Izzy says. "We've got to practice our barrel pattern. Right?"

Steve beams at her. "Atta girl."

"But don't you think you should watch that?" I ask. "It's not like—"

Steve drops one hand on my shoulder. "Abby." He grins. "It's okay to let go sometimes. The world won't break."

In that moment, part of me worries that it already has.

"But—"

"No buts. Come with me." His hand slides down my arm and his fingers interlace with mine.

I need to tell him. Even if we'll fight about it, he has to know. He's going to find out eventually, and. . . The words just pop out. "I can't ride," I say. "I'm pregnant."

It's not cute little cookies. It's not a cake with a baby on it. It's not a poem, or a scavenger hunt, or any of the other hundred ways I contemplated when I was thinking of how I could tell him. The kids are even all here, watching.

And I'm not even telling him all the things he should know.

But when Steve processes what I've said, it's as if the sun is rising. Its rays light up the entire world.

"You're *what*?" He drops the picnic basket on the floor, the contents rolling all over the room like beads from a broken necklace. His hands drop to my waist and he lifts me up into the air, spinning me around in a circle. "That's wonderful! The best news ever!" He drops me to the ground and kisses me.

And I pull away just in time and throw up all over the hardwood floor.

"I'm so sorry," he says.

I wipe my mouth, staring at the splatter of disgusting-ness that just evacuated my body. "Morning sickness isn't just in the morning," I whisper.

Steve's laughing now. "I really am sorry about that—I'm sure you wouldn't have puked if I hadn't spun you all around and then cut off your air supply. But I'm just so excited."

148

Izzy's already rushing over with a towel, a sponge, and a bowl. Gabe has grabbed the Lysol spray and he's dangling it from his finger.

"Wow," Ethan says. "Just, wow."

"You ready to be an older brother. . .again?" Steve asks.

"I'm ready," Gabe says. "Finally someone I can boss around."

Steve laughs.

It's been weeks since anyone has laughed in this house. I didn't notice the absence until I hear the rare sound. Mandy's death has cast a pall on the entire family, and it feels like this new little baby might have the power to lift it a bit. In this moment, for just a breath or two, I let go of my fear and my anxiety and my confusion about what to do or say, and I just revel in the news that our family is going to grow by one more heavenly little person.

I can always tell Steve the rest later.

## 13

### DONNA

When I was in elementary school, I prayed every single night for a sister. Since I lived in Podunk, USA, that lasted for like seven years. And by the time I went to 'high school,' all my friends with sisters pretty much hated them.

But even so, when I hit my knees every night, after praying that my dad would stop hitting my mom, I would beg God for a sister. "I'll keep her safe," I promised. "I'll make sure that nothing bad ever happens to her."

I forgot about that promise eventually, of course. God clearly disagreed with me that our family needed another victim. My desperately-longed-for little sister never came. He was probably right, really, not to send any more children to our broken family. Or maybe Mom was the smart one and she took measures to make sure it didn't happen. Who knows? They certainly never talked to me about their plans. But as an adult, that longing clearly held over.

I've always wanted a daughter.

I'm delighted with Aiden of course, but the idea of dressing a little girl up in frilly dresses and adorable shoes and boots, and the idea of taking her shopping and out for ice cream. . .it has always appealed to me.

I gave up on having a sister.

Then I gave up on having a daughter.

Thanks to my parents and Charlie, I gave up on almost everything I dreamed about having. When Beth asked if she could live with me here, I almost said no. I worried about how Will would react. I've been fretting that Aiden might be upset, too.

But now that she's here, and Will doesn't mind, it's almost like one of my childhood dreams finally *did* come true.

I chuck the pillow at her head. "Shut your mouth."

"Look, I'm just saying that while Edward may be powerful and broody or whatever, Jacob's hotter, and I don't know. He's just better for Bella."

"I can't believe you're team *Jacob*," I say.

"To be clear, the whole series of movies are kind of badly made," Beth says. "But if I had to choose, I'd go wolf."

"He's so, I don't know," I say. "Rapey."

"Oh, please." Beth rolls her eyes. "Like Edward's constant insistence she can't become a vampire isn't trampling all over her right to choose."

"It's all a little problematic," I admit, "from a parent's perspective." I could probably never binge the series with a daughter, at least, not without spending a lot of time explaining that I don't approve of any of the plot elements. But with someone who feels like the little sister I never had?

It's so fun.

"I know no one asked my opinion," Will says. "But I actually think that Mike—"

We both hit him with a pillow at the same time.

"Mike?" I can't help scoffing. Then I make a puking sound.

Beth groans. "He's so awful."

"He's a human boy, and he likes her legitimately," he says. "I'm just saying that—"

This time, I nix the pillows and just attack him. Beth, however, is still chucking pillows, many of which are now hitting me.

"I surrender," Will says. "Geez. You two are relentless."

"You're just mad you're not a werewolf *or* a vampire," I say.

"And yet I still managed to get the girl." He tugs me closer then and kisses me right on the mouth.

"Eww, come on," Beth says. "Cut it out."

"Bedtime for all the kids," Will says.

"I'm eighteen now," Beth says. "Legally not a kid anymore."

"Oh." Will pulls me onto his lap. "Did I fail to clarify? Bedtime for anyone who's not old enough to drink." He wiggles his eyebrows. "Nighty-night, little one."

Before I can stop him, he stands up, pulling me up with him. "Your aunt and I have some adult things to *discuss*."

"Fine, fine." Beth makes almost the same retching noises I was making earlier. "Whatever. I have homework to do anyway."

"It's a Friday night," I say. "Just turn on the next movie. Will may be sick of us oohing and aahing over supernatural men with glowing golden eyes, but we have two more movies to go."

Will groans. "What happened to adult time?"

I shove his shoulder. "It's overrated."

"Then I'm going to go work on the Camaro I just got."

"Be careful."

He collapses back on the edge of the sofa. "Are you kidding? You're just letting me go? That was a bluff."

"And I called it." I smile. "But if you're not really leaving, can you make some kettle corn?"

"We ran out," he says.

"Right." I slap my forehead. "I forgot to say that in order to make it, you'll need to drive into town, buy some kettle corn, and *then* you can microwave it."

Beth's giggling as she taps through the buttons to bring up the next movie.

"And while you're there, if you see anything that says 'werewolves suck,' or, like, 'vampires rule,' you should grab that, too."

I had no idea that picking at the people you love could be so much fun, but here we are. Watching Will and Beth squawk makes my whole night better. I thought, when I saw I was losing the ranch forever, and again when I signed on to take care of Beth, and then with Aiden being gone, and then Mandy dying, that this would be the worst summer of my life.

But I video conference Aiden most nights, eventually. Losing the ranch hasn't really made me sad at all. Beth's a hoot. And Mandy's loss has been horrible, but even that hasn't wrecked my life.

I'm beginning to think that, when you have a stable group of people who care for you, nothing can level your life.

Abby. Amanda. Will. Beth. Aiden. Even my boss isn't half bad. The list of people who support Donna Ellingson keeps growing and growing. Even Will's parents called a while back and apologized for not consulting me before putting an offer in on that ranch.

Will's just leaving for the kettle corn when my phone bings.

"It's David again, isn't it?" Will shakes his head. "That guy's the worst. Hasn't he heard of a weekend?"

"Have your cows heard of a weekend?" I ask. "Because

the last time I wanted to go shopping out in Salt Lake, you said you couldn't leave until all the chores were done."

"That's different," Will says. "Animals aren't nine-to-five, but business stuff should be."

It is David, though.

NOT A RUSH, BUT WHEN YOU GET A CHANCE, I SENT THE PROPOSAL FOR THE COVERED ARENA. CAN YOU TAKE A LOOK AND TELL ME WHAT YOU THINK?

Normally, I'd text him back right away, but just because Will was complaining, I put my phone down. "You can start the movie," I tell Beth. "David can wait."

Will's chuckling when he heads out.

The biggest surprise of all to me is how I feel about the prospect of David Park buying our family ranch. He sat me down last week and we walked through his plan for the ranch as a day-long getaway for city-folk. It's not half bad.

Most of them know absolutely nothing about cattle or horses, chickens or goats. It would be a snap to have a few of each of those things, and then to let the visitors help with some of the basic chores. Depending on the time of year, they might even be able to go home with some fresh eggs or some goats' milk.

I also convinced him to let Jeff and Kevin have a small ownership interest, if he wins the bid. It's an interesting model, because our profit doesn't rely in any way on the price of beef or the health of the cows. David agreed to give them eighty percent of the profits on the ranching operation as long as they cooperate with his tour plans.

Since moving back home, I've really learned a lot about win-wins in business. It all makes me admire David Park more and more, which makes Will more and more annoyed with him. Not that my hot, kind, generous boyfriend has anything to worry about. My crush on David Park had everything to do with how unavailable he was to me.

At least he appears to have given up on Amanda.

I bumped into Amanda at True Value a day or two ago, and she was wearing a clean shirt and pants for the first time in a while. It seems like we're all healing from Mandy's tragic loss in our own ways. It helps me feel less guilty for being happy again, truly happy, so soon after her death.

Will's back and he's just finished popping the popcorn when Aiden calls.

"I can pause this," Beth says.

I shake my head. "Not at all. I've seen it an embarrassing number of times. Keep watching. I'll be right back."

Will offers me the popcorn bowl, but I wave him off, too. "You guys eat it. I'll be back out in a minute."

Aiden's a sweet kid, and he really does want to talk to me every day, but he's only seven, so he never wants to talk for very long. Once he's told me about his day, asked me a few questions, and commented on how I look, we're about done.

"Hello, angel!" I can't help beaming. He comes home on Monday, and then everything in my life will be perfect.

"Mom!" Aiden's face is covered with something messy, but that's more a state of being for a little boy than anything else, so I don't comment.

"How has your weekend been so far?"

"Weekend?" Aiden blinks. "Oh. Yeah. It's hard to know what day it is when there's no school."

"Do you miss school?"

He shrugs. "I miss Gabe."

Close enough. "I saw him a few days ago. He just got some new monster trucks, and he can't wait to show them to you."

"Monster trucks?" Aiden's eyes light up. "That's so cool. Are they remote controlled?"

I shrug. "Not sure. I bet he can tell you next week."

"Today we got ice cream," Aiden says. "And I got to see Peter and Holden."

"That's great," I say, frankly shocked that Charlie was willing to drive that far. They live on the other side of town from his parents. When we lived there, he wouldn't even ride in the car with me when I went to drop Aiden off at Holden's house. "Was it fun?"

"So fun," Aiden says. "And I get to see them tomorrow, too."

"Why are you getting to go see them so much? Is Dad dropping you off? Is he doing a lot of work?"

"No," Aiden says. "He stayed and talked to Holden's dad."

That's unlike him, but I force myself to be glad and not suspicious. The more active role he plays in Aiden's life, the better. Holden's family is really kind, so hopefully he won't tick them off or lie to them or cheat them in some way.

I hate that it's a real possibility, but sadly, it is.

"How's Mister Will?" Aiden asks.

"He's great," I say. "He can't wait to see you again. He just got a brand new red Camaro, and he said you can help him with the brakes."

Aiden winces, but I'm not sure why.

"Are you alright, honey?"

He shrugs. "I'm fine."

"Do you have your stuff packed up? Are you ready to come home?"

It's so small I almost miss it, but he frowns before he looks down at something off screen that I can't see.

"Aiden?"

He mumbles something I can't catch. ". . .until. . .Holden. . . maybe."

"Sweetie, you have to look up and speak loudly or I can't hear you."

156

"I'd rather stay here." He glances up then, and hurriedly looks back down. "I don't want to go back to your house."

The words are like a dagger to my chest. Aiden doesn't want to come *home*? He doesn't want to live with me? "Honey, I think I misheard you. Is there something going on? Did you want to stay with Dad for another day or two? Maybe go to a ball game or something?"

He bites his lip.

"Your son is worried you'll cry." Charles' face looms in front of the screen, far too close and a little distorted. He looks like something out of a Tim Burton cartoon. "He wants to stay here and live with me. Permanently."

The words are like cannon fire, aimed right at my heart. "Aiden."

My son looks up then, his eyes wide and weepy. "Don't be mad, Mom, okay?"

"Do you really want to stay with Dad?"

"I miss my friends here," he says. "I miss my school, and I like the restaurants. Plus, Grandma and Grandpa are here."

I can barely breathe.

How stupid have I been? My life isn't roses and sunshine and butterflies. My life is blow after blow after nasty blow. I should've known something like this was coming.

"Aiden, how about you stay another week or two?" My voice is wobbly and unsure. I clear my throat, like maybe that will fix the problem. "You can see Holden and Peter, and you can go to lunch with Grandma and Grandpa, and then you can still come home before school starts." Why am I speeding up? If I keep going like this, I'll sound like an auctioneer any minute. "In fact, if you get your school clothes shopping done there, you can even stay for three more weeks." My voice breaks again at the end, at the thought that he'd rather do that with Charlie.

"Mom." Aiden's lip wobbles. "I love you so much. I wish you could just come back out here."

He's serious. He doesn't want to come back home. . .at all.

"Your dad and I need to talk, sweetheart. Can you go watch some television?"

"Okay." Aiden waves as he walks off.

When Charlie's face reappears, he looks like he's just robbed a bank. "You're always saying that all you care about is what's best for Aiden, but have you ever really stopped to think about what that is? What he wants?" He's so smug I can barely stand it. "I trust he was plenty clear."

"The court makes these decisions," I say. "Not our seven-year-old. No matter how much ice cream you give him—"

"Is that really what you want?" he asks. "To be the mother who hauls her son back to Hicksville against his will, so he can get a shoddy education and be raised with toothless hillbillies?"

"If you—"

"He'll hate you for it eventually," he says. "If you make him come back, he will hate you. And in another few months, I can make a motion for reconsideration, and the Court will ask him his opinion. I've had him meeting with a child psychologist, by the way. He agrees that Aiden's needs would be better met here, by me and my parents. We have the funds to provide for Aiden anything and everything he might need."

He leans even closer to the screen, so grotesquely close that I can see his nose hairs.

"Even if you drag him back, you're only delaying the inevitable. He's *my* son, a Windsor. And Windsors may fumble a battle now and then, but we never lose the war."

## ❧ 14 ❧

## AMANDA

For years, the only friends I had fell into two categories: real life or social media.

My Instagram friends were low risk. We were more business companions than actual friends. We networked for each other. We referred business to one another. We jointly promoted items and places, and we helped each other to grow and develop new opportunities. Of course, some of them *got* me and some didn't. But by and large, even the annoying ones were considered 'friends,' and I could put up with most anything.

Because I never saw them.

My other type of friend in New York were the socialites I knew physically who lived in Manhattan. We bumped into one another at parties, at the PTO, and at restaurants. Sometimes we'd even go out on a date or two before realizing we'd been out with the same guy.

If I'm being honest, they were really all frenemies. I never sat down and had a real or honest conversation with any of them. I spent more time worrying about who wore it better than I did about whether they were doing alright.

Actually, when I found out they weren't doing well, I'd usually either laugh or gloat or both.

Admitting that, even to myself, isn't easy.

Now that I have real friends, it's amazing in ways I didn't predict. I always have someone I can call with issues. They tell me when I'm way off base. They bring casseroles and drink wine and shop and share clothes that don't quite work.

That's more my role, but still.

The one downside is that they also call me when they need help.

"Amanda?" Donna sounds practically frantic.

"Yeah?"

"Thank goodness you answered. The last twenty-four hours have been a constant freefall, it feels like."

"What's wrong?"

For some reason, that simple question reduces her to tears.

I'm not sure what to say. If we weren't on the phone, I'd put an arm around her and let her cry. As it is, I just wait, awkwardly, until she pulls it together enough to speak.

"Charles is threatening to take Aiden, and he wants to stay in California."

"I thought he lived there," I say.

"No," she says. "*Aiden* is saying he wants to stay."

"Oh no, that's terrible," I say. "Summers are the worst."

"What?"

"This happened with quite a few of my friends' kids," I say. "Every year, their dads would spoil them and badmouth their mother the entire time they were there, and then the kid would decide he or she wanted to stay."

"Are you serious?"

"Yes," I say. "I'm sure that's what happened. And it's hard, but try not to worry. The court order says he *has* to come home, right?"

"But I don't want him to resent me," Donna says.

"He's *seven*. He'll resent you for a day or two and then he'll forget about it halfway through an episode of *Ninjago*. That's why courts make those decisions, not elementary school kids who have been plied with ice cream and basketball games."

Donna doesn't say a word.

"Hello?"

"I'm here," she says. "And. . .I hope you're right. It's just that, Charles isn't your average father. He's more of a diabolical mastermind. He says he'll sue for custody over and over until he gets it."

"But you have a secret weapon he doesn't," I say.

"What?"

"She wears stilettos and crushes men's . . .you know. . . with her fist. For fun."

She laughs. "Abigail. You're right."

"Tell me you've called her."

"Not exactly."

"Donna, I'm great, and I'm always happy to talk to you, but when someone starts threatening legal action, *call the terrifying lawyer first*."

"Right, you're right. And I will call her next, but. . ."

"But? Is there something else?"

Donna clears her throat. "The thing is, my hot water heater also died. And there's still a leak in that guest bathroom, which is not that big of a deal, but Will hasn't had time with the calves to look at it and. . ."

"Now Mandy's dead, you don't know who to call." My voice is flatter than I mean for it to be, but I'm a little tired of everyone calling me about this stuff. I got nothing, but people still think I'm made of answers.

"I'm so sorry," Donna says. "The thing is, I have my rent check, but I'm not sure where to send it, and I thought you—"

"Mandy left me nothing," I say. "In fact, everything she owns is going to some horrible woman named Lacey. Some kind of third cousin or something. I was actually supposed to be evicted last week, but Abby called the court and they said I don't need to go until the estate is processed. She's got her final probate hearing next week or something, I think. For now, I'd say hold onto that rent check. Maybe replace the hot water heater and offset the cost against your rent. But again, I'm not the expert on lease stuff."

"Abby."

I grunt. "Yep. I'd call Abby about that, too." I feel a small twinge of guilt at the idea of piling things on top of Abby. I know she won't let Donna pay for any of it, and it sounds like the issues with Aiden might be extensive. . . "Look, I have to call Lacey today anyway, so I'll ask her about what she's doing with the rental house, okay?"

"Thank you so much."

"But my guess is that she's going to sell it like she's selling everything else. She just wants as much money as she can get for, I don't know, liposuction and filler, and then she's out of here."

"Which means I'm about to get tossed out on my ear."

"You have a twelve-month lease," I say. "Again, ask Abby, but I bet she can't throw you out. She'd have to sell it to someone subject to that lease."

"Poor Abby," Donna says.

"It's her literal job," I say. "So she has no one to blame but herself for having to slog through all that boring legal stuff."

"I guess," Donna says. "Well, thanks."

"Oh, and by the way."

"Yeah?"

"I know it's been a bad few days for you, and I won't lie and say the last few weeks have been great for any of us.

But." I tap on my phone until I find the photo of Eddy and me. Then I click send.

"Amanda? Are you still there?"

"Check your messages."

"What's this?" Donna's voice ratchets up a notch. "Amanda Brooks, tell me what this is!"

"We got back together."

And now it's just screeching and hissing sounds. Old Amanda might have been annoyed, but new Amanda's beaming. "If only Mandy could see me now," I whisper. "She'd be screeching and dancing around, too."

Somehow, it makes it harder, after thinking about Mandy and how pleased she'd be with my decisions right now, to march into the Grill downtown and meet with Lacey Lease. She's wearing a stunning Altuzarra suit that I'd have said would make anyone look epic.

I was wrong, of course. The clothes don't make the woman. The woman most definitely ruins the clothes. If I posted that it would most definitely take off on social, not that I want to be known for being catty and hateful. I force myself to think happy thoughts.

Eddy and me sharing a milkshake last night.

Maren showing me her new cheers.

Emery reading me a story she wrote. It had a beginning, a middle, a longer middle, a side plot, an almost-the-end, then back to the middle. Then there was another side plot. And then it meandered. I fell asleep and snapped back awake as it took a sharp turn into fantasy, and then finally, ended. But still, her first story!

The great disaster's talking, and I realize that I totally zoned out on her. She's looking up at me, and again, holding out a manila envelope. Is that her job back home? Does she make envelopes?

"—list, and if you could just check over it and make sure everything is on here."

She wants me to help her with her theft of all Amanda's stuff.

I sigh.

"I'm not an expert on Amanda Saddler's property," I say, realizing as I say it that it's a lie. Even the ones I wasn't too familiar with, I now know everything about. I combed through every one of her documents looking for a will that named me before giving up. No one knows her properties like I do.

And I promised Donna I'd advocate for her, so I have to play nice right now. I force myself to sit down and order a coffee. "Black," I say.

"You usually want cream and sugar—"

I interrupt the waitress, whose name I should remember, but I just can't today. "Black."

"That boyfriend of yours is rubbing off on you." She winks as she departs.

A little warmth creeps down the back of my neck, and I try to remember that my life is blessed. Mandy's death and even Lacey's appearance don't change that. I pick up the list and scan it, figuring I can use this to segue into a question about Donna's house.

But it's not on the list.

"What about the little rental house that's a few months into a one-year lease?" I rattle off the street name. "The tenant was asking me about it today."

Lacey blinks.

"It's been recently remodeled," I say. "Much of the work was done by the tenant's boyfriend, and the lease terms reflect that."

Lacey opens her mouth, and then closes it with a click.

"The thing is, she's having some other issues. The hot water heater died, and there's a leak."

"If you mean the three bedroom here. . ." Lacey hands me a sheet of paper with property stats at the top.

I squint, making sure it's the right one. The photo's old, but the address and property details are right. "Yes, that's right."

"It was transferred by Amanda Saddler about ten days before she died."

"Transferred?" I don't understand. "What does that mean?"

Lacey huffs. "Gifted to the tenant."

"But wouldn't Donna know if that was the case? She'd have to sign something—"

"Look, all I know is the Court told me they had already given it to the tenant. Ellingson something."

Mandy *gave Donna a house?*

I'm really trying to not be selfish. I'm trying to unlock my inner peace, and care about others, and do good things instead of focusing on the bad. But it really stings that I was uninherited, while Donna got a house free and clear, and Abby got an office building *and* a ranch. I'm left with nothing because I didn't immediately get back together with Eddy?

What the?

My coffee shows up just in time to stave off my stupid tears. I glance over the list, nod my approval, and then bolt my coffee. It burns my throat, and I don't even care. "Alright, I gotta jet. Best of luck." I stand up and grab my purse.

"I have a buyer, you know," Lacey says.

That stops me in my tracks. "Excuse me?"

"The court said the paperwork will go through in the next two weeks, and you have to be out then. I can't give you any more extensions. My buyer's ready to close, with cash, immediately. The second the court approves the inventory."

Helen.

It has to be Helen.

165

And I'm just angry enough to march myself over to her house and demand that she work with me. She may laugh in my face, but it feels like I'm out of options.

So that's what I decide to do. My hands tremble on the steering wheel as I drive, my resolve crumbling a little more with every mile.

I've just reached Steve's house, where Abby said her sister's staying, noting the black Porsche really is parked right outside, when the last dregs of my confidence wash away. What am I doing here?

There's always Eddy's offer. He's been badgering me to just move the girls over to his house. He said he has plenty of room, and we know Roscoe and Snuggles get along. At least I'd have somewhere comfortable, close to the school, and *safe* to make a plan for my next steps.

My hand grabs the knob to throw the car into reverse when Helen appears outside my window.

"Amanda?" She's peering at me, and she sounds unsure.

Could I still peel out? Deny I ever came by? She'd probably recognize my license plate. She's too smart. I grit my teeth and roll my window down.

"Are you here for Abby?" She glances over her shoulder. "Because she and the kids live at the ranch. I'm staying here so I can take work calls without kids shrieking in the background."

Yes, that's why she's there. It's not that she drives them all up the wall. Her lack of insight actually makes me laugh. "I didn't realize she wasn't here," I lie.

"Alright, well, I'll tell her you came by, but she's probably home by now if you just head on down the road."

"Why are you here?" I surprise myself by asking.

"I just said," Helen says. "So I can take work calls—"

"No." I shake my head. "In Manila, I mean."

"Oh." Helen frowns.

"Wouldn't the meetings and calls be easier in New York? Isn't that usually where you live?"

"I needed to be here," Helen says quietly.

It's not a very clear answer, but something about the way she says it makes me believe it's the truth. I'd never have imagined Helen, the well-armored, well-*armed*, sister of Abigail, could be so vulnerable, especially to me.

And isn't that how I felt, after a summer with Abby? I needed to be near her? I needed her strength? I needed her support. I can't fault Helen for needing the same thing, even if she does seem like King Kong, saying she needs an emotional support bunny.

"I wish I hadn't turned you down," I say, so quietly that I'm almost sure she didn't understand a word.

"Interesting," she says. "Come inside and we can talk about it."

She didn't laugh. She didn't mock me, either. I still want to drive away, but I think about Helen for a minute. Not myself, not what I need, not Abby or her family or Eddy or Emery or Maren.

Helen Fisher.

She's not married or dating as far as I know. Her parents are a nightmare. She's rich as Croesus. Which means she's probably very, very lonely. Maybe that's what she needs more than anything else.

I've always needed money and stability. She clearly doesn't need that, but maybe her longing, and her need, maybe they're just as real as mine were. Maybe they're just as legitimate.

Maybe what she really needs is family.

"Alright. Maybe I will." Eddy calls as I'm walking inside. "Hello?"

"Are you okay? Why are you whispering?"

"I'm at Steve's house," I say.

"Why? Isn't he living at Abby's, now?"

"I know," I whisper even softer. "I came to chat with Helen."

"Helen?" Eddy pauses. "Why are you—"

"Can I call you back later, hon?"

"For sure," he says. "And you can explain then what's going on."

"Will do."

"So you're back with the rockstar." Helen's smile is broad. "He sure looked good making a scene at Abby's wedding."

"I'm so sorry about that," I say.

"Don't be. Usually I'm the one ruining things for Abby. It was so nice that someone else was to blame, mostly, for the mess that day."

I'm reminded then, that it was her date who picked a fight with my date, so we're kind of both at fault. Poor Abby. Her sister and her sister-in-law are both hot messes.

Helen sits on the far left of the sofa, right by one of the two wing chairs. She gestures for me to sit down.

I do. "What exactly did you want to talk about?" I'm literally cringing my way through every single word. What was I thinking, coming here?

"You said you regretted turning me down," Helen says. "Could you elaborate?"

She's a smart woman. She must know what I meant. I shut her down, and then I realized I literally had no other choice. I wished I'd been more level headed. Maybe I can run with that. "Mandy's death really threw me for a loop."

"You were robbed. Not once." She holds up a finger, and then swipes up another. "But twice." She leans back in her chair. "As I understand it, Abby's ranch should have belonged to you, at least in part." She lifts her eyebrows. "You helped remodel it. You watched kids and generally pitched in, and then when the court took it, Amanda

Saddler bought it and gave it to Abby instead." She whistles. "That must have ticked you off."

"At Mandy," I say. "Not at Abby."

"Really?" Helen lifts her eyebrows. "Not even a little bit?"

I contemplate my next words carefully. Helen's smart. She'll probably be able to sense whether I'm lying, so I have to assume she will also feel my sincerity. "I'm a selfish person. I think we probably share that particular flaw. When I first moved out here, I thought if I could just copy what Abigail did, I could be like her. I could have a charmed life, people who adored me, and guys following me around like lovesick puppies."

"And?" Helen's practically smirking. "Did it work?"

"Of course not," I say. "It would be like wanting a lovely wedding cake in a fancy boutique shop window, and then making cupcakes from a mix you bought at the local grocery store and trying to frost them with a ninety-nine-cent tub of frosting and wishing they looked like that cake."

"I don't understand."

I huff. "I'm not Abby, okay? My analogies don't always make sense. But I realized recently that the reason everyone loves her is that *she loves them*. It's not because she's so lovable that everyone's desperate to help and bless her. It's that she's always *loving* other people, and they can feel it."

"I don't get it."

"All I did was think about myself," I say. "I wanted to change myself so I could have what she had. What I should have done was change myself so I could *be* like she *is*."

"But that's hard," Helen says. "We can't change who we are. Leopards don't become tigers. And they certainly don't become housecats. Or waffles."

Waffles? That analogy went off the rails fast. I try to

169

refocus her. "We're all cats, though," I say. "If we retract our claws and play nice, we can coexist in a house."

"You have nothing to offer me," Helen says. "I've seen your business plan, and I'm already buying Amanda Saddler's place. I know why you regret turning me down—I was doing you a favor by inviting you to work with me, and I only did it at Abby's incessant insistence."

I should've known.

"You turned me down, and I got credit from my sister for being generous. It was a huge win for me, honestly."

"Then why did you invite me in today?" I'm suddenly furious. "Did you just want to gloat?" I can't believe her. "You really are the devil."

Helen's lips turn up at the corners.

"You're even worse than I thought."

"I invited you in because I thought it might be entertaining." She stares at me without a hint of guilt. I wonder how she manages that. "But now that you're here, being all honest and insightful and contrite, and maybe even a little hateful, I think maybe I was wrong."

"Wrong?" I ask. "About what?" The world may tilt on its axis, if Helen's admitting she's wrong.

"Maybe you do have something to offer." She twists around on the sofa and grabs a black briefcase. She reaches inside it and pulls out a red folder, and then she slides it across the coffee table toward me. "Here."

"What's this?"

"It's the agreement I had my people draw up before I approached you."

I look at it, but I don't touch it.

"You should take a look. Abby already reviewed it and made a lot of changes to get it into that form."

"Abby's one of your people now?"

Helen laughs. "Yeah, right. She's one of *your* people."

That floors me. "You're saying she negotiated this on my behalf. . .without even telling me?"

Helen shrugs. "Are you really surprised?"

No. Actually, I'm not. "I'll sign it."

"You haven't even looked at it."

"It says we're partners in developing Gold Strike? That we'll make decisions 50/50 and split profits 80/20 or something. Right?"

"You know Abigail fairly well," Helen says. "And apparently you know me better than I thought, too."

"Except it's forty-nine, fifty-one," I say. "Because you'd never agree to anything that could gridlock a deal."

Helen shakes her head. "Abigail was adamant that it had to be fifty-fifty." She laughs, and then she speaks in a singsong voice that's clearly a mockery of Abby. "'Any partnership must be equal or it's not really a partnership.'"

"Huh."

"'If it's not a partnership,' I asked her, 'then what is it?'"

"What did she say?"

"'A dictatorship,'" Helen says, her eyes dancing. "'And you know we can't have that."

I pull a pen out of my purse, flip to the last page, and sign my name with a flourish. "Gold Strike is back in business."

"It appears that it is," Helen says. "And the first thing we need to do is discuss the name. How about we change it to Strike Gold?"

This time, I'm the one laughing. "That's one of the few things I will never budge on. You see, Amanda Saddler insisted it be Gold Strike."

As I walk out the front door an hour or so later, I realize that Helen basically owns me now. If she says jump, I better hope I can get that high. It's almost eerie how Eddy calls the second I walk out.

"What's going on?" he asks.

I fill him in on the broad strokes.

"So you're not moving in with me?" His voice is practically plaintive.

"Not yet," I say. "And that's good news. The idea of moving right now might have killed me."

"I suppose," he says. "But you could at *least* come over for a sleepover now and again."

I laugh. "I'll run it past Roscoe and see what he thinks."

"How will it be, working with Helen, do you think?"

"I thought she might be a cyborg," I say. "But now that we've spent a bit of time talking, I think she may actually be a friend. . .disguised in the devil's skinsuit."

The words sound insane as I say them, but I realize that I believe them. Some of my closest friends started out as enemies, or at the very best, frenemies.

Who knows? Maybe Helen will be next.

# 15

# DONNA

When Aiden's old enough to be making career decisions, I'm going to steer him away from being a lawyer. What a terrible job. Case in point: I'm calling Abby at eight forty-five on a Friday night.

I'd like to say that I'm an anomaly, but I feel like a lot of her friends call her with legal questions and emergencies. In fact, we're only friends now because she has such a big heart that even after I was trying to screw her, she helped me with an emergency. . . late at night. Her husband's a doctor, and I imagine they get a lot of late night medical calls as well. Between the two of them, it's a wonder they're willing to have any friends at all.

Just when I think I'm about to go to voicemail, she answers. "Hello?"

"Abby." She can't see me, but I cringe as I say her name.

"Is everything alright?"

"Not really," I say.

"Please tell me that moron isn't threatening to keep Aiden?" Only a stellar lawyer would be able to keep track, on top of managing her own busy life, of when my son is due to return home from California. "Gabe has the date of his return circled on the calendar and he's made a little countdown chain with paper rings that gets shorter every day, so he has to come back Monday, or I'll be getting an earful."

I laugh, and for a split second, it's not even forced. "Aww, Gabe. Have I mentioned how much I love him?"

"What's going on, Donna?"

"Can he win if he sues for custody a year after the court assigned me as custodian?" I know we've talked about this before, and she helped me feel way better. I'm counting on her doing the same thing again.

"I mean, I'm not licensed in California, which is where I assume he'd try to bring the claim, but if I remember right from when I looked it up, their criterion were like, the age and health of the kid, emotional ties to parents, parental capacity, and maybe a history of abuse? There was one more element. . .I think it's ties to the community, school, and home or something like that."

Criterion? Ties? Capacity? "What does all of that mean?"

"To bring a claim at all, he'd need to show something significant had changed, and then he'd need a compelling reason to bring a suit in California again, after a judge transferred to Utah."

"Like?"

"You losing your job, him getting a new one, evidence of the child failing to thrive, that kind of thing."

The child psychiatrist or therapist or whatever is making more sense.

Aiden's doing fine in school, thankfully, but he has said he misses his old school and friends on several occasions. Other than Gabe, he hasn't made many new pals here. It's partially my fault. I don't really have time for many other friends, so I never take him to see anyone else.

"He used to be in soccer and basketball, and I haven't done anything like that here."

"That alone is pretty weak—"

"My job here's ending," I say flatly. "Although I think I'll have another one lined up with a spin-off company."

"Okay."

"And his dad did get a new job—quite a high paying one."

"That's his real motivation," Abby says. "They'll do a re-up, or you could, on how much he pays in child support. So if he can get Aiden back before that happens, he won't have to pay you a truckload of money—in fact, you'd owe him. I don't know this for sure, but based on what I have seen of his personality, he would really like that."

"He's also always wanted to win at anything and everything he does," I say.

"I'm sure that's part of it, but don't underestimate the motivation of money."

"But you're saying he *could* petition for a change."

"With all that going on? For sure. Would he win or even get jurisdiction moved? I doubt it."

She doubts it. But she's not positive. My husband, who walked away without a backward glance after stealing millions is threatening, and. . . I'm not reassured.

I'm terrified.

"Donna, try not to worry. There's nothing you can do about it, anyway, so it doesn't help to fret."

"If he claims Aiden's better off in California? With his old friends and school and activities, and a doctor agrees with him?"

Abby sighs. "Courts have gotten much more progressive, which by and large is good for kids. Plenty of dads are great, and they take excellent care of their children. It's good that they don't automatically award the kids to moms as a matter of course. But it does make things like this harder. We may have to work to show why he's better with you, even in a school with fewer activities and resources, and even if the transition may have been difficult for him. Certainly we can find a physician who will argue that the difficulties may stem from his parents' recent divorce, or his father's time in jail."

The words feel ripped from my very soul. "He also says that he wants to stay with his dad."

"Oh, that must've hurt," Abby says. "I'm sorry he said that, but try to remember that he *is* only seven. Gabe's eight and he told me yesterday that he wants to be a trash collector when he grows up. Kids evolve and change. I don't spend much time worrying about what they say to me once or even twice. A judge won't be utterly swayed by it either, even if they do allow a consultation at his age."

In spite of her attempts to calm me down, it's a very, very long weekend. I'm still fretting when I get to work on Monday. I'm not even supposed to be here, since I had the time off for Aiden's return, but I don't know where else to go.

Charlie texted me this morning at eight a.m., informing me that he will not be bringing Aiden home. When I sent the screenshot to Abigail, she squeed in response.

Apparently this is the *best* thing that could have happened for us. Failure to honor the court order is not taken lightly. But I know Charlie. He doesn't make stupid blunders, so he must have some kind of ace in his back pocket.

I'm definitely preoccupied when I open the front door of our little planning unit. When David Park shouts "Hooray" and uncorks the champagne, it nearly hits me in the eye.

I dodge just in time. "Whoa."

Champagne's bubbling over the side of the bottle. At nine in the morning.

"What's going on?"

I glance around, but no one else is here.

David points at a screen. "Talking to my sister—but now you're here too, and I won't have to drink this alone."

"Why are we drinking champagne?" I try not to sound judgey. "At breakfast time?"

He brandishes a jug of orange juice at me. "Hello, mimosas."

I can't help chuckling at his enthusiasm. "But why?"

"Apparently there was some stiff competition on the dude ranch," a voice from his computer screen that I assume is his sister chimes in. I can't help noticing that she has an accent—which is only noteworthy because David doesn't. "He's quite pleased to have won."

"Oh." I'd almost forgotten about that. "So you are buying my family's ranch?" I take a few steps so I can see the screen on his computer.

"Wait, it's her ranch?" His sister's absolutely gorgeous. Pale, luminescent skin. Full lips. The roundest almond shaped eyes I've ever seen, that are a deep, textured brown shade. "You didn't say you had an in."

"Her brother owns it, but they aren't close," David says. "Believe me, it's still a triumph."

"Helen Fisher didn't get it?" I didn't think Abby's sister would ever back down. I felt like she'd pay any amount to get what she wanted.

David shrugs. "We went back and forth a few rounds, but then she just bowed out."

I wonder why. I mean, I should be delighted. Without this ranch, I could be unemployed soon. This guarantees my ongoing employment, and even though Patrick had his reservations, I think with my guidance, David will do a decent job. Or at least as decent a job as you can do with a working cattle ranch that's forced to host tourists.

It's going to be really strange to go back and work at my

own home, especially with it being run by strangers. Why can't everything in my life be fine at the same time? My love life is finally going well, and I have actual friends, so I guess I should've expected my job to end and my son to decide he wants to live with his dad.

David eyes me sideways, but doesn't say anything. All day long, he keeps shooting me strange looks, but every question he asks has something to do with work, including a lot of questions about the resumes he's sent me to review for my replacement, the new resort manager.

"What's wrong with you?" David finally asks, half an hour before quitting time.

I shrug. "Nothing."

He frowns. "Weren't you supposed to have the day off today? Or was that tomorrow?"

"Today." I can't help my sigh.

"We didn't have anything that couldn't wait," he says. "So why are you here?"

He may not have noticed my ragged sigh, but he definitely notices when I burst into tears. Poor David. He's a really good guy. If Amanda hadn't been so clearly destined for Eddy, I would've gotten over my ill-advised crush and encouraged that. He deserves someone good. He's patient, calm, and supportive as I recover from my bawling and explain what's going on.

"Abby will get it under control, I'm sure," I say. "It's just scary, that's all."

"Have you made a plan?" he asks.

"A plan?"

"About what you'd do, heaven forbid, if the court did rule for your ex?"

I can practically feel the blood draining from my face.

"I'm not trying to scare you," David says. "But as someone with a lot of business ventures, I can tell you that the court is always a single person, and that means that no matter how good your legal representation, and no matter how solid your case, the results are always a bit of a wild card."

Any calm I'd managed to find evaporates like spit in the Sahara.

It hits me then, after hearing David say that the court is a *person*. Charlie or his parents must know a judge. Through Golf. Church. Somehow, they have a contact they're reasonably certain will take their side. I'm sure of it. Otherwise, why would he suddenly start insisting on this? How would Charlie be comfortable ignoring the court ruling and keeping Aiden if he didn't have some kind of backroom deal?

David's right.

I need a plan if things don't go my way. If Abigail can't work her miracle, what then?

"You may not want to hear this, but I'm only trying to be helpful, alright? I know you're happy here. I know you grew up here and have friends here. You have a boyfriend too, and he seems to be making you really happy."

Where's he going with this?

"But if the worst happens and the court thinks it's better for Aiden to be in California, I can give you a job there easily. A lot of my business is based out of California. I'd even offer you a substantial raise—to address the much higher cost of living, obviously."

And now I'm bawling. Again.

"I hope that means you're touched," he says. "Because if I upset you again, I'm so sorry. You for sure have the job offer here, working on the ranch I'm buying from your lousy brother. Maybe it'll all go your way, and then I'm just the jerk who upset you over nothing."

"No, this is gratitude," I finally manage to say. "For sure."

I'm driving home when Holden's mom calls. Normally,

I wouldn't pick up. My 'friends' from California showed me exactly how close we were when Charlie went to jail. They all, as if they were on some kind of group message or something, closed ranks and dropped me like a hot potato.

But she just saw Aiden, and she might know something helpful. I can't afford to screen her call out of residual rage.

"Karin," I say. "How are you?"

"I can't believe how long it's been since we last talked," she says. "Aiden has grown *so* much. He's taller than Holden!"

He was always taller than Holden. Her kid's a cocktail shrimp. "I'm so glad Charlie took the time to get the boys together."

"He's been amazing," Karin says. "I can't believe you let him get away."

*Get away?* "He embezzled millions of dollars."

She laughs, like I'm making a hilarious joke. "I bet you're wishing you'd stood by him right about now instead of believing all that nonsense."

Nonsense? Oh my word. I'm about one inch from telling Karin just how I really feel about her, so it's probably better to change the subject. "So what did the boys do?"

"Yesterday?" she asks. "Or today?"

Why's Aiden playing with Holden so much? Something weird is definitely going on. "You saw him yesterday *and* today?"

"I watched them while Charles went to another fundraiser. Your ex has just been absolutely indispensable for Spencer, you know."

He's a politician. I almost forgot about that. Last I checked, he was just an assemblyman. "Is his term almost up?"

"He's running for mayor soon," she says. "And based on

current polling, we think he'll be a lock. People just love him."

Which still doesn't explain. . .

"And Charles and his parents and their friends have set up a dozen different fundraisers already. It's an absolute crime, but the political party hardly provides them anything these days. They have to come up with all their own campaign money, at least at this stage."

"Wow, I had no idea Charlie even had an interest in politics."

"Neither did we," she says, "but we bumped into him at the movie theater, of all places. My brother was with us, and we all had gone to see that ghastly cartoon—you know, the one with the flying dogs?"

Luckily, I don't know. "Your brother." Something about him's familiar, but I can't place quite what. "Have I met your brother?"

"He's almost never around," she says. "Judges just don't have much free time. Between their full dockets and handling administrative things, they practically work him to the bone. But he just *loves* it. I don't get it."

There it is.

"Well, anyway, I just wanted to say how delighted I was that Aiden plans to come back. School hasn't been the same for Holden without him."

I grit my teeth.

"When things start up again, we really need to get together. With the number of ladies buzzing around Charles, if you don't act quickly, you may lose him for good."

If I were the Hulk, I'd be shredding my clothing and the interior of my car as I smashed the phone to bits. But the devil inside of me stays tucked right where it belongs. My hand's not green. Not even my eyes change, judging by the reflection in my rearview mirror. "When I get back, you'll be the first person I call. Thanks so much for filling me in," I say.

"Of course, girl. I mean, my husband is all Team Charles, but I've always had your back."

Yeah, just like Judas Iscariot had big J's back. "That means so much."

"We should make shirts to wear to PTO events." She's practically gushing. "Oh, what an amazing idea! I wonder what lettering we should use. Team Donna. And I'm not the only one, I swear. All the moms are pulling for you."

"Really?"

"Well, all the married ones, anyway." She giggles then.

If I did have to relocate back to California, the only thing worse than dealing with all the PTO moms would be seeing Charlie all the time.

I wouldn't even have Will around to support me.

That thought has me pulling over to the side of the road to practice breathing techniques I haven't used since Aiden's birth. Why does my life always go like this? Normal people don't have to make these choices, do they? Because if things don't go my way, the only path left to me that has Aiden in my life every day will require me to move to California.

And my boyfriend runs a ranch, so he can't follow me there.

Which means, if I can't figure out how to stop this runaway train, I may soon have to choose between Will and Aiden. I already know who I'll pick if it comes to it.

It's the first time in my life that I've really regretted being a mother.

# 16

## ABIGAIL

The first time I ever set eyes on an ultrasound machine, I swear, the imaging of the fetus looked like a blob. The tech pointed out Ethan's arms, and I could make those out. But when she started pointing out other things—heart, lungs, bladder—I was lying when I nodded along and said, "Oh. Neat."

And when they started talking about the gender?

Yeah. I definitely saw nothing that would tell me male or female. I didn't have a lot of confidence that Ethan wasn't really going to be Elena instead.

But they were right.

After four babies, I got a little better at making sense of what I was seeing. And today, the guy holding my hand for this ultrasound is trained in reading them. He looks positively radiant about the images on the screen.

"Your estimate and ours line up perfectly," the tech says. "In fact, you're only one day off from our projected due date."

"How does it look?" Steve asks. "Are the sizes all where they should be?"

"Well, at sixteen weeks and five days, the head is

supposed to be. . ." He clicks and moves the mouse, and then he clicks more. "Yep, right on."

Steve's beaming. He almost hasn't *stopped* beaming since I told him over the weekend. He must've pulled some major strings to get us in for an ultrasound this fast.

"What about the gender?" His look's almost sly. "We don't want to wait to find out."

"Are you sure?" The tech taps the screen. "Because I'm not really supposed to tell you. The radiologist will read it, and then—"

"Oh, please." Steve rolls his eyes. "You know already."

Flattery is absolutely the best way with this guy, I can already tell. "I mean, when you've done this for a certain number of years—"

"It's a boy," I say.

Both their jaws drop.

"It's not my first ultrasound either," I say. "And it's not my first boy."

"Wow," the tech says. "The mother almost never notices on her own, but yes. She's right. It's most definitely a boy. Either that, or he's growing a third leg."

I try not to let my cringe over his joke show on my face. He's really trying to be a friendly guy, and I appreciate it. "Let's hope it's not a third leg."

"That's my boy," Steve says.

"Oh, for the love—"

Both the guys are laughing so hard, I don't think they even noticed the OB came in. "I'm assuming the ultrasound looks pretty decent?"

"Nothing concerning I saw," the tech says.

"Great. Let's head back to an exam room, and I'll complete my exam. I like for all the mothers to get a pelvic and—"

"I have a meeting, actually," I say. There's no way I'm about to let her do a breast exam, and if she's insisting on a pelvic, that could definitely be next. "This whole thing was amazing—that you could get us in so quickly. You have no idea how much we appreciate it. But if we could shift whatever else we need today to the next appointment, that would be amazing."

"Oh." The OB frowns, but she doesn't argue further. "Well, I do have plenty of other patients waiting, since I squeezed you in."

"Yeah, see?" I pull my shirt back down over my barely-there belly and button my pants. Then I stand up. "We so appreciate it, but we don't want to impose even more."

"Alright," Steve says. "The front desk can hopefully find us another time, and we'll get all those Ts crossed then."

"Perfect." She extends her hand. "So nice to meet you, and congratulations."

"There's not a better obstetrician this side of the country," Steve says. "The hospital was pretty delighted when she transferred out here. Dr. Heaps actually ran the maternal-fetal medicine program in Seattle for a decade before coming out here to be near her parents. We're darn lucky to have a perinatologist at all, much less one of her caliber."

"I've had four easy pregnancies in the past," I say.

"But now that you're over forty," Dr. Heaps says, "we just want to keep a little bit closer eye."

Great. I'm like a banana that's too spotty—any little anomaly and everyone worries. If they want to wrap me in bubble wrap now, imagine if I told them about my lump. I feel better and better about my decision to hold off on saying anything.

Unfortunately, the lie I concocted about a meeting means I have to drive right over to the office the second we get back. It's especially unfortunate because I feel sick as a dog and really just want to lie down and sleep.

Instead, I force myself to work through the pile of misery that's always waiting for me. The first few briefs I wrote were almost exciting. I felt like I would make a difference in the world. But somewhere between then and now. . .the magic all went out of it. I suppose that's how most jobs are.

I'm finalizing the inventory for the Eugene estate for the five millionth time when the door to my office jingles.

"Hello?"

The only sound I hear is a bit of shuffling in the front room.

I'm not at all big yet, but for some reason, it already feels hard to stand up. I ignore my aching feet and creaking knees and hop up and walk through the back door into the front room.

Coincidentally, it's Mr. Fred Eugene, my cute-as-a-sharpei client. I haven't seen him in a while. Mostly his fiancée, Brooke Dailey, calls or comes by on his behalf.

"I was just finalizing your inventory with the updated valuation. I think the court will finally approve it, and we can be done. What can I do for you?"

Mr. Eugene grimaces. "The thing is. . ."

I duck my head a bit, hoping to get a better view of his face. "Is everything alright?"

He glances up at me and then quickly looks back down again.

"Why don't we go to my office?"

He follows me slowly, and I honestly worry that he may be having a stroke or something. I watch him carefully, one of my hands ready to whip out my phone and call Steve.

"Here, please take a seat." I perch on the edge of my desk, because standing for long periods of time leaves me a little unsteady right now. I've always had way less energy in the first part of pregnancy, and this one's no exception.

He collapses onto one of my wingback chairs, and finally he looks up at me. "Can you draft a prenup, and then tell my fiancée that you're insisting on it?"

I couldn't be more shocked if he told me his first wife was back from the dead. He always seems so happy with her. "A prenup?" I wonder whether he really knows what he's asking. "Why do you want one?"

"Don't they tell the person you're marrying that they can't have any of your money?"

Or. . .maybe he totally gets it. "That's a common misconception," I say. "Entering into a marriage is basically a contract. You're joining two people as one, legally, for a lot of things. So the prenuptial agreement can literally cover any aspect of that agreement. It certainly *can* say that she can't have any of your money. Is that really what you want to do?"

He swallows slowly. "I'm a little nervous that she only wants to marry me to get my first wife's money."

I'm very proud of myself for not reacting to that obscenely obtuse comment. Once, when Ethan was very small, he hopped on Nate's treadmill and turned it on. He was flung off onto the ground, and afterward, he said, "I shouldn't have done that." I managed to keep a straight face then too, but it was just as funny a statement.

"She's just so much younger than me, and sometimes she acts like she really loves me, but other times she seems. . .frustrated with me."

"Aren't you getting married in like a week?"

He sighs. "Is it too late? Does it have to be done a month before or something?"

I shake my head. "You could do it an hour before and that would be fine, but these kinds of things often cause fights. You should be prepared for that."

"Well, that's why I want *you* to be the one insisting on it." He looks so hopeful, so pathetically hopeful.

"Mr. Eugene, I can't make you ask for anything like this. She'd immediately know it wasn't me, or if she didn't understand, she'd insist that you fire me." I clasp my hands together so I have something to focus on. "Couldn't you just be honest with her? Ask her outright whether she really loves you?"

He sighs. "It's hard to be honest with someone you love. Sometimes your love blinds you."

"But if you can't talk to her, if you can't be honest, and if you can't trust her—" I was about to say, *why are you with her?* But then I think about me and Steve. I love him so much, and I love this little baby, too. But I'm afraid that if I'm honest with Steve, it may harm the baby.

And our relationship.

Maybe things aren't as easy or as clear as I wish they were.

"Sure," I say. "I'll draw up a prenup, and I'll tell her we found a letter from your dearly departed wife saying she wanted you to get a prenup if you ever remarried. How's that?"

His eyes light up. "That's perfect!"

"What are you hoping will happen with this?" I need to know, if only to be sure how to draft it.

"I want her to look at the prenup and say, 'I'll sign anything. I just love you so much! Who cares whether I get money.' But I'm afraid that if there's a prenup, she'll just walk away."

"So it's a test?"

He thinks for a moment. "I suppose it is."

Let's hope she's not smart enough to see that coming and call his bluff. "If she agrees to sign, will you make her do it?"

"No way," he says. "Agreeing to do it will be enough."

After he leaves, I think about how nice it would be if there was something like that I could do to see how Steve would react. I'd certainly sleep better at night if he knew the truth, but I'm afraid that I'm past the stage where I can test things out. I've already put a ring on it, and as a doctor, his opinions are pretty firmly baked.

Once I've made my way through a respectable amount of my to-do list, and I've drafted a middle-of-the-road prenup, I print a copy and drop it in the mail for Mr. Eugene, along with a letter explaining that it should conform with the details of his wife's wishes, per her recently discovered letter. That should do the trick, I hope.

By the time I get home, I really need a hug. Or ten.

Steve's outside, making use of the last of the light to teach Izzy and Whitney a lesson. I'm surprised Emery and Maren aren't here as well. I stand and watch for a moment before they notice me. I'm considering giving up and heading inside when little arms wrap around my midsection.

"Oh, hey." I turn around to the sight of Gabe's little round face, smiling up at me. The faint freckles across the bridge of his nose stand out in this light, especially when he's beaming. "Mom. I love you."

"Are you saying that because you want to watch an episode of *Ninjago* and you're trying to butter me up?" I quirk one eyebrow.

His smile widens. "I mean, I do want to, but I also love you." The mischievous glint in his eye is one hundred and ten percent Nate. It used to pain me to see it, but now it's a light spot in my day. Isn't it funny how loving someone new can free you to remember the love you had before with fondness?

I thought I'd feel like I was betraying Nate, but instead, now that I've found Steve, I just feel safe again. I lean over and press a kiss against his squishy little cheek. "Fine," I say.

Again, I'm blessed with a ragged-toothed smile. Eight's an awkward age—the handful of adult teeth crowding out the kid ones. The baby teeth are too small, the adult teeth too big, and their bodies are starting to stretch to become something more, but they're overbalanced and over-energized and they fumble and bumble everywhere they go.

I love every minute of his coltish awkwardness.

"One more squeeze," I say.

His arms tighten again around me, and then he kisses my face one last time. "Love you."

"Love you, too."

"What about me?" Steve's riding at the same time as he trains the girls now, deeming them good enough that he can train a green horse while he's teaching them. There are very few things in this world hotter than watching my husband teaching a young, goofy horse how to be a better animal, but watching him do that *while* he teaches my kids to be better people?

I guess that is.

"Nope," he says, "you still need softer hands, Izzy. How'd you feel if I yanked on your face like that?"

Izzy's at the age where she's starting to argue with everything. "But—"

"Iz, first you ask nicely. You only yank on them if they've ignored you, just like your mama does."

Luckily, she still knows when to back down. "Okay," Izzy says. "Sorry."

Steve's horse is tossing his head and pawing on the ground. He tightens his reins and starts tugging to get him to pay attention and quit, but he's not too distracted to correct my other kid, too. "And Whitney, sit up straight and still. I can't tell anyone I taught you if you fling yourself around like a bobblehead. I'd be too embarrassed."

"You guys almost done?"

Steve smiles. "We'll be in soon. I smoked a roast—it should be ready when we get inside. We'll feed the horses and be right in." He swings sideways and encourages Gus forward. He was a real mess last month, but he's starting to shape up now that Steve brought him over here and rides him for every lesson with the girls. When his lips draw near, my heart kicks into gear, and my belly flip-flops, but not in a bad way.

In the way it does during the best parts of a good romcom.

I thought this kind of thing never lasted, but so far? It has with us. His lips finally cover mine, and miraculously, Gus stands perfectly still. He's making me like him more already.

With Steve's mouth against mine, the rest of the world disappears and I'm peaceful. Calm. Joyous.

When he finally straightens up and heads back to the center of the paddock, I sigh. Life shouldn't be like this—bad things to balance out the good—but sometimes it just is. I had a lot of good years with Nate, so I'm resolved to appreciate whatever amount of time I have with Steve.

The smell when I walk inside the front door is beyond heavenly. I immediately begin to salivate.

"You're home late," Helen says from where she's curled up on the sofa.

"Aw dang." I toss my keys on the table. "I went to the wrong place again."

Helen rolls her eyes and sits up. "Izzy texted and told me Steve was making roast."

"And you thought that was an invitation?" My lips twitch from suppressing my smile. "Or are you like a dog—can't resist the smell once you've caught the scent?"

"Is that a briefcase?" Helen tsks. "Home late, and brought stuff with you. I thought I was the workaholic in the family."

"Right now, I think you're the unemployed one." I can't help teasing her. I'm a lawyer in a tiny town, making a third of what I was making back in Houston.

If I'm lucky.

The fact that Helen's between acquisitions hardly leaves her unemployed. She owns several huge companies and manages all her investments to boot, but I can't miss the chance to needle her. Especially since I've essentially always been a pincushion to her ribbing.

"Actually, I struck a small deal today. Izzy's text was perfectly timed." She stretches. "I'm back in the saddle."

"I'm not sure you can use the phrase that way," I say. "It means to get back to something you used to do. If the deal is what you mentioned before—working with Amanda to make her and Mandy's dream come to life—that's not really back to what you've ever done in the past."

Helen waves her hand through the air. "Pish posh. The point is that I'm out there in the business world again, doing what I do best. Making things happen."

I doubt she knows a single thing about the hospitality business, and she knows even less about this region. "Are you sure this isn't just because you're mad at David Park?"

Helen jumps to her feet. "That jerk only offered on the ranch because he heard I'd done it. It makes *no* sense for him to buy one this far away from his stupid resort in Dutch John. There are plenty of places closer that he should have bought."

She's never mentioned that before, but it makes sense. "I wonder why he did buy the Ellingson place."

"To piss me off," she says. "Ever since that stupid fight at the wedding, he's been even worse than usual. I swear, that guy was unbearable in business school, but the real world hasn't taught him a thing. He's absolutely insufferable now."

"He's not bad looking, though," I say.

"Sure, he's hot enough—"

"So you *do* find him attractive." I can't help gloating a bit.

Helen rolls her eyes. "You're just trying to distract me."

"Distract you?" I frown. "From what?"

My big sister points at the coffee table, and for the first time, I notice what's covering it. Blue baby booties. Blue baby socks. Blue bottles. Blue blankets.

It's a whole blue baby explosion.

"I went shopping today, and it was so fun I almost changed my mind."

"Changed your mind?" I'm having so much trouble keeping up with her today. I can't decide whether she's being particularly bizarre, or whether I'm dealing with pregnancy brain-fog.

"I've decided to throw you a baby shower." She crosses the room, grabbing my arm as she passes me and dragging me toward the window. Her arms sweeps across the entire thing. "Imagine this."

Oh, dear.

"A huge circus tent. Clowns, maybe? I haven't decided. Photo booths. Waiters with trays serving the funniest, cutest little blue things my chef can come up with. Maybe a baseball theme? We could have the Yankees come sign balls for everyone." She pauses. "People here probably hate them. Who do they like? The Mariners?"

I scrunch my nose.

"Ooh, or maybe tiny doctor stuff!" She goes all starry eyed. "That's it. It'll be so cute. Tiny scrubs. Tiny stethoscopes. We could have the wait staff dress like doctors and write prescriptions for drinks." She claps. "This is going to be so stinking cute." She pauses again. "But is that big enough?"

*Big* enough? "Helen, where do you think you are? We're not in New York or Chicago or L.A."

"Do you think Steve would wear scrubs and, I don't know, diagnose people, but in a funny way? The internet says guys actually come to these, now." She shakes her head and waves me off. "It doesn't matter. Look, the point is, it's going to be amazing. The nicest baby shower anyone in this teensy speck of a town has *ever* seen. Even your snooty Amanda will be bowled over."

"Why?" I ask. "What's the point?"

She drops an arm around my shoulders. "Because, dear sister, I'm finally going to be here for once when you have this child. I want to be part of it! I want to welcome him into the world, and by golly, he's going to *love* his Auntie Helen the most."

"Tell me you haven't mentioned any of this to Mom and Dad."

This time, it's Helen who scrunches her nose. "I mean, Mom said she'd never been to a shower, either."

"There's a reason," I say. "Can you even imagine her at a baby shower?" I groan. "It wasn't bad enough to have her here for the wedding?"

"She didn't even know you were expecting," Helen says. "I had to make up some bogus story about how you were waiting until twenty weeks so you'd be sure the baby was viable."

I close my eyes and rub my hand across my forehead. No wonder she called me three times today. "And is she coming for the shower?"

"Of course. She's making you a blanket." Helen's lips are twitching.

"I mean, at least that should be interesting." I can't even imagine what a blanket made by Mom will look like. Wow, lately every time I think things can't get stranger?

They do.

# 17

# AMANDA

Some dogs get along with everyone. They wag their tails and lick hands and even jump up on any person they meet. Some dogs make new friends easily and follow them around, as devoted as can be.

Border collies are often hailed as one of the friendliest breeds. They're hardworking for sure, but also social and generally welcoming.

Roscoe? Not so much.

And since Mandy's death, he's become practically feral. It's like, in his mind, she helped keep us safe, and now he's on his own. When the mail lady comes, he snarls like a rabid lunatic. I've honestly been worried that he might go through the window that's next to the door and attack her.

When Ulysses comes in his tractor to cut the lawn, I have to make sure he's locked up, or he'll race after him, snapping and barking and growling like a wild animal.

"I'm not sure what to do about it," I say.

Eddy's grinning. He doesn't look concerned at all.

"What if he bites someone? What if they insist we put him down? Why aren't you taking me seriously?"

He wraps an arm around my shoulders and yanks me

against him. Then he pats the sofa next to him and Roscoe hops up and curls up next to me.

"All dogs may have originally been domesticated from the wolf, you know. A lot of people believe that. Or maybe not. But these days, all the different dog breeds exemplify different traits. Why do you think Roscoe picked you, of all people, when you moved here?"

I snuggle up next to him, leaning my head against his shoulder. "Because I'm wonderful?"

"Obviously he liked you," Eddy says. "But something about you drew him to pick you specifically."

I wait a moment, but when he doesn't keep talking, I poke him. "What, then, Mr. Smarty Vet?"

"Border collies are working dogs. They need jobs. They're exceptionally smart—quite possibly the smartest breed of dog on earth. You can teach them hundreds of commands, ranging from oral to visual, and they keep them all straight."

"I'm pretty smart, too. So that's why?"

Eddy laughs.

He *laughs*.

"Then he'd have picked Abigail."

I can't help laughing with him. "Fine. Then what's your point?"

"Believe me, if you'd met Jed, whom he loved before you, you'd see the humor in you suggesting he chose you for your intelligence. Jed—the person who he bonded with from when he was a pup—was a deeply broken person. He needed love and guidance, and he lived alone here."

"Broken?" I sit up, and I start to get really offended. "Now, what exactly—"

He presses a finger to my lips. "Just listen for a minute, before you get your dander up."

I huff. "I have no dandruff."

"Wow, you're a genius. Dander, not dandruff." He's

laughing again, and I'm laughing too. "Jed was independent, but also lonely. He was in love with his next door neighbor his entire life, but too proud to do anything about it."

This sounds a little uncomfortably familiar. "I didn't wait for decades and do nothing with you."

Eddy's million dollar smile is so distracting, I almost forget I'm annoyed. "My point is that he needed to find someone he could love, someone he could trust, and someone he felt needed his help."

"You're saying I'm his *job*?"

"It's an honor, you know, to be chosen by someone like Roscoe."

He hears his name and his head lifts, his ears perk up, the one on the right flopping down at the tip like it always does. Then he tilts his head. I reach around my stupidly hot boyfriend and ruffle the fur on top of his head.

"I think he could tell that after Paul, and after no success finding someone new, and in an unfamiliar place, you needed someone to love you."

My heart contracts a bit. "He wasn't wrong." I'm not crying, but I swipe at an errant bit of moisture anyway. "I mean, he has saved me."

"From the cougar?" Eddy drags Roscoe onto his lap and rubs him all over. "Or from your loneliness?"

"Both?"

"And he's not very social, but look." Eddy pushes Roscoe back to his corner of the sofa, and then he leans over and pats his ankles. "Come on, Snuggles. Come on, girl."

She eyes me sideways, and then she looks out both of the front windows intently, and only then does she trot over to the sofa. She puts up with me, but she adores Eddy, and she likes Roscoe pretty well, too. Once she's been petted enough, she curls up on the floor at the edge of the sofa, just below where Roscoe's lying.

"She likes no one but me."

"And Roscoe, apparently," I say.

"Wolf dogs usually only like one person," Eddy says. "I think she tolerates you and the girls because Roscoe has made it plain that she has to."

"Good job, Roscoe," I say.

And again, after hearing his name, he's up and trying to crawl over Eddy's lap to lick my face.

"Since Mandy's death, Roscoe can sense your pain. He's doing double duty now, keeping you safe like he always did, but also trying to make sure no one can threaten you now that Mandy's not here to protect you."

"That's why he keeps trying to hop into the car everywhere I go?"

"Exactly," he says. "He's not being annoying. He's trying to be helpful."

"But now that you're around all the time, will he level off?"

Eddy shrugs. "I suppose it depends on whether he thinks he can trust me."

"He's a smart dog."

As if he knows we're talking about him, Roscoe whimpers and drops his head on his paws, his gaze alternating between me and Eddy.

"He is." Eddy drops his voice. "But I'm not going anywhere. He'll eventually figure it out." He's talking about Roscoe, but he's looking at me.

Which makes me think about the day he came back—Abigail's wedding. He proposed to me that day, but he hasn't breathed a word about it since then. Does he think we need to work back up to that level? It's a sensible plan, but it makes me wonder whether he's having second thoughts about it.

Does he regret asking me? Or is he afraid of being

turned down again? We've been dating again for weeks, and so far, he hasn't even said 'I love you.'

I haven't either, but still.

We've been tiptoeing around the words as if they're some kind of landmines planted by the enemy in a past war. It started as something kind of awkward—I wasn't sure whether I *should* say it, and then I *didn't* and I could tell he noticed, and then he didn't say it either.

It feels like we're at some kind of bizarre impasse.

Even Maren asked me about it yesterday. "Do you still love him?"

"Of course," I said. "Maybe more than before. It's one thing to have a crush on someone, and quite another to find someone who's willing to wait and work through things with you."

"Then why don't you ever tell him?" she asked.

I had no idea what to tell her.

Why's my teenager more insightful than I am?

"Maybe just say it," she said that night, after ruminating on it for hours, apparently. "The next time you think it, just blurt it out."

She's braver than I am, too.

"I better go." Eddy groans a little as he stands up. "It's so nice being able to pop over for lunch, but I have a bunch of vaccinations to do, and they won't give themselves, sadly."

"I should really finish up the plans I promised Helen."

"How's that going?"

I stand up, too. "Eh."

"At least it's not horrible."

"Only because I'm so easygoing."

Eddy's laughter isn't small, and it isn't polite.

"Hey, mister. What's all that carrying on about? Are you saying I'm *not* easygoing?"

"I didn't say a single word. I'm not that stupid." He pretends to zip his lips.

I roll my eyes, and the words spring into my mind. *I love him.* Eddy makes me laugh. He calls me on my nonsense. He helps remind me when I'm being too narcissistic, but not in a rude way. In a way that says, *I adore everything about you, but other people might think this is a bit much.* I've never had that before. Past boyfriends belittled me. Paul ignored me.

I've never had someone who really *got* me, but at the same time, strived to help me improve.

But before I can say the words out loud, they choke up in my throat. "See you for dinner?" I ask instead.

I'm such a coward.

He grimaces. "Actually, tonight I'm supposed to do this really dumb thing."

My eyebrows rise on their own. "Dumb thing?"

He inhales dramatically. "It's just—the contract I signed when I left said I'd do a few events via livestream, and I agreed to write a few original songs each year."

"Why would you—"

"The money's good, and I figured if I had a high maintenance—" He coughs. "I thought that if I had a girlfriend with good taste, she might appreciate a few nice gifts from time to time."

I can't help my smile. "Well, when you put it that way. . ."

"I'm supposed to play the new song, acoustic, tonight."

"New song?" I had no idea he was composing at all.

"It's not a big deal," he says. "It's kind of been knocking around in my head for a while, actually. It felt great to get it down on paper."

"Play it for me," I say. "Or just sing it, maybe, since you don't have your guitar."

He shakes his head. "No time right now."

"Well, at least invite me over to hear it live along with a billion of your closest and most devoted fans."

"Amanda," he says. "Be realistic. I don't have a billion. Just ten million."

"You ridiculous divo," I say.

"Divo? What's that?"

"It's a diva, but of the male variety."

He's chuckling when he leaves. "I'm supposed to do it at six p.m. If you want to be useful, maybe you can video-tape it."

"Useful?" I bat my eyes. "You sure do know how to sweet-talk a lady, Dr. Dutton."

Eddy blows me a kiss on the way to his truck. "Wear something nice, and we can announce that we're dating. Maybe some of my billion fans will go follow you, too."

"Or maybe they'll send me flowers with razor blades hidden in them," I mutter under my breath.

His worshipful fans are the worst.

But as long as they aren't kissing him, I suppose it's fine. He can take the money they spend on his music and spend it on something nice for me. It's almost like recycling, or composting, or whatever. Taking their poop and turning it into flowers.

Eddy's whistle interrupts my musings and I barely shift in time to avoid being knocked over like a bowling pin when Snuggles races past and launches into his truck bed, tongue lolling.

"I think she'd have stayed with you if I hadn't called her." Eddy pats the frame of his truck. "Making progress."

More like, she almost stayed with the handsome Roscoe. He's standing at my side, scanning the horizon to check for threats.

"Take care of our girl," Eddy says.

Roscoe tosses his head as if he's answering.

The rest of the day crawls past miserably slowly. Helen

hates all my plans, or at least, finds them all wanting. Mandy used to mostly rubber stamp my ideas. Helen keeps asking question after question, and then follows up by telling me why they won't work.

"Maybe we should hire someone," I say.

"If we hire someone to work out these details, then what will you do?" She tilts her head.

"Not to do this stuff," I say. "To mediate when we disagree, which feels constant."

Helen leans back in her chair and folds her hands in her lap. "Which of my suggestions was wrong?"

I review her questions and objections in my head. She wanted me to have a designer come out and do an efficiency study before we task the surveyor to set the platting for the new retreat and the barn so that we don't overlook anything important, like sun position at various times, or kitchen location relative to sleeping times so the staff won't wake up the guests preparing breakfast. She wanted us to do a pollen assessment for the area so that our sensitive guests who either aren't used to the outdoors or the area can be prepared. She also wanted me to put together a more comprehensive list of suppliers for the various things we'll need once we're up and running. Mine was pretty bare bones.

When I think about it, none of her ideas were bad. She wasn't even rude in how she told me to go about doing them. She just made me feel bad at my job, because she's so dang good at hers.

"What *is* your job, exactly?" I ask. "It seems like all you do is poke holes in the work I'm doing."

Helen slings her purse over her shoulder and smiles as she stands up. "What did you think management was?"

I've worked my way through a quarter of one of my new tasks when I realize I need to feed the girls something for dinner, and I've barely got time if I want to make it to

Eddy's a few minutes before six. When I shoot out of my bedroom, I come to a complete halt.

Emery's leaning against the kitchen counter, smiling and telling some kind of story. She's also scraping things off a cutting board and into a bowl.

Maren's pulling something out of the oven—something that smells like *heaven*.

My girls are making dinner.

Together.

While smiling.

I glance around, searching for evidence as I approach. "What's going on?"

They both turn toward me at the same time, wearing identical looks of surprise.

"Mom? We're not quite done," Maren says.

"Did aliens come?" I narrow my eyes. "Are you a creature from outer space that's wearing a Maren-suit?"

Emery laughs. "Please. Any alien that tried to take over her head would run away screaming."

"You're the one—"

That's more like it. "I just can't believe you made dinner."

"It's a frozen pizza and a bagged salad, Mom," Maren says. "Don't get all weepy on us."

"Yeah, Abby's kids have a rotation. They're split into pairs and they have to do dinner four nights a week." Emery points. "Ethan does frozen pizza a lot when it's his turn, and we figured we could handle that much."

A month ago, hearing about how Abigail's perfection, and by extension her kids' perfection, inspired my children would have set me off. But today, I'm just happy about it. Being close to them is inspiring my kids to grow up, to get along, and to try new things.

"This is probably my carbs for the entire week." I lean

over and breathe in the smell of the pizza. "Actually, just breathing that makes me feel more full."

"Do you really care?" Maren asks. "I mean, you've got the guy. Double your carbs—so what." She's smirking at me, but I don't really mind.

And she might be right. It's not like I'll blow up like a balloon because I ate a slice of pizza. What's a little extra cellulite? Eddy won't care, especially if the pizza makes me happier.

*A moment on the lips, a lifetime on the hips.*

My mom's voice springs into my brain, like a trained assassin waiting for the perfect moment. I haven't seen her in more than five years, but she still lives in my head, rent free. I shake it off and slide a slice of Maren's meal onto my plate.

I'm determined to stop letting my past haunt my future.

"Thanks, girls."

"Of course," Maren says. "We can't have you being late to watch Eddy's livestream."

"Wait, you knew about that?"

Emery waves her phone at me. "We're teenagers. We've known for more than a week, ever since his agency announced it."

"A heads up might have been nice."

"You didn't know?" Maren frowns. "You're an *influencer*, Mom. Wouldn't you think that you might keep up with your own boyfriend?"

"I've got a totally different job right now." Plus, it's relatively new to me since Mandy's death, this getting out of pajamas and showering and working thing. Not that long ago, I was lying on the sofa all day, languishing. I don't feel the need to remind them of that.

We didn't say a prayer over the food, I realize, when mine is almost gone. Well, I can't turn into Abigail overnight. Surely God understands I'm grateful without me always saying it, right?

"How was school?" I ask, not really directing it at either of them in particular.

"Fine," Maren says.

Emery shrugs.

Baby steps. At least I'm moving in the right direction.

"Please tell me you're not wearing that?" Maren's entire face scrunches in a way I haven't been able to for years, thanks to Botox.

"What's wrong with this?" I glance down at my black yoga pants and Lololime heart tee.

"Other than the pizza sauce spots on the front of it?" Emery points.

I swear under my breath.

"Also, your boyfriend's a literal rock star," Maren says. "A little glam so his fans realize he's well and truly taken couldn't hurt."

This is coming from the same person who just told me to stuff my face now that I've got a boyfriend. I don't growl, but I want to.

Instead, I scramble to my feet, and I don't argue when the girls insist on accompanying me to my room. They help me choose a nicer outfit—a clingy green tunic and pleather pants with a chunky pair of buckle-adorned boots—and then they help me pull my hair into a quick updo. Maren even helps me touch up my makeup.

"It's like I have two stylists," I say.

"A stylist," Maren says slowly. "Maybe that's what I want to do."

"What you want to do?"

She shrugs. "The counselor at school's bugging all of us. The other girls want to do things like be moms, or run shops, or I don't know. Like, waitress. Meanwhile, I have no idea what I want."

I could totally see her bossing people around and telling them how to wear things. "We can definitely look into that more."

She's actually smiling at me as I head out the door.

When I turn back around, Emery's holding a whining Roscoe by the collar. "Have fun."

"You guys can come," I say. "Let him come, too. Snuggles loves him."

"Yeah, you might want to tell Eddy to get her fixed," Maren says. "I think if they love each other any more, we may wind up with puppies."

I laugh. "He's a vet. I'm sure that's taken care of." I reach the car door, and I gesture for them to come.

Maren shakes her head. "I have homework, and Emery has a paper to write."

*My kids* are doing homework? Without being asked? "You are aliens, aren't you?"

They're both laughing when I pull out of the driveway, and a pang of guilt creeps over me. It's probably the very happiest I've been since Mandy died. Does that mean I've done something wrong? Should I be this happy when she's not here?

"I miss you, lady." I know she can't hear me. I'm not even sure there really is a god, much less an afterlife, and given how seldom I remember to pray, that might be the best for me. But I still send little thoughts out to Amanda Saddler from time to time. "In case you can hear me, being happy doesn't mean your absence isn't making me sad."

When I get to Eddy's it's less than two minutes until the livestream, but I still take thirty seconds to clean up under my eyes and reapply concealer. Grief's a real witch.

I waltz through the door to a snarling Snuggles right at six on the dot. She gives one more half-hearted growl when she realizes it's me, and then flops down on the floor by Eddy's black-boot-clad feet.

206

"Sorry I'm late!"

He points at the wall, where his phone's mounted on a black stand. "Hello, fine fans. I'm Eddy Dutton, and I'm so glad you could make it to my first livestream. I know people were sad to hear that I won't be signing on for another album anytime soon, but I hope the new songs I'll be sharing and then releasing as singles will help bring a smile to your face."

The comments box under his video's going wild.

I hate that all those idiots are in love with my boyfriend.

And I kind of love it, too.

I know it's juvenile, but having the toy that everyone else wants was great back in preschool, and it's still kind of awesome now. So when Eddy gestures for me to walk over to him, I do.

And I'm doubly glad that Maren and Emery made me put on something more glamourous.

"I want to introduce all of you to someone. This woman right here is Amanda Brooks. She's insta-famous as Champagne for Less, and if you're not following her already, why not?" He grins. "But I really do want to just say how much I adore her and how happy she makes me. If you want to see me smiling, make sure you show her that same kind of love." He presses a kiss to my temple.

"But for now, I'm sure everyone is as excited as I am to hear this new song."

Eddy points at a chair that's just behind the video. "Humor me and sit there, by the camera, sweetheart? I miss doing live shows. The energy, the fans, it really adds something. But with you right there, I can see my favorite face in the world while I'm singing."

I'm totally blushing like an idiot when I walk off the screen and sit. I have no idea how he does this, being all vulnerable and stuff on air. He's strumming his guitar and tuning it a bit when I sit down.

"You know, for years, I looked and looked for the right person," Eddy says. "That one person who would fill my life with joy." He glances at me. "If you've found someone who makes you that happy, make sure you don't take him or her for granted."

And then he looks down and starts to strum.

It's a slower song than I expected, and I haven't heard him play acoustic since that Fourth of July barbecue when Abigail fell into the river.

But his voice is deep and rich and sure, and I could listen to him forever. I see why his fans were so sad that he wasn't going back on tour or recording another album right away.

☙❧

O ur first ideas,
    *Of love are formed,*
*When we watch our parents,*
*From the day we're born.*

☙❧

B ut mine weren't joy.
    *They were more sad,*
*It made me a boy,*
*Who thought love was bad.*

☙❧

U ntil, until, until the day...
    *Until, until, until the way.*
*You showed me love.*

*You showed me life.*
*You gave me something*
*That I just couldn't find.*

F*rom the day,*
  *I found you,*
*I knew that love,*
*Just might be true.*

Y*our face was light,*
  *Your voice was peace,*
*You changed my heart,*
*You were a thief.*

U*ntil, until, until the day...*
  *Until, until, until the way.*
*You showed me love.*
*You showed me life.*
*You gave me something*
*That I just couldn't find.*

A*nd then I wrecked*
  *The gift I'd found.*
*I took our love,*
*And dropped it on the ground*

I realized too late,
    What harm I'd done.
But now you're back,
Please be the one.

✦

U ntil, until, until today...
    Until, until, until I met you,
I've never married,
Or even wanted to.
But you gave me something
That I just couldn't find
Please be my wife forever,
My always valentine.

✦

A nd then Eddy drops down on one knee. In front of the camera, in front of all of his fans, but his eyes stay trained on me. He reaches beneath the sofa and pulls out a tiny, bright blue box.

"You'll be proud of me," he says. "I had my agent call Tiffany's. I told them I was about to propose to the most beautiful influencer in America, and that her brand was a perfect fit for theirs. I asked them if they'd give me a discount if I said how great they were to work with live, during the release of a new song."

"And did they?"

He laughs. "Not a chance. But the shipping was free."

I'm laughing too, but I'm also crying. Why didn't those useless girls make sure I put on waterproof mascara?

Eddy's still on one knee, but he shuffles toward me.

Snuggles, not knowing what's going on, creeps along next to him, licking his elbow and whining.

He stops so that he can still be seen on camera, but he's close. Right next to me, in fact. "That song was a little cornier than my usual, but it was also the easiest I've ever written any song."

"Oh yeah?" I look into his very earnest, grass-green eyes.

"I love you, Amanda. You changed my life. You changed how I look at love. I can't imagine any bright future that doesn't have you in it. Please, please, please marry me."

I bite my lip. "I'm sorry, Eddy, but this is all wrong."

His face falls. His arms droop, the gorgeous diamond solitaire angling downward.

I lean over and brace my hands on his shoulders. "Your fans should really be able to see the whole picture, don't you think?"

His laughter is off-kilter then, but it's practically saturated with relief. "Yes," he manages to choke out. "Yes, let's do that."

I walk into view of the camera, and then I shift so there's room for him. He and Snuggles shuffle over again.

"You are a phenomenal woman," Eddy says. "No matter what life hands you, you may throw a little tantrum as divas are wont to do, but then you dust yourself off and turn to rally the forces and attack. You're resilient, brilliant, and brave, and I love you. Please marry me." He leans closer and whispers, "I don't think I can handle being rejected three times."

I laugh this time. "That was hardly a rejection right there."

"What would you call it?" He snorts. "You said, 'I'm sorry, but this is all wrong.'"

"It was a joke, you big baby," I say. "But I won't reject you a third time, Edward Dutton. I was always team Jacob, but I guess it's time I reconcile myself to the fact that I'm winding up with Edward after all."

Eddy stands up. "Who the heck is Jacob?"

I pull his head down and kiss him. And when we finally stop, he slides the beautiful, non-discounted Tiffany and Co. diamond onto my finger.

It may have taken a while to get here, but it's a perfect fit.

# 18

# AMANDA

oments after Eddy closes down the livestream, there's a knock at his door. Instead of looking surprised or annoyed, he grins.

"What's going on?"

He heads for the laundry room, dragging Snuggles along with him. "Be patient."

"Forget patience," I say. "Tell me who's here."

"Who isn't here?" He winks, and then he jogs to the door and swings it open.

Maren. Emery. Abigail and all her kids, and even Steve. Donna and Will and her niece, Beth, I think. They all stream inside, along with a few women I've gotten to know in town. Jeff and Kevin shuffle in, and to my great shock, so does Helen.

For some reason, it really hits me how sad it is that Mandy's not here. It may not be an official engagement party, but she would've been the first to hug me. The first to call me Mrs. Dutton, long before it's really proper.

Appallingly, probably also the first to tease us about the wedding night.

"Congrats!" Abby squeals as she rushes toward me, arms outstretched.

"Who would've thought a year ago that we'd both wind up getting remarried in this tiny town?" Tears roll down my cheeks. I must look like a zombie by now, with all the ugly crying I've been doing.

"I miss her, too," Abby whispers.

Four words and my quiet tears mutate into wracking sobs.

The others fall quiet, but I can't seem to let Abby go. "She's happy for you, wherever she is."

I know that's true. "I'm happy for me, too."

"And me." Eddy thrusts his arm between our faces and starts to pretend to pry us apart. "But you really can't be so close to Amanda, Abs."

"Why not?" she asks.

"Yeah, why not?" I frown.

"Because Steve says she's pregnant," he whispers. "And I hear that kind of thing's contagious."

I laugh through my tears, then. "Yes, get thee hence, foul breeder. None of that around me."

"Or at least, not yet." Eddy's eyes are sparkling.

"Whoa, I hope you know that you're buying a vintage edition," I say. "I really hope you're not planning to put it through something as traumatic as childbirth, because I can't survive that again."

He rolls his eyes. "I don't want a kid if you don't, but if you do, then I do. I just do as I'm told."

I laugh at that. He seems to be sincere about it. "Then keep that baby stuff way away."

"I didn't think I wanted another one either." Abby pats her nonexistent belly. "But here we are."

"How far along are you, exactly?" Eddy asks.

"Seventeen weeks," Abby says.

"Just over that," Steve says. "And it's a boy."

"Oh!" I hug Abby again, squealing all over again. "That's so exciting! Now you're unbalanced, though."

"No, we're perfectly balanced," Abby says. "Steve has a daughter."

"Steve has three daughters," Steve says. "And he also isn't sure why he's talking about himself in third person, but he's already started it, so now he's just staying in the saddle."

"Your husband's very odd," I say.

"Says the woman whose fiancé just proposed on a livestream in front of millions of fans." Abby releases me and steps back, where Steve's waiting to slide his hand into hers.

For the first time in a very long time, I don't have a pang of envy while watching them. I'm just happy for her. Her perfect, pristine marriage, complete with a new little baby-on-the-way, brings me nothing but joy. It's nice to find happiness in your own life.

It really makes it easier to be a better person.

Or at least, I hope it is.

"Congrats, Mom." Emery always gives the best hugs. She grabs you and clings on like a baby koala, determined never to let go.

"I have a bone to pick with you," I say, partially as a joke, and partially as a defensive mechanism so I don't spend the rest of the night wearing an Emery.

"What?" Her eyes are wide as she releases me.

"And you, too." I glare at Maren as sternly as I can.

"What did we do?" Maren's brow furrows.

"You didn't tell me to use waterproof mascara." I scowl. They both laugh.

"It would've given it away," Maren says.

"I don't think that anything would have tipped me off to the fact that my rocker boyfriend had written a song to propose to me, live."

"A song that will probably pay for the wedding, judging by these stats," Donna says. "That video is *trending*."

"But it's the sales of the single that really bring the money in," Eddy says. "Let's hope when it releases officially tomorrow that they're just as good."

"Oh, I think they will be, at least for a while," Donna says.

"It's a pretty corny song, though, man," Will says.

"Oh?" Eddy puffs out his chest. "I'm engaged, dude. How about you?"

Will chucks him on the shoulder. "My girl's flighty. Don't scare her off, or I'll hold you accountable."

"Haven't you heard that song?" Eddy asks.

"Huh?" Will glances at Donna. "We just heard the song he's talking about, right?"

She laughs.

"No, this one." Eddy scrunches up his face in the way he always does before an impression, and when he sings, it's in a pronounced falsetto. "If you love it, then you shouldn't put a scare on it."

"Those are not the lyrics," I say.

"Didn't you know that quoting lyrics in a written work, like a novel, can get the author sued?" Eddy asks.

"Oh, are you writing a book now?" I ask.

"Who knows?" he asks. "My girl's amazing, but she's high maintenance. I'll do anything to bring home the bacon —or designer high heels—she needs."

The rest of the night's almost as silly, but it's light, it's happy, and it's fun.

Which is just what we all need.

But even so, there's still a ragged hole where Mandy should be. I wonder how long it will be until that goes away. And how dark will my world become if my longing for my friend ever does truly fade?

# 19

# ABIGAIL

No matter how she feels about him, Mr. Eugene's definitely afraid of his wife-to-be. I mailed him the prenup, along with a clear letter he could have used, and he still hasn't done a thing with it.

Instead, he showed up out of the blue to demand an emergency meeting.

"But all you have to do is hand it to her," I say.

His face is pale, and his hands are shaking. "But I thought you could—"

"Mr. Eugene, tell her I drafted it, and that I'm insisting, and that you—" My office door jingles, and my mouth snaps shut.

That better not be Brooke Dailey. On the phone, he assured me he wasn't bringing her. He told me he just needed me to walk him through some things.

"Oh, sweetheart," he says, his voice unsteady.

"Freddy." She beams at him. Then she turns toward me, her eyes becoming flinty. "Mrs. Brooks."

"It's Archer now," I say. "I was married recently."

"Right."

She should remember. She was in my office yelling at

me on the day of my wedding. "How wonderful to see you." I don't even try to make my voice sound sincere. If she doesn't bother, why should I?

"Freddy tells me that you need to talk to me?"

I glare at him.

He immediately ducks and looks at his loafers.

I sigh. As a lawyer, I could easily tell her that I have nothing to say and insist that I'm not sure why he asked her here. I could also tell her that he asked me to draft this, and that he's afraid of her.

But as a person, this poor man clearly needs my help. His test may be misguided, but it also might work. It's a bit more devious than I expected from such a small, retreating man, but that only makes me more proud.

Or I would be proud, if he wasn't forcing me to be his unwilling foil.

"Yes, thank you so much for coming in." I force a smile. "Please, follow me." I snatch the manila envelope off the counter and carry it into my office. I circle my desk to sit in my chair and gesture for them to take the wingbacks.

Poor Brooke keeps trying to catch her fiancé's eye, but he's got his gaze glued on the floor. At least he won't fall and break something this way.

"I'm sure you're just busting with curiosity about why I needed to see you," I say a little too sharply.

As I'm speaking, I'm also noticing that she's now wearing much more expensive clothing than she was the last time I saw her.

A Gucci bag. Manolo Blahnik pumps. And if I'm not mistaken, that's an Alexander McQueen suit. My boss was obsessed with them, and I think they're only carried by Nordstrom. I wonder where the closest one of those is located in relation to sleepy little Manila.

I clear my throat. "As I was going through some of the papers from the safety deposit boxes for the inventory, I found a letter from the late Mrs. Eugene." I drop my hands to the desk so I don't fiddle with anything as I embellish upon this ridiculous story. "She requested that her husband, to whom she never disclosed her great wealth, remarry and find joy if she predeceased him, but she also requested that he be sure to draw up a prenuptial agreement that leaves all of her wealth to a charity on his death, seeing as it wasn't really his to begin with."

Brooke blinks.

"I know this may come as a bit of a shock, but I've drawn up the prenup as she requested, and—"

"That's not a will, though." Her voice is flat. "Surely it's not binding."

"Well, of course it's not," I say. "But Mr. Eugene wouldn't have a dime more than his pension were it not for her leaving him everything, so he wants to honor her wishes."

Brooke stands up. "That's ridiculous."

"Excuse me?"

"What charity?" She starts to pace at the front of my office. "What charity gets all your money?"

I forgot what charity I put in the prenup. Crap, how could I forget? Oh, maybe because it's all *fiction*. It's not like authors remember the colors of the eyes or hair of their *invented* characters, either, I'm sure.

I try to open the envelope without being obvious, but Brooke's eyes are sharp as a hawk's.

"Surely you recall what charity's supposed to receive more than twenty million dollars on your death?" Brooke rounds on *Freddy*, no beaming smile this time. "And how could you spring this on me, with *that woman* telling me what will happen to my money?"

"Your money?" My voice is light, but I seem to keep from smirking.

She rounds on me next. "I'm sure you put him up to

this. You've hated me since the day we met. It must be hard to watch a woman only ten years older than you, who looks legitimately younger than you, marrying someone with so much money. I hear you have four kids." She narrows her eyes at me. "You want that money for yourself, don't you?"

"Do you have any idea who my sister is?" I ask. "I'm guessing you don't, because if you did, you wouldn't ask me stupid things like that."

Brooke frowns, but I can see when she decides to change tactics. "Is there really a letter?" She spins back toward Mr. Eugene. "I want to see it, this letter your wife supposedly left."

Mr. Eugene's spluttering.

"I'm going to have to ask you to leave," I say. "You're not behaving calmly or rationally in my office, and I can't have you accosting my client or myself."

"Your client?" Her voice started out shrill, but now it's practically shattering the glass in my back window. "He's not your client anymore. You've caused all of this with your interference, so you're fired."

I pick up my phone. "I've been more than polite. You can leave, or I can call my husband and have him pop on over and escort you out." It's a bluff, of course. He's working in Green River.

Luckily, it works. Her nostrils flare, and her designer-shoe-clad foot stomps, but she finally storms out.

"Well, I guess you know what she was after." I'm deep in my gloat when I glance over at Mr. Eugene and realize he's bawling.

For me, this was merely a confirmation of what I always knew. But for him? It destroyed all his dreams and fondest feelings.

I'm a bad person. Maybe not Brooke Dailey bad, but quite possibly puppy-kicking-when-no-one-is-looking bad. I drop into the seat next to him and drape my hand across his. When he turns his over and squeezes, I can't help thinking about what stupid Brooke said.

That I want his money for myself.

The icky feeling that washes over me has me pulling my hand free. I want nothing to do with *that* kind of insinuation, in any way, shape, or form, but I do want him to feel better. I just can't handle him bonding to me, or imprinting, or whatever that's called. He does remind me of a baby bird. They tend to imprint on anything that brings them worms.

Good heavens. What am I supposed to do with him now?

In the end, it takes me almost three hours to extricate myself from the sob-fest I helped create. I sink into my chair afterward and wonder how I can possibly frame this interaction on the bill.

First, I have to consider whether I *can* ethically bill him. I mean, I wanted nothing to do with this. He came to me and begged me to help. I did exactly as he said, and then he ignored me and brought her here. I should fire him for turning my office into an episode of *Maury Povich*. Any way I look at it, it's fair that I should be paid for my misery in this trainwreck, but now I'm back to how to write it down, exactly.

Held client's hand while he sobbed. 3.1 hours.

That won't work.

Helped eliminate a greedy, gold-digging—

Nope. Too unprofessional, even if it's true.

How about. . .

Consulted regarding impact of failed engagement. 3.1 hours.

That could work, maybe?

I lean back in my chair and close my eyes.

Of course, my phone starts to ring like a madman. It's not a kids' ringtone, and it's not Steve's tone, so I ignore it, but whoever it is calls back. I groan, but I do pick up, reluctantly.

"Hey there," an irritated person says. "Just confirming that someone's presently onsite and that we can bring the dry goods delivery? I have you down for flour, oats, chocolate chips, and two kinds of sugar?"

"And molasses, right?" I ask.

"Yes, molasses, and a few other things like soda."

"Perfect," I say. "I'm here, but they can just drop it off. The door's open."

I should pack my bag and head home, but I need just a moment to recover from the emotional vampire named Freddy. I close my eyes again.

Fate thinks it's funny that I want a break, apparently, because three or four minutes later, my phone starts ringing again. I almost ignore it this time too, but at the last second, I pick up.

I regret it immediately.

"Mrs. Brooks?" a perky voice asks. "This is Rebecca from The Women's Center of Utah. The doctor ordered an image-assisted core-needle biopsy several weeks ago, and we don't have the results back yet. Did you have one set up with another physician in a different location? Should we transfer our medical charts there?"

I used the last name Brooks with them, so that no one would realize who I was, on the off chance any medical people might recognize the name of Steve's new wife. The medical world's uncomfortably small—you never know. But it does feel strange having her use my former married name for a health scare while I'm pregnant with Steve's baby. I hit the speakerphone button and lean back in my chair so I can close my tired eyes.

"Mrs. Brooks? Are you still there?"

"Um, yes." I cringe, but I'm a bit distracted by the door opening out front. It's just the dry goods delivery people, and thankfully I told them to just go ahead and drop things off. "I'm here."

"Have you set up the procedure elsewhere? Or do we need to call someone to encourage them to share the results?"

"Um, not exactly," I say.

"Have you had the procedure or not?"

"Not," I say.

"Mrs. Brooks, I hope I don't have to remind you that this is a procedure meant to rule out the risk of cancer. It's not something you should delay."

"I don't have cancer," I say. "And even if I do, it's *me* who has cancer, not you. So you don't need to chastise me about it."

"I'm just trying—"

"You're trying to do your job," I say. "I do understand that, but let me assure you. I'm a career woman, a bright lady, and I have my reasons for waiting. When I'm ready, I'll schedule the biopsy. I'd appreciate if you wouldn't call me back again."

I hang up the phone.

That's when I notice Helen standing in my doorway, her shoulders drooped, her mouth dangling open.

I've never seen her look that dazed in my entire life.

This is not good.

I force a laugh. "These people keep calling me over and over, insisting I need to go in for an annual exam. Ridiculous."

"You said you don't have cancer," Helen says slowly. "And then you said, 'even if I do.'"

I hate how smart she is sometimes.

"You know doctors," I say. "Always jumping to ridiculous conclusions."

"You wouldn't have said that if there wasn't something that made you believe that you *might* have it."

"Helen," I say, "trust me—"

She steps closer, her head tilted, her eyes trained on mine. "But I don't. Not about this. You're exactly the kind of moron who would try to be all noble and not make us sad after Nate and Mandy. You'd stick your stupid flamingo-like head in the sand—"

"Steve will make me abort the baby." I set my jaw, and I don't look away from her gaze. "If I do have cancer, if this dumb test comes back positive, he'll make me abort him." I bring one hand over my stomach as if my hand can keep him safe.

"So will I." Helen's eyes are flinty. "And I'm a lot more terrifying than Steve."

This time I can't help looking at the wall in frustration, and then I plant my hands on the top of my desk. "I'm an adult, Helen, and I can make my own decisions."

"But you're making bad ones," Helen says. "Monumentally stupid ones." She rushes toward my desk. "Your kids have already lost one parent. Nate may have irritated me, but he was a great father. Do you really want them to lose their mother, too?"

"It's not—"

She presses her hand across my mouth. "Stop talking. I'm not one of your imbecile clients. I'm smarter than you, and I'm perfectly capable of impersonating you if it comes down to that, and then I'll see all your ridiculous records for myself. If that fails, I have a team of investigators who will discover anything else I want through any method necessary. Now, tell me what is going on, and don't leave a single, solitary thing out."

I collapse back against my chair and exhale in defeat. I start at the beginning, and other than glancing down to click a few things on her phone from time to time, she never looks away from my face. By the time I finish, she looks much calmer. Maybe I've convinced her that I'm right.

"Abigail, you're going to do exactly as I say."

"I'm not a toddler, and you can't order me around."

"If you don't do everything I say as soon as I say it, I'll call Steve and then our parents, in that order."

I hate her. "Fine. What do you want?"

"First, my car's right outside."

"So is mine."

"I drive much faster and my car makes it fun," she says. "We're headed for that local airstrip outside of Green River."

"What?" I shake my head. "Izzy has—"

"Ethan's helping with her project, and Steve will be home to make sure the kids all get to bed. I told them I'm flying you out to make some critical decisions about the baby shower that can't wait."

"This is ridiculous."

"No, Abigail. Gambling with your health when four tiny people and one teensy baby all depend on you is what's ridiculous. Actually, it's unconscionable. That's a word that, as a lawyer, you should know. I've called in a few favors, and you'll be getting your core-needle biopsy today."

"It's already after five p.m."

"And that matters. . ." Helen tilts her head.

"Nothing is open," I say.

"For you," Helen says. "For people like you, nothing is open. For people like me, nothing is ever really closed. Now, get up and let's go."

I really hate her. "If the results come back positive—"

Helen leans closer. "You better pray to that God you love so much harder than you've ever prayed in your life. Because the only way you're getting out of this alive is if you don't have cancer. If you do, I'll kill you myself for being an idiot."

Something about her diatribe breaks the walls I've built to keep myself sane through all this, and I start to shake uncontrollably. My horrifyingly scary sister circles my desk, pulls me to my feet, and hugs me tightly. "It's going to be alright, Abs, I swear. Helen's here."

For a brief moment, I let go of all my fear, all my worries, and all my anxiety. For my baby, for my kids, for Steve.

And for myself.

Because as brave as I may try to be, I've been really scared, too. My voice wobbles when I whisper, "I don't want to die."

"I know," she says. "And if money can save your stupid life, then you won't."

She wasn't kidding about how fast she drives. After a few moments of white knuckles, I finally complain. "You know, dying in a car crash might be more exciting than cancer, but it's still dead."

She laughs.

"I'm not kidding."

"Neither am I." She doesn't slow down until we reach the hangar.

"Where are we headed?"

"Where do I have the most connections?" She shrugs. "New York, of course."

The flight feels longer than usual, but of course that's all in my head. There's no security to clear, and there are no extraneous stops. We fly straight to New York, land in a private airstrip, and then a driver takes us right to a local hospital.

It's quite late by the time we arrive, but no one seems to have told Mount Sinai it should be closed. Apparently the city that never sleeps has also spawned a medical center that never sleeps. I've barely changed into my gown when they come for me with a wheelchair.

"Is this really necessary?"

Helen waves her phone at me. "Do you really have to protest every single thing?" She taps the screen and swivels it toward me. It's a phone number that's been saved as Stone Cold Cowboy Hottie. "Because my finger is itching to call your husband and tattle on you."

I sigh, but I don't complain any more. In fact, thinking of Helen saving Steve as a stone cold hottie makes me smile.

The biopsy's quick, relatively speaking, but it's not at all pleasant. After sitting through all the appointments where Nate was poked and prodded and jabbed, I'm pretty familiar with being on Helen's side of things.

It's my first time being the patient, and I don't like it any better.

Finally, it's done, and the nurse, the doc, and the orderlies are on their way out the door.

"How long until we know what the results are?" Helen asks.

"A few hours," the doc says before he disappears.

Helen folds her arms. "Now, we wait."

# 20

# ABIGAIL

An awful lot of our lives are spent waiting.

We wait when we pick up our kids from school. We wait on prescriptions. We wait on the weather. We wait on new books. We wait on our favorite show to release a new episode. We wait for loved ones to forgive us. Of all the things we wait on, test results might be the worst.

Helen's checking her watch, so I know I'm not the only one who's annoyed.

"I'm sorry."

"It's about time you apologized to me."

Our family isn't one that apologizes easily. Then again, we don't make it easy when someone finally does say they're sorry, either. "You're so gracious at accepting."

"I have exactly one sister," she says. "And you've met my parents. If you leave me alone with them, so help me, I'll—"

The doctor peeks his head in the door. "Is now a bad time?"

When Helen stands up, I can't help noticing that her hands are shaking. She balls them into fists, and I watch her straighten and swallow. "No. Please come in." She looks more strung out than I feel, and I'm the one who might be sick.

The doctor steps inside the room slowly, holding a clipboard with papers stacked on the top. He looks down at them, adjusting his glasses. As if my life's unfurling before me like a spool of thread, I'm reminded of the moment the doctor came in with Nate's results. We had gone to the emergency room because his eyes had turned yellow, and we knew that meant something major was wrong. We were still hopeful, in that moment, that it might not be something very dire.

But I will never forget the deep and soul-drenching fear that gripped me at that point in time. It was like I couldn't breathe, and like the world had gone black, and like the Night King was coming for me, all at the same time.

Battling with that fear was a desperate and valiant hope.

No matter what the doctor says, I owe Helen an even bigger apology, because I know what this moment is like. I've been through it before, and I should've known how scared she was. Instead of sulking in the corner and whining and complaining, I should've hugged her. I should've told her it'll all be okay. I should've reassured her.

"The results of the core-needle biopsy are preliminary, but I've consulted with the radiologist, and we both feel—"

"For the love of all that's holy, doc, spit it out!" Helen looks like she's going to strain something any second.

He smiles. "It appears to be benign. The incidence of false negatives is less than four percent. We'll want to do some follow up testing, and if it's a cyst, you may want to drain it, but it should be a very minor procedure that won't interfere with your pregnancy."

Helen sinks into her chair.

I collapse into mine and drop my face in my hands. All these months worrying. . .for nothing. I place my hands over my belly. "It's going to be alright, little guy. Mom's fine."

Once the doctor has said his piece and gone, I really lose it. Helen's not doing much better, and we're in the middle of bawling and hugging and blathering when my phone rings.

It's Steve.

There's no way I can talk to him right now. I'll have to call him back.

Ten seconds later, he texts me.

WHY ARE YOU IN THE HOSPITAL? CALL ME. RIGHT NOW.

My heart stops in my chest.

"How does he know where you are?" Helen's peering over my shoulder.

It's probably not the best time for me to lecture her on the etiquette violation of reading over my shoulder, but I'm annoyed. "We installed this software because Ethan's always losing his phone. Once, it fell in the pasture and got rained on." I groan. "If you really can't find it, even with a ping, you can check its last known location."

"And?"

"When you boot up the program on the laptop, it shows the location of every device that's linked to our account. He must have been looking for Ethan's and noticed mine."

"So?" She tilts her head. "Just tell him what happened. You don't have cancer, so he can't get too mad."

"Oh, I'm definitely not telling him that I thought I *might* have cancer."

"Oh." She frowns. "Well, I think you're going to have to, now."

I pick up my phone like it's a viper that might strike. "I guess so."

"Is it really that scary? The man adores you."

I groan. "But that's *why* he's going to be so angry."

She shrugs. "Not my problem." She points at the door. "I'm going to call our car."

I nod, and then my finger hovers. I know I should hit talk, but I can't bring myself to—

The phone rings and I nearly drop it.

It's Steve. Again.

This time I force my finger to stop trembling and I swipe talk.

"Abigail?"

"I'm ready to confess," I say. "I'm having an affair with a doctor at Mount Sinai in New York."

"Very funny," he says. "Is the baby alright?"

Right. The baby. Of course he'd assume this was about him.

"Helen's exactly the kind of person who would whisk you away to have things checked out without me."

I can't help my chuckle, even though it's wildly inappropriate. "Yeah. So, actually."

"What?"

"I might have found a lump."

"A *what?*"

"In my breast," I say. "A while ago."

Dead silence.

"But don't worry," I rush to say. "We got a core-needle biopsy just now, and it's benign."

Still nothing.

"Are you there?"

"You found it *a while ago*? What does that mean, exactly?"

"I was worried that if the news wasn't good, you might. . ."

"I might what?"

"Make me—try to—well, argue with me. About the baby."

"You're the most articulate person I know, and you can't talk?"

"I was worried, after the conversation we had about that woman, that patient, that you might insist I abort the baby for treatment."

"I'm not a monster."

"No, I know you aren't."

"Do you?"

"I do, Steve. I love you. But I also know that, as a doctor, you see things differently than I do, and sometimes we don't agree."

"We could have worked through those differences, if you had told me what was going on."

"I know. I should have."

"When will you be home?"

"It's Helen's plane. I guess we can come back tonight."

"Stay at a hotel," he says. "Staying up all night's not great for the baby or for you."

"Okay."

"We can talk when you're back."

"Are you mad?"

"I'm choosing to focus on the fact that I'm relieved," he says. "Have that doctor email me all the results, please."

"You're actually not angry?"

He sighs. "This is hard to do over the phone, Abby, but we're brand new. You haven't known me that long. I'm choosing to believe that this is just a product of our limited time together. I may have my medical opinions, but I also respect you and your body. I wish you'd trusted me enough to tell me, and I suppose that failure may be partially my fault."

"No," I say. "It's not your fault."

"Alright," he says. "Like I said, we can talk about it when you get home."

"You're really not angry?" Why can't I stop asking that?

The answer surprises me: I'm afraid. I didn't expect to find someone like Steve, someone I love even more than I loved Nate, if I'm being honest. Someone who takes care of me, someone who *gets* me, someone who adores and is patient with the kids. A hard worker who's also generous and thoughtful.

A stone cold cowboy hottie who I love to kiss, even now.

And if my lack of trust causes unhappiness between us, I'll never forgive myself. I'm scared of losing him precisely because of how much I love him. Maybe that's part of why I hid this from him in the first place.

"I'm disappointed in myself," he says. "It would be really hard for me to be angry with you. You've given me everything."

And then I'm crying. Again. "Don't worry." I hiccup. "I'm fine. It's just the hormones," I say.

"It's been a really long few weeks." He sighs. "I can't wait until you're back and I can hug you. I love you, Abby."

"I love you, too."

Helen's rolling her eyes when I hang up. "Don't even tell me. I heard." She makes a gagging sound. "Of course the perfect man isn't mad at the perfect woman, even when she's a complete moron."

I'm lucky. I get it. "That's what I have you for, making sure I know just how stupidly I've behaved."

"Darn straight."

"Steve says we should get a hotel."

"I own a penthouse here," she says. "And I own a very nice hotel, as well. But I recommend the penthouse."

How did I forget that she lives here, most of the time?

She spends the next forty minutes, as we head to her posh apartment that I've never seen, berating me for making poor life choices. But once we're in her apartment,

233

and I'm wearing her obscenely expensive pajamas, and we're both brushing our teeth, she just. . .stops.

I take that as my sign to retreat. Quickly, before she finds her second wind. As I'm darting toward the guest room, she says, "Abby."

"Yeah?" I turn to face her.

"I love you."

We Fishers don't apologize much, but we say 'I love you' even less often.

"I love you, too."

"I'm sorry."

Whoa. Two apologies in one day? And she's telling me she's sorry? Will miracles never cease? "For what?"

"If I were less abrasive, or if I were around more—basically, if I were a better sister, you'd probably have told me. I wouldn't have had to overhear, and then you'd have been spared all those months of worry."

"Thank you for flying me out here, thank you for taking care of everything, and thank you for being here now."

She trots across her gorgeous, hand-scraped hardwood floors and practically accosts me by plowing into me. Then she hugs me so tightly in that moment, that it almost feels like Mandy's back. No one else has ever hugged me quite as tightly as she did, until Helen, tonight.

As if she's trying to show me that she's here now, really here, Helen spends the next week expanding the prior plans for the baby shower even more. I'm worried that it's going to be the most outrageous baby shower the world has ever seen, but after the secrets I kept, I find it very hard to tell her no. How am I supposed to rein her in?

When I know where it's coming from. . .

Life's short. It's uncertain. She's missed a lot of it already.

But she's here now.

There's a beauty in the desire to show someone that,

and it's healthy to want to celebrate the moments we're all sharing while we can. After losing Mandy, I think we're all a little more aware of that blessing, celebrating the now.

Just before the shower, Donna receives a summons from a California court. The judge is apparently someone she knows—or she knows his brother and sister-in-law, anyway. I've never seen her so frantic.

"Donna."

"He violated the court order, and he won't release Aiden to me. You said to let him go over, as long as I was documenting my attempts. Well, last week we drove all the way out there, and he still refused to let me see him, much less bring him back home, and now he's started school out there."

"Did you call the Sheriff?"

"They said the court order isn't really very clear, and it's from another jurisdiction."

That's absurd. I wonder whether her fink of a husband knows the Sheriff as well.

"So you've sent letters, made calls, contacted the local law enforcement, and physically demanded his release yourself."

Donna nods. "David Park offered me a job out there, and I don't want to go, but I'm almost to the point I feel like I have no choice."

I can't help my smile. "Ah, Donna. That won't be necessary. You said your ex knows this judge because his brother's running for office? The elections are in a few weeks, right?"

She nods.

"It's finally the right time, and a good friend of mine should be getting off work right now." I pick up my phone and hit talk.

"Abby?"

"Jacob," I say. "It's been a long time."

"It sure has been. How are the kids?"

"Ethan's running a ranch, if you can believe that."

"For some reason, I'm not surprised. But that wedding announcement you sent me broke my heart."

Jacob's a real ham. He's happily married and has been for years. . .to my cousin. "Tell Ashley I said hello."

"I'll tell her that, but what am I supposed to tell my brother? He was trying to build up the courage to ask you out, and then you went off the market again before he could."

"I imagine he'll get over it." His brother's funny, smart, and pretty good-looking, but he's also a war correspondent. He's never loved any woman as much as he loves the adrenaline of traveling to war zones, and I'm pretty sure he never will.

"What can I do for you?"

"It wounds me that you think I'm calling for a favor," I say.

"You're not?"

"Well, maybe I am. But I'm also calling because I may have a story you won't be able to resist."

"A story?" His entire family report news in various places and formats, all over the world. "I'm all ears."

"What if there was a mayoral candidate for San Francisco—"

"I'll do it."

"You don't know what I need."

"You had me at mayoral."

I laugh, and then I ask him whether he'd be incensed to find out that a candidate was using his brother—a judge—to harass a mother and her child over whom he didn't even have jurisdiction.

"The very second you go on record, I'll be sure to run it."

"Perfect," I say.

"As a newscaster, I really hope it goes badly for you," he says. "But of course, as your friend, I hope using the threat of me works."

"Same."

When I hang up the phone, Donna's staring at me like we've never met.

"What?"

"Will it work?"

"Let's find out," I say.

It takes me two calls to get the judge's phone number. Technically, I really shouldn't call him after hours, and I *really, really* shouldn't call on his personal line. But then, I'm not licensed in California, and he's not *my* judge.

And he *never* should have tried to take a case he had a personal interest in—especially when it's at the behest of his brother, who wants a favor for a campaign donor.

"Judge Atkinson," I say.

"Who's this?" a woman asks.

"I'm a lawyer in Utah," I say. "And you're going to want to pass the phone to your husband, or he just might wind up calling you from jail this time tomorrow."

"Excuse me?"

"No, you should be excusing yourself. If you're considering hanging up on me, you should ask your husband something before you do. Ask him whether he's approved any motions lately that he shouldn't have, as a special favor to his brother. Ask whether he's taken cases he had no jurisdiction to take. Then, when you watch the blood drain from his face, when he stammers or stutters or looks at his feet, hand him the phone. I'll wait."

She swears under her breath once. Then again. "Who are you?" she finally asks.

"I'm his last hope of a get-out-of-jail-free card," I say, "And I'm losing my patience fast."

After a strange kerfuffle and some low murmuring, a man answers. "Hello?"

"Judge Atkinson," I say. "Your last name has a nice ring to it with the word judge in front of it. I wonder whether they're nice to judges in federal prison. What do you think?"

"Who is this?"

"I'm the lawyer for the mother of Aiden Windsor. You recently approved—"

"What do you want?"

"I think you should know that, in addition to being an ethical lawyer, I also have quite a few connections to both politicians in your area and the media. So far, they've all been very, very interested to know more about the conversation my client had, and recorded, with your sister."

Donna's waving at me as if I don't know that she didn't record the call. I ignore her.

"Apparently, that crazy Karin had a lot to say that helped Aiden's mother make sense of what exactly was going on. But my friend's an anchor for the six p.m. news and he was practically salivating as I walked him through how much her ex helped with your brother-in-law's campaign efforts. He was as shocked as I was to discover that you'd bizarrely insisted you had jurisdiction for a child custody case that your very court already passed off to Utah. Our entire conversation was off the record, of course, but he is literally waiting, with bated breath, for my call after you hang up."

"I'll take care of it."

"See that you do. Let's say you have forty-eight hours to return Aiden to my client, and impress on your dear friend the importance of never doing something like this again. I keep meticulous records, and the statute of limitations on stuff like this is federally mandated, so as you can imagine, it's not short."

Donna's still in my office, a little incredulous, when her ex calls.

He swears a lot more than the judge's wife did.

I'm able to extrapolate from what he says that Aiden will be home in the morning.

Donna's beaming when she hangs up. "Thank you, so much. Again."

"I'm sorry you had to fret for so long, and that Aiden has started school there. It's just that we had to give Charlie enough rope to hang himself." I pause. "And also, I've had a stressful few weeks. It's a long story, but it's resolved now, and I'm back to bringing my A game, I promise."

"Even your B game is pretty scary," Donna says. "But I'm happy to see the bazooka's firing full speed again." She stands up. "Please send me a bill this time, or I'll have to come up with my own amount to pay you."

I laugh. "Alright. I do have a lot of baby things to buy. All of them, really."

"I have a feeling a lot of that is about to be taken care of." Donna's smirking.

"Helen's a little out of control."

"You can say that again."

"Whenever you can, try to put the brakes on her ideas, will you?"

"Officially, Amanda and I are supposed to be co-hosts, but unofficially?" Donna sighs. "Every suggestion I've made has been vetoed, and then she's made some notes, and then she's told her assistant to handle it."

"That sounds about right," I say.

"Was there ever a hurricane Helen?" she asks. "Because if there was, I feel like it would be a doozy."

"Alright, well, keep trying."

"You know she had us call the Harlem Globetrotters yesterday," Donna says. "She was obsessed with the idea of having them come and perform privately, just for the shower."

I sigh. "Alright, I'll try and talk to her myself."

Donna's face as she leaves has me all kinds of nervous, because Helen has been getting cagey about details, but there's not much I can do at this point, other than wait. And hope.

She knows Manila's tiny. Surely Helen won't get *too* carried away, right?

# 21

# DONNA

I hate shopping for gifts. Lately it's been a little easier, because I no longer have a husband who questions me —no, interrogates me—over every purchase, and I have a job that pays me a decent salary. That, and Mandy gifted me *a house*, so I no longer have a rent payment to make. That frees up a lot more disposable income.

But even without the stress over how much to spend and how to pay for gifts, selecting the right one still freaks me out.

Figuring out how much should I spend is the first hurdle, and it's often confusing and it seems to be ever-changing. Twenty bucks used to be an appropriate figure for most everything. Anything less was stingy, and much more and you were showing off. But now that's all turned on its head. There's almost nothing decent you can buy for twenty bucks, for one, but beyond that, other people routinely spend more on things for me.

It's just hard to know *how much* more I should spend.

And even if I settle on an approximate amount, I'm terrible at deciding what to buy for someone else. Take this stupid baby shower. Abigail already has four kids, so even if she's being greedy and having yet another child when I have only one, I really am happy for her.

But she's also loaded. And her sister's richer than Kylie Jenner, so what on earth could I buy her that she won't already have and that she might actually want?

I get why she didn't register. It's not like there are a lot of Bed Bath and Beyonds around here. Babies R Us went under. What are her best options? The closest Target is in either Salt Lake City or Casper, Wyoming.

If I was only crafty, I'd be all set.

I've tried, but I cannot make *anything* that looks even somewhat presentable. That leaves me reliant on Amazon, where she *did not* register, and because I ordered late and we live in Manila, two of the things I ordered haven't come yet. That's why, when Will breezes through the door, I'm staring at a very small, very sad-looking blue hamster that looked much, much better in the online photos. "What are you doing? We're going to be late."

"I may not go."

"To your best friend's baby shower?" He frowns. "Aren't you hosting?"

I stomp my foot and point. "Look."

"What *is* that?" He crouches down and peers at it. "You bought them a baby Tasmanian devil?"

"It's supposed to be a hamster," I wail.

"It looks like a blue poop," Aiden offers.

Will and Aiden descend into a laughing fit. The man is several decades old, but poop jokes still slay him. Maybe it's a Y-chromosome thing.

"What's going on?" Beth peeks her head around the corner. "Do you think this will work?" She slowly steps into the hallway.

She's wearing the cutest baby doll dress that I have ever seen—blue, with white eyelet trim.

"Whoa," Will says. "Who are you trying to impress?"

"Shut up." She disappears again.

"What's that about?" I ask.

"She clearly likes someone." He grins. "No way a teenager takes that much time to get ready unless she's after a guy."

"Or a girl," Beth yells.

"Except you're not gay," I say.

She steps back out and this time, she's holding a gift bag. "No," she agrees. "I'm not."

I fixate on that gift bag like it's my lifeline. "What's that?"

She tucks it behind her back. "It's a baby shower. I have to take a gift."

"I know." I'm descending again into the Pits of Bleak Despair.

"You can have our gift," Aiden says, "to keep for yourself, if we can put our name on yours."

He's a smart kid. Now that we have him back, not only do I not have a giant hole in my heart, but he also keeps us laughing. "Yes, what he said. Look how *cute* our gift is. Will said it looked like a baby Tasmanian devil." I slowly shift my hands to frame it up. Maybe with a little encouragement, she'll actually want the hamster.

"What in the world is that?" Beth leans closer and flicks it. The blue demon poop flips across the table, end over end, and slides off, finally coming to rest in front of the trash can. "Quick. Someone shove it in there and tie the bag."

"If we feed it after midnight, we'll all be in trouble," Will says. "Or if it gets wet, right?"

"Shut up," I say. "What did you get that's so much better, anyway?"

"Literally anything would be better than that," she says. "I can't believe you bought a little stuffed animal."

"It's not the only thing I bought, but it's the only thing that arrived."

"Still, what were you thinking?" Beth shakes her head.

"The ad for it confused me," I say. "The kids playing with it were having so much fun."

"With *that*?" Beth looks utterly incredulous.

"It didn't look like that in the ad," I say. "But stop changing the subject. What's your gift?"

Beth clutches the bag to her chest like it holds the medicine she needs to cure her best friend's terminal cough. "No way."

"Those crooks on Amazon charged me thirty dollars for that monstrosity."

"Oh, man," Will says. "I can't believe you paid thirty bucks for that." He sits on the sofa and crosses his arms. "If we don't have a gift, then I'm not going either."

"I also bought a box of diapers." I point. "But I don't see you with anything, so don't blame this all on me."

"I'm a guy. It's a given that my date's going to pick out a gift for us both. If you want cash, I'm always happy to contribute."

My niece is trying to sneak back into her room when Aiden sounds the alarm. "Where are you going, Beth?"

"She's trying to hide," I say. "Just tell us what's in the bag, Beth." I begin to circle her like a hyena stalking a gazelle.

"What are you going to do about it?" She quirks an eyebrow, but she keeps moving away.

"Will."

He hops up, always willing to lend a hand, and pretty soon, the four of us are all jogging around the kitchen. Beth's holding the bag over her head and shrieking. Aiden's squealing with joy. Will's jogging half-heartedly, clearly not sure what he'd really do if he caught her. I'm the only one lunging for the gift bag with real intent.

"Just show me," I wheeze. "Holding it up is stupid. It's basically eye level for Will, right?"

As if it just occurred to him to peek into the bag, Will's eyes light up. "It's a blanket!"

NO way. "But you can't knit!"

"It's definitely a blanket," Will says. "And a cute one, too. Blue clouds with little gold stars in between them."

I point at her. "Where'd you get that?"

"You know that rose lady?" Beth squares her shoulders and inches her chin upward.

"Dolores Jenkins?"

Will's eyes widen. "She hates everyone."

"She likes Amanda," Beth says, "and she likes me."

"No way she made you a blanket," Will says.

"She loves to crochet, not knit, and last year, I helped her cover her roses before the first freeze. She said she owed me one." She shakes the bag at me. "One."

"It's mine," I shout. "You're going down, you little freeloader."

Beth, always a devious little vixen, stops circling and darts out the front door.

I sigh in defeat. "We're doomed."

"You're Abby's best friend," Will says. "Just take the diapers. She knows you well enough to know that you don't knit or sew."

"You could give her babysitting coupons," Aiden says. "Like I give you coupons for free hugs."

It's an indication of how bad I am at gifts that I actually consider that. "No, it's fine. Will's right—Abby won't care, or be surprised, probably. Let's just go." Still, I feel glum as I watch the scenery pass on the drive to the Gorge. Of course, Helen insisted on picking the best venue in the area —a place most people use for weddings—for a baby shower.

"Why the Gorge?" Will asks. "It's not like they're

strapped for space. Between Steve's place and Abby's, they have thousands of acres of land where they could've held this party."

"I actually think she's holding it out here so that Abby couldn't see all the stuff she was planning."

"Will there be balloons?" Aiden asks.

He's become strangely obsessed with them since his trip to California. "I'm not sure, honey; maybe."

"At least it's not raining today," Will says.

We're probably both thinking about their disastrous wedding. It's still one of the most beautiful—no, it was the most beautiful wedding I've ever been to, in spite of the unexpected weather. But that rain was a rotten twist of fate.

"I hope it stays clear," Will says. "I didn't bring a change of clothes."

I look at the wide blue skies and laugh. "I think we're good."

But as we pull up, I worry that rain's not their biggest problem. "Abby asked me to do one thing a week ago, when she saved my life by terrifying Charlie's judge into sending Aiden back."

"What?" Will asks.

"Abby scared Dad?" I keep forgetting he's here, now that he's back.

"Uh, no, that was a joke," I say. "But she asked me to rein Helen in. I was supposed to make sure she didn't go overboard."

Will whistles. "I think you might have failed, spectacularly."

"Whoa!" Aiden unbuckles and presses his face up against the window of the car. "Is that an elephant?"

It is. There's an elephant walking in front of us.

An. Elephant.

A string of ponies with bright, colorful blankets on their

backs prance ahead of it. A dozen bouncing dogs follow. And the people milling around are wearing the most fantastical costumes I've ever seen in my life.

"This is *amazing*, Mom! Is it all real?" Aiden's eyes are wider than coasters, and his head's swiveling like a compass that can't find its bearings.

"What on earth is all this?" Will sounds the way I feel.

Beth, on the other hand, bounds out of her car next to us, oohing and aahing loudly. "Whoa!" she gushes. "This is so cool!"

Ethan meets her at the edge of the madness, and they embrace.

They're embracing? What's going on? Ethan finally lets her go, but I'm positive he held on for too long.

"My Aunt Helen's something else," Ethan says.

Wait, is *Ethan* the guy Beth's trying to impress? Focus, Donna. That's a problem for another day.

They're still chatting as they wander off, following the other guests who are forming a queue in front of the giant tent up ahead. Forget the gift issue—Abigail's going to kill me. As Will, Aiden, and I follow the other party guests toward the tent entrance, I can't help noticing the sign. Because it's ten feet tall and it's gleaming.

Royal Hanneford Circus.

This is so much worse than the basketball team or fake doctors performing mock miracles. I cast around for the person who made this mess.

Helen's talking in a rather heated tone to someone on the side of the tent, pausing intermittently to wave at people as they arrive. "Come in." She smiles broadly. "Yes, you're in the right place. This is Abigail Archer's baby shower. Please come on in!" Someone else is murmuring something, and she doesn't miss a beat. "Of course. That's why the invitation said 'children welcome.'" She waves them on.

"What did you do?" I ask, when we finally reach her.

"They were practically driving through anyway," she says. "You would not believe the deal I got."

"On a *circus*?"

Helen leans closer. "They were about to go under a few years back. I could have—" She extends her index finger and pretends to poke something. "—toppled them. Instead, I saved them. They owed me one."

Royal Hanneford Circus owed her one? Who in the heck is this woman, really? "But this is a baby shower."

"One that no one will ever forget!" Helen's beaming. "Right?"

People are starting to pile up behind us, so I stop arguing. Obviously it's far too late for me to do anything other than enjoy it. I just hope Abby's doing the same.

Aiden's pulling on my hand so hard, I'm worried he'll remove my fingers from my body. We finally amble in, and one of the ushers asks us our name. Apparently, even though she's crazy, Helen's organized.

"As a co-host, you have reserved seats on the front row."

I hate admitting it, even to myself, but that makes me feel really special. I'm beaming as Will, Aiden, and I take our seats. Abby's right in front of us, and she doesn't *look* upset, so hopefully it's fine.

Cirque performs a full show as far as I can tell—which literally none of us have ever seen before, so I guess there's no way to know. An elephant does tricks. The ponies and dogs do as well. And the humans flip and fly and swing and bounce and tumble.

It's pretty breathtaking.

The music's amazing, and people keep coming by and passing out free popcorn and sodas. All in all, I have no idea what something like this must cost, but I can't fault Helen's showmanship or hospitality.

Meanwhile, I got a blue demon poop.

I'm trying to enjoy it, but as a co-host, I've been pretty badly outdone.

"This is my first baby shower," Will says. "But I must say, it feels like I've been missing out up until now."

"Yeah, this is what they're usually like."

Perhaps most impressive of all is how many baby jokes the performers manage to make. It can't be part of their normal script, but they really do keep the focus on Abby, inasmuch as a circus puts the focus anywhere but on themselves.

In the grand finale, Gabe gets invited to ride the elephant, and as soon as he's sitting in the little box on its back, he whispers something to the driver.

"Sure, young man. Your wish is my command." The elephant's boss turns to face the audience. "Is there an Aiden Windsor here?"

Aiden leaps to his feet, his hand practically pumping the air over his head. "Me, oh, me, that's me."

My heart swells as he runs down the platform steps and zooms into the ring. He gets to sit next to Gabe, and a monkey sits right next to them. Talk about a good best friend.

But finally, even this ends.

I still think this was ridiculous as part of a baby shower, but I can pretty much guarantee no one from around here will ever forget this. Anyone who wasn't invited or failed to show will regret it forever.

As quickly as this all started, we're suddenly being ushered out. I should have known, when the invitation only mentioned a starting time, that this would *not* be an over-in-two-hours kind of thing. As we exit the tent, we're led across the back plaza to the entrance of the same room where Steve and Abby had their wedding reception. The shocking part to me is how much Steve and Abby appear to be enjoying it. I'd have assumed Abby would be stressed or furious or annoyed.

But they just look. . .happy.

So I stop worrying, too, and I don't try to prevent Aiden from peeling away and taking off after Gabe like a heat-seeking missile.

"Welcome," Helen's voice is amplified so it's easy to hear. She's standing on a raised platform at the front of the massive room.

Something about her greeting, or perhaps her location, reminds me of how Mandy and Steve presented Abby's wedding gift not too long ago. The thought makes me sad. As crazy as this entire event has been, no one would have enjoyed it more than Mandy. She wasn't one of those older people who hates new and different. She embraced it. She'd probably just have been upset that she didn't think of this herself. Though I doubt she was rich enough to bleed money quite like this.

Now all her wealth is being blown on who knows what out in Los Angeles. I still get really frustrated when I think about that. It couldn't have been what Mandy really intended, but then, none of us would have thought she might die when she did either, so I can't fault her.

"First, I should say that the children with us today are welcome to head over there." She points at a door on the far wall. "There's a smaller room with tables just like these. A separate meal's being made for them in the same room where they'll be eating. The chefs I brought in to make their food will also teach them how to make it at home."

The kids all over the room start squawking.

"I think they'll find it to be both fun and educational, as well as delicious. If the kids will head out that way. . ." She points.

Since she suggested it, I just wave when Aiden and Gabe fly out.

"And now that it's only adults, I can tell you that today's meal is being made by a team led by a chef who has earned several Michelin stars, and I hope you'll all enjoy it. The theme of today's shower is 'Things that start small often become epic.'"

I can't help chuckling. Nothing about today started out small. It's been epic from start to finish. Separate food for kids and adults? Someone else to watch my kid? A circus? A meal made by a Michelin star chef?

"In accordance with that theme, the food portions will be tiny at first, but don't worry. There will be nine courses, to represent the nine months of work my sister's doing, growing that adorable little nephew of mine. And near the end, like her child in the last few months, the size of the portions will increase."

Abby laughs, so the rest of us do as well. Right after Helen gives the staff the green light to start serving, I notice movement from the back of the room.

It's David Park, coming in late. He beelines for our table, and snags the seat next to me. "Phew," he says. "I was worried I'd miss the whole thing."

"Not a chance," Will says. "Though you may have missed the best part."

"Was that an *elephant* outside?" He widens his eyes. "What on earth. . ."

"Helen might have gone a little overboard," I say.

"Helen Fisher's doing all this?" He shakes his head. "I'm surprised I got an invite. Steve must have sent it."

I shrug. "Maybe so?"

"After the wedding fiasco, I figured I'd be *persona non grata*."

Helen walks past our table just as the waiters are bringing plates with the most beautiful arrangement of fruit made into the shape of an orchid that I've ever seen. "Hello, David. Glad you made it."

"Helen." His eyes widen. "Um. Yeah."

"When I invited you, I figured you might not come."

"*You* invited me?"

"You've surely heard the phrase that begins with, 'keep your friends close?'"

He rolls his eyes. "I'm a rival, maybe, but calling me an enemy might be a little strong."

"I never said *enemy*." She smirks. "That was all you."

"I didn't say you're an enemy either," David says. "I said that was strong."

I've never seen him so flustered, and his cheeks are flushed red.

"This is a shower for my sister," Helen says, "and the purpose of a shower is to celebrate, but also to outfit the parents with baby gear." She leans closer. "I figured being rich and all, at least you'd bring a decent gift." She lifts her eyebrows.

"Oh."

"Cash is fine, if you're not prepared." She winks over her shoulder as she walks away.

"That woman is the devil," David says.

I can't really argue with him, though Abby and her parents and kids seem to be having a good time at the Devil's party. The other people from town appear to be completely bowled over by everything, and I don't blame them.

"If she really is sticking around here, at least you'd be free of her in California," David says.

"In where?" Will asks.

I close my eyes.

"What's going on?" Will sounds upset.

David's been out of town, so I haven't had a chance to tell him that Aiden came home. "Nothing," I say. "I won't need that job, as it turns out."

"What job?" Will asks. "Why isn't anyone explaining?"

I drop my hand over his. "When I was worried Aiden might be stuck in California, David offered me a job there, so I could be close."

"You never told me that," he says. "Were you really that worried?"

I shrug. "I'm a mom. We always worry."

"But would you have gone?" he asks.

"If Aiden had been stuck there, yes," I say.

"Without even talking to me about it?" Will looks almost angry.

This isn't coming out right, and that's not helping, but why's he so mad about this? "Look, it didn't happen, okay? I didn't have to choose between you and Aiden."

"But it's good to know where I stand."

"You couldn't really have thought she'd pick her boyfriend over her son," David says. "I mean, what kind of mother—"

"It would be nice if she *thought* about it for thirty seconds," Will says. "But, whatever. You may not be a very emotional person, but I am, and I find it upsetting."

"The offer?" David asks. "Or the fact that she was wisely contemplating it?"

"You know, you can bag on Helen all you want," Will says. "But you're the one who keeps poking in where you aren't wanted."

"Wow," I say. "Look at that."

The second course has arrived, and thankfully that distracts the two stags from continuing to slam their horns against each other.

"What is it?" Will asks.

"It appears to be a cheese puff," David says. "The smaller balls and the garnishes are also edible, however. Mushroom cheese puffs, I would guess."

Will's lip curls. "I don't think I want mine."

"Afraid of new things?" David shrugs. "A small town problem if ever I knew of one."

"Listen," Will says.

"No, you two both need to listen." I make eye contact with Will, and then I swivel my eyes and glare at David, too. "If you can't stop fighting, I'm moving to another table."

"Fine," David says. "I apologize. I shouldn't be baiting bears."

Will grits his teeth and huffs, but he doesn't say anything else.

"I'm proud of my big rancher bear," I whisper.

And then he kisses me, almost as if he feels the need to claim me in front of David, who never had any interest in me in the first place. I should laugh, but when Will kisses me, I always lose track of everything else.

A loud commotion behind us breaks us free, and we both turn around entirely in our chairs to see what it is.

"I was gonna wait til the end of the shower to do this," a loud voice from the back of the room says.

I turn, along with everyone else in the room, but I can't make out who it is. She's backlit by the bright daylight outside, so all I can make out is the silhouette of a woman in some kind of skirt.

The woman continues, her voice quite loud. "But that food looks so darn good that I just can't wait. Is there an extra spot for an old lady?"

Amanda Saddler's wearing a baby blue sundress and strappy, flat sandals when she saunters through the door and stops in the center of the room.

If you'd told me this morning that something at the baby shower would top an elephant ride, I'd have called you a liar. But you'd have been right.

The pandemonium that ensues thereafter is practically deafening.

## ❧ 22 ❧

## AMANDA

Paul and I had a lousy marriage. When the police came to my door to notify me that he had died in a car accident, I recall feeling guilty as they offered condolences. Grieving widows should be wrecked. They should be hollowed out. They should be destroyed by the loss of their spouse.

But my first thought when they told me was that this was sure a lot simpler than navigating a messy divorce. The only downside was, no child support.

It didn't feel as though I deserved the sympathy I received over the next few weeks. His death made me profoundly sorrowful, but I didn't think I deserved to mourn. That left me longing for an escape, and with two very young children, I didn't have one.

Once I realized that I was also suddenly broke, everything became much harder, and the only respite I found was in having a few drinks. Sometimes more than a few. But downing beer felt too plebeian. And pounding wine felt. . .too mournful.

The only thing I could bring myself to drink was champagne. It's so bubbly, and so bright. The first date Paul and I ever had was to a fundraiser, and after several boring hours, he grabbed us both flutes of champagne and took me outside. On the beautiful granite steps of the capital building, still wet from a recent rain, I had my first sips of champagne, and my first kiss with Paul.

Finding a nice bottle always reminded me of that evening, and also, for some reason, freshly baked bread. Perhaps because it's celebratory. Like, hey world, the worst has happened, and I'm all alone, but *I'm fine*. Or at least, *I have faith that I will be fine*.

But decent champagne, the crisp kind with tightly knit bubbles and a creamy, soft feel, isn't cheap. And I had very little money and no plan to make more. At the time, my Instagram account was nothing more than a lark. I had some followers, sure, a few thousand. Mostly they were suburban housewives, curious about the lifestyle of a wealthy New York City mother.

Most influencers can tell you all about the one post that changed their life. They may laugh, or they may gloat, or they may blush, but the story is almost universal.

I've heard the same thing over and over and over.

"I was a nobody, essentially, and then I had a video/post/story that just *exploded*, and everything changed."

For me, it was when I discovered an amazing deal on cases of champagne through a small internet site and shared my excitement on Insta. I still recall the exact details.

I was holding up a flute of sparkly gold bubbly, and it took up most of the shot, but my smiling face was show-cased behind it. The caption was: Time's limited. Celebrate every single moment, but don't break the bank doing it.

That post exploded, and the wine distributor reached out and offered me my first paid deal. I changed the name of my account to Champagne for Less that very week. Kind of stupid, in retrospect, but I thought I'd be selling champagne forever.

The night it took off, starting only moments after I posted, I was practically glued to the post, wide-eyed, as I watched the likes, comments, and shares tick up, up, up. At first I was trying to respond to comments, but I quickly gave up. My follower count took off as well. I didn't sleep until well after three a.m., so in awe was I of the spectacle.

I'd have thought that seeing Amanda Saddler again would remind me of her death, or the death of my husband. I'd have guessed it would bring to the forefront of my mind all the times I dropped down on my knees after Amanda died—me, the most agnostic of agnostics—and begged God to bring her back.

But as I stare at Mandy, beaming in the center of the room, and very, very alive, I can't help but think of that post.

People are rushing toward her. They're calling her name. They're asking questions. They're gushing and shouting and crying. It feels, in some inexplicable way, like watching that post go viral. The likes and shares and follows were utterly outside of my control. I was excited and unsure and confused about what was happening.

And now I'm excited and unsure and confused about what's happening in front of me again.

Mandy clearly didn't burn in that fire.

Was she injured, somehow, and crawled away, only to be found amnesiac by a passerby? But somehow, they didn't hear about Amanda Saddler's funeral and put two and two together?

Doubtful.

Which means she must have planned the whole thing. She must have intended to fool us.

To fool me.

In that moment, when she turns toward me and our eyes lock, I'm filled with an unspeakable rage. The person I trusted to keep me safe more than anyone, other than perhaps Abby and Eddy, caused me to feel unimaginable grief. She knowingly put me through utter misery.

If she's already legally dead, would I be in trouble if I killed her? Because I'm genuinely considering it.

The only thing stopping me is my almost equal and opposite joy that she's alive. For months now, I've felt like a half-person. I've felt like I finally found my home, and then it was yanked away from me. Even if she caused this pain knowingly, even if I'm furious with her for doing something so misguided, I'm also unfathomably happy to see her.

I stand up, and I start to walk. People who have crowded around her murmur and elbow and jostle everyone else until an aisle opens between us. I don't run. I don't whoop for joy, but I also don't stop moving.

Not until I've reached her side.

She looks less sure than I've ever seen her in my life. Her eyes slowly pan up my body until they reach my face, and then they stop. Wide. Uncertain. And she swallows, slowly.

She forces an unsteady smile. "We're here to celebrate new life, remember. It would be a very bad time to end someone else's."

I throw my arms around her and hug her tightly. "You're alive." Tears are streaming down my face, and I'm not sure when they began. "You're alive."

"I'm alive." She pats my back a few times, and then she returns my hug. "I'm here, now. I'm sorry I ever disappeared."

Her words from before circle back around in my brain and I remember why we're here. We're celebrating Abby and Steve's baby. I already hijacked their wedding with

Eddy's return, and David and that business guy fighting over me, kind of. I really need to not wreck this, too.

I'm trying my best *not* to be a narcissist, but here I am, taking all the space again.

"What a marvelous way to celebrate the importance of life," I say loudly. "To have a beloved family member back from the dead." I clear my throat. "I hope you brought a really nice baby gift."

"I would never come to a joyous party like this empty handed." Although, now that I've released her, it's clear that she *is* empty handed.

"Umm, you look pretty empty handed, though."

She rummages around in her tiny purse as though it's a carpet bag, and finally she triumphantly extracts a piece of paper. She unfolds it slowly, and waves it overhead. "I know how much Abby loves that pampered palomino. What do you call him? Leo?"

"That's the one," Abby says. "But he's not pampered. He's just perfect."

Mandy laughs. "Right, right. How could I have said pampered?" Her eyes turn toward Steve. "You love horses more than anyone I know, and you have quite a few. But other than Leo, to my knowledge, none of yours are particularly fancy or expensive. Before you went to medical school, do you remember what you told me?"

Steve's head tilts, and then he shrugs. "Not a clue." He chuckles.

"You told me you would never succeed in reining at a top level, because the champion horses always come from champion bloodlines, and you can't justify spending that kind of money on a horse." Mandy's smile widens. "Well, you may not be able to justify it, but I can."

"Is this a gift for the baby or for Steve?" Abby smirks.

"This baby will occupy all your time for the next year or

259

so," Mandy says. "You'll both be exhausted. You'll be crabby. You won't have time to brush your teeth, much less break a horse. Knowing that, I preordered one instead. This little foal's mother is Andiamoe, daughter of Gunnatrashya and Wimpys Little Chic. She's not available as a broodmare, of course, but I paid through the nose for an egg." Mandy beams.

None of what she's saying means a thing to me, but Steve looks absolutely floored.

"The sire's your Leo's grandfather, Hollywood Dun It. He's not alive anymore, but I figured if I'm going in, I may as well go all in. The broodmare, due in six months or so, but confirmed pregnant, is on her way here already."

Steve takes Abby's hand and beams.

"Once your little boy's old enough to play and feed himself, it'll be time for you to break that little foal. And your new little son can watch as his dad competes with exactly the right bloodline for the win he's always wanted. You can teach him to dream big, and then once he's old enough to ride, you can give him lessons on his very own, very expensive horse from a champion bloodline."

"That's an amazing gift," Abby says. "Thank you so much."

"It's not only from me," Mandy says.

"It's from me, too." Donna stands up across the room and starts waving. "Remember when we were talking about this?" She looks at Mandy with the craziest eyes I've ever seen.

"Uh." Mandy frowns. "Sure." She glances sideways at me.

I shrug.

"Right, well, it's from me, from *Donna, apparently,* and also from Amanda Brooks."

If she thinks signing my name to her present is going to

get her back into my good graces, she's crazier than I thought.

But it's a decent start.

The next course is being brought out by the army of wait staff, and I realize we've definitely stolen the show. Helen's going to be annoyed at the least and furious at the worst. "Well, Mandy's going to join us at our table." I gesture. "And then we'll hand the reins for this show back over to its host. Helen Fisher."

"It's not a show," Helen snaps. "It's a *shower*."

All evidence to the contrary...

But Helen's not done yet. "And there aren't any reins. We're all just enjoying a nice meal."

Most of the people in this room have never had anything nicer than the food served at the Grill or Brownings. A catered nine-course meal served by a Michelin starred chef? It's probably totally wasted on people who would rather have macaroni and cheese with bacon on top.

Nevertheless, Helen waves the waiters and waitresses forward. "I swore I wouldn't announce each course, but I thought I'd just mention that this course is an artichoke and black truffle soup. It was made famous by Guy Savoy at his first restaurant in Paris, but he still serves it in Vegas to this day, and our chef was trained by him."

"Artichokes?" Eddy's eyeing the crystal dishes askance as Mandy and I sit down.

"Fancy food isn't always amazing," Mandy says. "But it has a much higher chance of it, in my experience. Even when it looks strange." She takes the first bite, and after she beams and goes for another, the rest of us dig in as well.

Not that there's a huge amount of soup. That's kind of the point of nine courses, I think. Once we're done, we just have to sit around and wait for the next course. It leaves me plenty of time to grill Mandy.

"So you planned your own death." I cross my arms.

"Yes." Mandy sits up straighter in her seat. "Let's talk about this here, where there are witnesses."

I'm angry, but somehow she's still making me smile.

Jeff and Kevin, who are seated opposite us at the table, and Eddy, as well as Ethan and Beth, who didn't have room at the main table, all shift in their seats and look away.

I suppose that's about right.

"You clearly did it for a reason. Care to share?"

Mandy's the one who looks confused now. "You don't already know?"

"You hate me?" I ask. "You wanted me to go prematurely grey? Or, wait, I know. You wanted me to appreciate you more?"

"Didn't you get my parting gift?"

I can't help balling my napkin into a wad in my hands. I'm actually beginning to shake a little bit. "Your parting gift? You mean the will leaving everything to me that you *destroyed*? Or did you mean your delightful cousin, about whom I knew nothing?"

Mandy laughs. "Oh, she's a fake."

"A *fake*?"

She shrugs. "You had to think I was gone, and if you were a little stressed, well, it gave Prince Charming more opportunity to help."

I can barely speak.

"Although, if Miss Steal-the-Show hadn't been around, it might have moved along quicker. You were supposed to be evicted."

"*Evicted?*"

"Helen Fisher had no business showing up and offering to buy my house and saying she'd let you keep living there."

"Showing up? Buying your—" If I don't get my feelings under control, I really will strangle her right here.

"I sent you that hourglass so that you would—"

"Hourglass?" My voice is much, much too loud and everyone in the room seems to be watching us.

"Yes, the hourglass I ordered on Amazon. I actually worried it might give me away."

"You mean the Toilet Timer?" I'm sure my face is red. My heart must be pumping a million beats a minute right now.

"The what?" Mandy pulls out her phone and starts tapping at it. Then she swears under her breath. "I had to make a whole new Amazon account, thanks to this faked death thing. The entire ordeal has been a major hassle."

"A hassle?" My voice cracks. "It's been a *hassle*?" I do stand up this time. "You broke my world."

"I saved your world." Mandy's smiling. "You were too stubborn to accept Eddy. We had gone round and round about it. You knew what you should do, but your heart could not let it go. Or was it your head that couldn't let go, while your heart knew? I'm not sure."

"You faked your own death so that I'd get back together with Eddy?"

"That's so sweet," Eddy says.

I glare at him, and as I do, I notice something.

The entire room is definitely listening.

"Those idiots," Mandy hisses. "The *toilet timer* was supposed to be a plain old hourglass. I was trying to send the message that our time is limited."

"I thought you were mad at me for taking your bathroom too often."

She slaps her forehead. "You're too much like me, girl. You always have been. You would've held it against Eddy forever that he left you here, unless something else intervened to show you that we don't have forever to waste." Mandy drops her voice to a whisper. "I wish someone had done this for me. I might have forgiven Jed before it was too late."

She looks so broken-hearted that my anger crumbles a little bit.

"Why would you think the toilet timer was about the bathroom? When did you ever use my bathroom?"

No one in the entire room is talking. They can all hear us.

"Because of that one time. You know." I widen my eyes.

"Oh! The leftover sushi?" She busts up laughing and slaps her knees. She laughs so hard that her eyes start to water. "Egads, girl, no. I just wanted you to figure things out before you wound up with nothing but a handful of letters that were never sent." She turns to look at Eddy. "From what I saw that day on the livestream, it looks like it worked."

"We're engaged." Eddy stands and grabs my hand, turning it to show her the ring. "Tiffany's."

"Atta boy," Mandy says.

"He made us all look horrible," Jeff says. "I'm not a vet. I'm definitely not a rock star. And I'm never going to be able to buy a ring from Tiffany's, so what am I supposed to do when I find the one?"

"Pick someone who's not as high maintenance as this one." Mandy snorts.

"Hey." I scowl at her, but in that moment, I almost understand what she did and why.

It wasn't just forgiving Eddy that happened while she was gone. I broke down badly enough that I realized my entire life was too focused on me. I saw what was getting in my way with all the people in my life.

Now I'm trying to fix it, because Mandy forced me to the bottom.

It wasn't fun. It wasn't pretty. It wasn't very kind. But parents don't have to be your friend. Their job is to keep you safe. To teach you. Sometimes that means they have to do the hard things no one else will do to make you grow up.

My parents never did that, and I hate the way Mandy chose to do it.

But maybe it wasn't totally evil.

It's not like she had a lot of training on the parenting front. Maybe, like me, she was doing the best she knew how to do.

"We can talk about this more later," I say.

"Of course." Mandy points at my seat and claps then, because there's another course coming out. "It's steak! Please let it be filet."

"I'm sure it is," I say. "What else *could* it be?"

Mandy's cackle is a sound I have missed more than any other. She's a horrible, evil woman for leaving me. But now that she's back, I can't stay angry with her nearly as long as I should.

I'm nearly done with my steak—it was filet—when Helen stops by our table. "I hope you're all having a great meal."

"Of course," Mandy says. "My compliments to your chef. This is tender enough, even for old, crumbling teeth."

I roll my eyes. "Crumbling? You have perfect dentures now, I'm sure. Because we found your melted ones, so they must be new." I'm torn between being choked up and being angry, thinking about that.

"I just wanted to mention how delighted I am at your return." Helen inclines her head like she's a princess or something. "I assume that means the sale of your ranch won't be finalized next week as planned?"

Mandy cringes a bit. "Yeah, that might have had something to do with my return today. Sorry to ruin your plans."

Helen shrugs. "These kinds of things happen in business. It's not personal."

"These kinds of things?" I ask. "Really? People come back from the dead and then you can't buy the ranch you had under contract?"

Helen laughs. "Well, maybe not quite like that. But deals fall through. It's kind of the nature of how things work."

"Well, I owe you a huge thank you," I say. "If not for you, I'd have had to relocate my girls and move. Thanks for mitigating this demon's plan for damaging me."

Helen's mouth curls upward in a half-smile. "You can thank me after you hear from my lawyer."

"Excuse me?" I blink.

"You signed a binding agreement," Helen says. "The sale of the ranch may not go through, now that the estate is no longer empowered to carry it out, but the agreement you and I signed, the one my lawyer drafted? That's ironclad."

"Are you talking about Abby?" I glance across the room.

She's opening gifts at the moment, from people who appear to be heading out. Not a great time for me to pepper her with questions.

"The contract clearly states that you and I are in business together, fifty-fifty partners, to develop Gold Strike."

"You kept my name!" Mandy beams.

"Focus," I say.

"Whether we do it on her land as we've planned, or on another local ranch, you're obligated to facilitate this deal until it's done. There's a specific performance clause with a fairly hefty penalty." She inclines her head again, this time at Mandy—which totally makes me hate her more—and then says, "Although I know you're well off, Mrs. Saddler, I doubt you can go toe to toe with me."

"No, I don't think that I can." Mandy sighs. "I suppose that means we'll all be partners. Unless you won't cut me in as an owner of the ranch?"

"You'd be willing to work together? The three of us?" Helen looks shocked.

"Why not?" Mandy asks. "It's been my experience that

the biggest bullies just need to be taught a lesson or two and they can become excellent pals."

"Are you saying I'm a bully?"

"Takes one to know one." Mandy winks.

I'm still furious with her, but I'm also deliriously happy she's alive. I slide my chair over and throw my arms around Amanda Saddler, and after I hug her, I don't ever want to let go.

## 🦋 23 🦋

# ABIGAIL

Lawyers can't predict the future. It would be *really* helpful if we could, but since we can't, we're stuck imagining every single scenario we can and trying to proactively address them. It makes for really long, really confusing, and really boring documents. People get angry about that, but they're the first to line up and yell at us when things go sideways.

"I took the time to review it thoroughly, like you asked, and I'm so sorry," I explain to Amanda, "but Helen's right. The modifications I made to the agreement were made to protect you from her in future business endeavors, but it never occurred to me that Mandy might have faked her own death." I can't help glaring at Amanda Saddler, just a bit. "Maybe next time, you let me in on the play."

"You're a terrible liar," Mandy says. "You'd have given me away immediately."

She's not wrong about that. "Be that as it may, my sister's correct about the specific performance clause, and while you could certainly choose not to develop the land Mandy owns, Amanda would still be obligated to help her locate and develop another property in this region."

"Well, that's too bad," Mandy says. "But maybe this will turn out better."

Amanda groans. "Have you met her? Helen's the worst."

I don't bother arguing. I'd rather file off the ends of my fingers than go into business with my sister.

"Well." Amanda sighs. "I guess that's all I needed to know."

"Then you're ready to head over to your surprise party?" I ask.

Amanda whips a small mirror out of her purse and touches up her mascara, her concealer, and her lipstick. "Now I am."

"You really are a horrible fiancée," I say. "Eddy worked so hard on this."

"Shouldn't *you* have been throwing it?" Amanda asks.

I shrug. "Pregnant."

"You can't use that to get out of everything."

"Oh, I think I can." I smile. "But I did offer to throw you a bridal shower."

"And I turned you down, because I'm not twenty years old, and I don't need three more blenders and a set of cloth napkins."

I laugh. "Who doesn't need a new blender?"

"Me," Amanda says. "The woman who's currently living in a seventy-five-year-old house with no pantry and tiny cabinets. That's who."

"You don't even like to cook," I remind her.

"But if you're upset about the lack of space, we can remodel," Mandy says. "You certainly know people."

"And we'd put the new pantry, where?" Amanda rolls her eyes. "As long as we don't have two blenders, it'll be fine. Like she said." She gestures at me. "I don't really cook."

"Says the woman who got me to bankroll a cookie company." Mandy huffs.

Maybe time for me to change the subject. "Will you be

living in the same place after the wedding?" I ask. "Or are you moving in with Eddy?"

Mandy stands up and stomps on my foot on her way toward the door. "Stop trying to kick hornets' nests."

"Ouch." So much for trying to change the subject. "I was just curious."

"We haven't totally decided," Amanda says. "Eddy would like us to move in with him, but I'm not sure how many years we have before Mandy fakes her death again."

I can almost hear Mandy's eye roll.

"Plus, it's so convenient to live onsite when we're building out a new resort," Amanda says.

"Convenient," I say. "And also loud."

"You sound like Eddy," Mandy mutters. She raises her voice. "And that's not a compliment."

"You're the one who was pushing them to get married," I say.

"They haven't even set a date yet," Mandy says. "So there's no sense in worrying about any details."

"Except this party," I say. "Do we know who all was invited?"

"Knowing Eddy?" Amanda asks. "Half the town."

"Half?" Mandy says. "Try all of them."

I'm laughing as we walk across the street to Brownings. But when we walk inside, there's hardly anyone there.

All ten people jump out and say, "Surprise!"

Donna. Will. Jeff and Kevin. Steve and my kids. Maren and Emery. That's it.

"This is the surprise party?" Amanda asks. "Are you serious?"

"What?" Eddy looks around, a little embarrassed. "Isn't this everyone you like? Should I have invited Helen?"

"You thought I'd only want ten people?" Amanda's hands have gone to her hips, and now I'm getting a little nervous.

"Or maybe I should have invited your ex, David Park."
Eddy's frowning. "And how did you even know about it?"

"You sent the time and date to our joint calendar,"
Amanda says. "I hardly went poking around."

I stifle a snort.

"You two are both a little pathetic," Steve says. "How
about this? I'll make a post on the town's Facebook page
and see who can make it."

"And I'll put a sign outside, announcing the engagement
party's here," I say. "And I'll write 'Come on in!' How does
that sound?"

"Sure," Amanda says. "Go ahead." But then she rounds
on Eddy. "Two days ago, we attended a baby shower. It had
a circus, a nine-course meal, and a guest who came back
from the dead. You thought our engagement party should
consist of my sister, my friend, my dearly departed friend, a
plate of fish sticks and a bowl of Doritos?"

"We don't serve fish sticks," Renita from Brownings
interjects.

Amanda shushes her.

"You said that baby shower was the most ridiculous
spectacle you'd ever seen," Eddy hisses.

"Hey," I say. "Helen might have gone overboard, but it
wasn't a spectacle."

Amanda casts an apologetic look my way. "That's not
what I said, well, not exactly, and it's certainly not what I
meant." She turns to face Renita, as well. "Sorry about the
fish sticks thing. It's not about the venue at all—it's about
the planning and the guest list."

The door to Brownings opens. Half a dozen people
walk in.

"Is this the engagement party?" Greta Davis asks.

"You're in the right place," Amanda says. "Welcome."

"I better get back to the kitchen," Renita says. "Looks
like I need to pull another bag or two of fish sticks out of

the freezer." She winks at Amanda. She doesn't look too upset, so hopefully it's fine.

"Fish sticks? I love those," Greta says. "Fish is good for the heart, too."

Maybe not so much when it's battered and fried. . . But I don't bother arguing. Only in Manila would we have these kinds of conversations getting crossed. As more and more friends filter in, including my darling sister Helen, Amanda relaxes. It's no Cirque show, but at least she's able to celebrate her engagement with a decent number of people.

It's always interesting to me how important our web of interconnected humanity is. Humans aren't made to thrive all alone. We need connection.

Lots of people I either don't know or have barely met show up, but the person whose attendance really surprises me is Mr. Eugene. Not because he barely knows Amanda—which is definitely true—but because Brooke Dailey's on his arm again, grinning from ear to ear.

"Hello, Mrs. Archer," Mr. Eugene says.

"Why hello, *Freddy*." I shouldn't use her horrible nickname for him, but I can't help myself.

"I'm sure you're surprised to see me," Brooke says.

"I am," I say honestly, watching Mr. Eugene to see what his reaction will be.

"You shouldn't be," Brooke says. "In your line of work, I'm sure you've seen quite a few people overreact."

"Overreact?" I stifle my laughter. "Sure."

"It took me a bit of time to come to grips with my jealousy over the demands of Freddy's first wife, but once I did, I found him and I apologized."

"She offered to sign the prenup," Mr. Eugene says, "and then I came clean." He's the one grinning like a fool, now. "I told her about your plan, to see if she really loved me."

*My plan?* In all the world, I don't know anyone as cowardly as Mr. Fred Eugene. "My plan, great."

"She passed the test." He's still beaming. He looks like someone the dentist gave a little too much laughing gas. "That's how I know it's true love."

At first, I'm almost incensed he's calling what they share true love, and I can't stop fuming. But I keep thinking about them for most of the party. It's all just ridiculous. Clearly that woman has latched on to him, a very old, very infirm man, who's only now discovered that he's absolutely loaded. She plans to cash in on a big payday someday soon, and beyond that, I'm not sure quite how their relationship functions.

But to Mr. Eugene, does it really matter why she's kind? If she *is* kind to him, and if she takes care of him, maybe that's all he needs. It's not as if she's stealing from his children—he doesn't have any. It's not as if she's planning to murder him, at least, I hope not.

So even if I find their 'relationship' gross, that's a little irrelevant. There are plenty of relationships in this world I don't understand, and plenty more of which I probably wouldn't approve.

As long as Mr. Eugene's happy, I should hold my tongue. In this case, that means that I won't call Elder Services and file a report. I'm still mulling my thoughts over when Eddy stands up.

"Thank you all for coming to celebrate with us, and to Renita for the amazing food. This isn't perhaps the most conventional way to do this, but I wanted to take this chance to ask—"

"Wait." Amanda hops to her feet and slaps her hand over his mouth. "Me first, remember?"

Eddy brushes her hand away and then threads his fingers through hers. "Fine, fine. Go ahead."

Amanda looks at me. "I wanted to take this chance to ask Abigail Brooks—er, Abigail Archer if she would be my Maid—er, Matron of Honor."

"Oh." I glance sideways at Steve.

"Will the wedding be before or after the baby?" Steve asks.

"We're flexible," Eddy says. "After? Would that be easier?"

"I'm coming up on twenty weeks now," I say, "which means I'll be large, but it might be nice to do it before I have to deal with sleepless nights and nursing around the clock."

"Better in than out?" Amanda glances at Eddy. "What do you say? Wedding in a whirlwind? Married in a slow flurry?"

"I'd marry you tomorrow," Eddy says. "In overalls. But this has to be your decision."

Amanda shrugs. "I'm an influencer. My whole life has been about the image, and you know what? I'm so happy that I don't care either. Let's plan a Christmas wedding. . ."

Everyone cheers.

"And on that note," Eddy says, "Steve, would you be my Best Man?"

Steve nods. "Of course."

"Excellent," Amanda says. "Then how about the two of you say something. You have the most perfect marriage I've ever seen, so we'd love to learn from your vast knowledge." She smiles at me brightly, and then she sits down.

She can't know, because I haven't talked to her about it, how Steve and I are doing right now. When I got back from New York, he had already reviewed all the medical reports and records. I waited for him to yell, to berate, or to lecture me.

But it never happened.

In fact, he didn't do anything other than hug me and tell me how relieved he was that I was alright. If it had been me who had been lied to, if Steve had kept things from me, I'd have been livid. I'd have taken my pound of flesh and then gone back for more.

I'm still nervous about the whole thing, to be honest.

But every time I've asked him about it, he's changed the subject.

Speaking to everyone about our marriage advice feels. . .disingenuous somehow. How can I tell everyone how to be deliciously happy when I lied to Steve for months? Honestly, Amanda has been really upset with Mandy. . .but I wasn't. I could totally see how she might have had the idea, started with implementation, realized it might have been a mistake, but decided to stick with it anyway, because it was already in motion.

There's definitely right and wrong in this world, and those things are very black and white. But there's a lot of grey out there, too. Sometimes it feels like the most important parts of life happen in the grey.

"Mom." Ethan nudges me. "Go ahead."

I clear my throat. "Well, I'm honored to be the Matron of Honor. I kind of thought, when I turned forty, that I would never have to do this again."

"You stuffed me in a bridesmaid dress not too long ago," Mandy says. "This is my revenge."

"Just like you, I imagine I'll enjoy it."

Mandy smiles.

Amanda and Donna and all our friends are smiling, as well. Even Helen looks pleasant. It's strange to me to think about how, two years ago, I didn't even know most of these people, and I was used to seeing my own sister about once every two years.

"When Nate died, I barely knew Amanda." Great, Abby. Start by talking about dead people. "As a mother, I'm always telling my kids to try new things. They balk at the thought of eating sushi, or Indian food, or anything new really, and I'm always right there, forcing them to taste at least one bite. Yet, I'd had Amanda in my life for years and never taken the time to try and get to know her. After we were thrown together, I discovered that she's delightful. She's funny. She's kind. And in a pinch, there's no one better to have in your corner."

Amanda's smile is genuine and it brings me joy to see it.

"When we both got here, we were both broken in our own ways. I'd lost Nate, and in doing so, I'd also lost my way. It's not that without a husband I had no purpose. It was more that, after losing someone I loved so dearly, I'd lost the bravery to try and love again."

Helen, of all people, is the last person I expect to be crying. Yet, there's a tear trailing down her cheek.

"I had a family before I came to the Birch Creek Ranch. I had parents, a sister, and I had four beautiful children. I had friends back in Houston. I still do. But there's something different here, and when we came for the summer, we put down roots. That was something I didn't expect would happen anywhere."

I glance around the room at Jeff and Kevin. At the Davis sisters. At Renita. At Eddy and Amanda, Maren, Emery, and Beth. Donna and Will and little Aiden. At Helen. Mandy.

"We were outsiders, but most of you welcomed us anyway. We had preconceived notions and applied them liberally." I glance down at my husband. "I thought Steve was a drunken horse trainer with a great six-pack, and I assumed he'd be a safe summer fling."

That gets me a few laughs, thankfully.

And a few hoots.

"No more mowing with your shirt off, by the way." I glare at the women who were hooting. "You're taken now. No more billboard ads."

"No more jogging in those tiny little shorts, then," Steve says.

Seeing as I've gained about ten pounds and I'm not jogging at all, that earns him a laugh.

"Thankfully, you all forgave us for our snap judgments. You also watered us, and you made sure we had enough soil and sunshine, and you waited for us to grow. I'm so happy I got to know Amanda. The growth I've seen in her while living with all of you nearby has been tremendous. She's learned so much about herself, about loving, and about family. I'm so happy she met Eddy—I think he's taught her a lot of those things. Certainly, since getting married, I've done a few stupid things."

People laugh, but I'm thinking of one thing in particular.

"The important part of marriage is apologizing when you make a mistake, and on the other side, forgiving the mistakes your partner makes. And then, if the two of you will continue to learn together, no one will ever be able to pull you apart." I sit down, hoping Steve sensed my sincere apology and will take it to heart.

I really try not to interrogate people in my personal life, an occupational hazard for a lawyer, but I also really need to believe that we're okay. Hopefully, after tonight, we can really talk about the way I kept that information from him, and whether he can forgive me for it.

## 24

# ABIGAIL

I've barely sat down when Steve pops up. Apparently he had his advice ready to go. "For the record, you guys really should have let me go first." He stares pointedly at Amanda. "No one should be forced to follow my wife for things like speeches. It's cruel and unusual."

Everyone laughs.

"You know, when I was a kid, my grandmother—my dad's mom—came to visit our family. She didn't tell my mom how long she'd be in town, and my mom thought it would only be a few days." He sighs. "A week later, Granny was buying things for the bathroom, and she bought a value-sized shampoo and a little plant. That's when Mom realized her mother-in-law wasn't leaving very soon. It didn't make Mom happy."

Quite a few people chuckle.

"I wasn't very old at the time, but I learned that month how quickly houseguests can wear on you and how much they can change a family's dynamic. In many ways, living in a small town is like being in a home with a bunch of unwanted houseguests. People you didn't invite over are always peering at you around the corner and judging your every move."

Now everyone's laughing.

"If you think that judgment isn't real, it is. And by the way, Gregory. That horrible yellow car's an eyesore, and it always has been." Steve glares at him.

Gregory laughs even louder.

"The best thing about family is also the worst thing—that no matter what, they're not going anywhere. My grandmother drove my mom up the wall during the seven weeks she stayed with us, but she also played gin rummy with me every day. We went for walks and rides, and we went fishing. She took me to school. She helped me do my math homework, which I've always hated. When she died, less than a year later, I'd made a lot of memories with her I would never have made if my mom hadn't put up with the misery of having someone in her house, telling her what to do."

I pat Steve's hand.

"The people in this room are just like that. Annoying. Irritating. In the way. And also brilliant and kind and caring. People have become who they are because of the things that have happened to them, and the choices they made in response to those things. We have to take them as they come, and we have to forgive their errors when we know they're trying to do better."

He squeezes my hand in return.

"A little while ago, my lovely wife had a scare. She found a lump that she worried was cancer. She went to a doctor without telling me, and that doctor told her she thought it might be cancer, too. She asked Abby to get a biopsy."

When Steve looks at me, he's nervous. I hadn't even told the kids, and here he is, telling the town. Strangely, I'm not upset. The only person I was worried about telling was Steve.

"Abby's husband died of cancer, you know, and her idiot new husband had just told her that if a woman gets cancer while she's pregnant, they should always abort the child and treat the cancer."

He sighs.

No one is laughing right now.

My kids look particularly wrecked.

"I'm fine," I say quickly. "I'm not sick."

Izzy exhales loudly, and Ethan closes his eyes.

"See, even now, I forget sometimes the trauma that dealing with a loved one dying from cancer can cause. Abby didn't trust me to be levelheaded and to be on her side. So she didn't tell me what she was dealing with."

He drops a hand on the top of my head.

"My darling wife has been worried ever since she finally confessed about her scare that I was upset about her hiding it from me."

He sighs slowly.

"I was upset." He pauses. "I was livid, really. In case you haven't noticed, I broke your blue bowl." He scrunches up his nose. "Sorry about that."

What blue bowl?

Probably not the point.

"But luckily, my wife was with her sister in New York, so I had a day to get it together before she came back. By the time she did, I'd thought it through. She was dealing with her past trauma, namely Nate's death. And I was dealing with mine." He looks around the room slowly. "See, the last time the woman I cared about was pregnant, she told me it wasn't mine. She left me."

Now people are murmuring. A lot of them probably remember.

"I got angry because of my past issues. I mistakenly put my past on Abby, but when I considered her issues, I was able to let it go. I never yelled at her. I never raged or grumped. I knew she did the best she could, and the best way I could show her that in the future, when scary things happen, I'll always be on her side, was to be calm, kind, and understanding."

He looks at Eddy now.

"If you want Amanda to trust you, you have to support her in everything, even mistakes. That's what marriage is. If I could give you just one piece of advice, it's this: forgive."

And now he's looking at me.

"Don't hold onto wrongs and hurt feelings. Let them go, and learn to love better. If you can do that, you'll change together. If you can do that, the more time you spend together, the better you'll get to know one another. And you won't be crawling the walls because of all the slights that have piled up and are bugging you."

Steve looks back at Eddy and Amanda. "My wife loves me, and she loves our children, and she loves that baby that's coming. She loves us all so fiercely that she'd do anything to keep us safe. I've watched the two of you, and you love each other just as much. That's why I'm team Eddy and also team Amanda. Go forth and show the world what your team is made of."

After he sits down, it's not only Helen who's crying.

When the party finally ends, I'm more than ready to go to bed. I've turned into a complete lightweight, now that I'm pregnant. It was hard enough when I was in my twenties and thirties, but now? Being pregnant at forty is horrible.

I'm so tired that I'm sleeping nine to ten hours a night and sometimes it still doesn't feel like enough. The second trimester's supposed to be the easy one, but I still feel drained. Steve points at his truck. "Let Ethan take your car home. I'll drive you, Rip Van Winkle."

"Hey," I say. "I haven't slept a hundred years—I wish. Lucky guy."

Helen's walking out right after us, and I hear her chuckle.

"The polite thing to do," I say, "is not to draw attention to how much a pregnant woman is sleeping."

"Sure, sure," Helen says.

"Bet we'll beat you home." Steve tosses my keys to Ethan. "I'm driving your mom." Then he ushers me into the passenger side and slams the door.

"You think we're going to beat my sister? Did you forget what she drives? Or that we're not going the same place?"

He laughs. "I just figured it would keep us from standing out there talking to her for five minutes, being polite. Who cares who wins?"

I love this man more every day. He drives quickly to get me home so I can sleep, but he doesn't even bother trying to beat Helen, or Ethan either, for that matter. They both pull ahead of us quickly.

But when we pass Steve's, Helen's car isn't there.

"Do you think she got confused?" I ask. "Did she think we were all going to my place? I do not have the energy to play games or anything."

"Don't worry," Steve says. "Once you go to bed, she'll disappear almost immediately."

When we arrive home, Helen is there, and I realize she may have had a reason to speed. There's a line of gifts laid out on the porch in front of the door. The first box is large, and then they get smaller, box by box, until a tiny one on the very end.

There are eight boxes, total.

"What's this?"

Ethan pulls up behind me, the tires of my car crunching against the gravel. The kids pour out, all of them reacting immediately with hoots and shouts and cheers. No one loves a present more than a child.

"I didn't get a chance to give you my gift at the baby shower," Helen says. "There was too much going on."

"You had the circus come," I say. "And you prepared a nine-course meal."

"Right, but none of that was an actual gift." Helen points. "These are gifts."

I can't help rolling my eyes. Helen has been essentially absent from our lives for twenty years, and it's like she's trying to compensate by dramatically overdoing everything. "Giving us something else is not only totally unnecessary; it's dramatically more than you should do—just like that shower." I can't help smiling, just thinking about it. I was too busy to interfere with her shower plans, and I paid for that oversight.

Or rather, she paid for it.

"Well, if you don't want yours, which is a mistake," she says, "because I'm great at picking gifts, at least don't turn your children's gifts down for them."

"Wait," Ethan says. "One of those is for me?" He's trotting up the steps a half second later.

"Ooh, which one is mine?" Izzy at least has the decency to turn back and shoot me a look of chagrin before crouching down to examine the tags.

Whitney and Gabe are like Roscoe when he's trying to be polite. They're shaking and twitchy and desperate to run up too, but they don't want to upset me.

"Just go." I wave them over and they're off like racehorses at the sound of the starting bell.

"Wait, wait. All of you have to open them *after* your mother opens hers."

"Is that tiny one the baby's?" Gabe asks.

"It is," Helen says. "So you can open that one last, since he's not here yet."

"Alright, Mom. Don't make us wait all night." Ethan's

standing behind a box that I assume is his, so I walk toward the far end. "Wait, Mom, this one is yours." He points.

I can't help wondering what might be inside. Helen hasn't exactly been very involved in our lives, so her presents are frequently not quite what we wanted. But she's not wrong about the quality of her gifts. Now that she knows us better, I'm curious what she chose.

"It's not a living creature, is it?" I eye the box. It's not huge, but it's big enough for a puppy. At least none of the packages are shifting or whimpering. Gabe has been pretty persistent in asking for one, but I definitely can't handle that while being pregnant.

"I feel like you have more than enough of those already." She scrunches her nose. She hasn't warmed to the cows, horses, chickens, and goats quite as well as the rest of us have. "The last thing we need is more critters who poop all over."

I smile, and I reach down for the box. Once I've picked it up, I have a decent guess. "It must be shoes."

Helen scowls, and I know I'm close. "Just open it."

I unwrap the thick, very expensive paper slowly, just to torture the kids.

"Mom." Whitney has both her eyebrows raised, and her eyes are wide. "That sloth on *Zootopia* moved faster."

"Oh," I say. "I didn't realize I was going so slowly." I slow down even further, barely peeling any paper back at all.

They all groan.

Except Steve. He thinks it's funny.

"But the sooner you unwrap it, the sooner you can sleep," Ethan says.

I rip the rest of the paper off, and it is a shoe box of some kind, but I don't recognize the name. I have no idea how to even pronounce it. Lucchese?

Judging by his whistle, Steve does. He practically dives for his box, and he wastes no time ripping the wrapping off.

"I thought this would be the best gift you got," Helen says. "Then stupid Amanda went and ordered some kind of designer horse." Helen hates being outdone.

"I think it's fine," I say. "You brought an elephant to Manila, Utah." I lift the lid on my box and resting inside is the most stunningly gorgeous pair of cowboy boots I've ever seen in my life. They're robin's egg blue, with a two-inch wooden heel, and there's a floral tooled overlay on the toe and the shaft with red, blue, and brown flowers.

"You have a spectacular horse," Helen says. "It's about time you looked as good as he does."

"What are these?" I ask. "Where did you find them?"

"I was told it's the best Western boot made," Helen says. "And you can open yours too, kids. I didn't forget about you."

Steve's got his box open, and he's already putting them on. His are made of something that looks like navy blue alligator on the bottom, with light brown shafts, and they look *good*.

"Are mine shoes too?" Gabe asks. "Because that's kind of—"

"Gabriel Lucas Brooks," Izzy says. "You close your ungrateful mouth right now, before I close it for you." She's glaring at him intently.

He huffs. "Fine. But Legos are way better. And if I had to, I could make shoes *out of* Legos, too."

"If I hear one more thing about Legos," Whitney says, "I'm going to bury you under them."

"Alright, alright," Ethan says. "Let's just open our gifts and see what we have." He tears his open, and they're the exact same style as Steve's, but they're grey on the bottom with black shafts.

"I thought you might want something a little less. . .

285

.showy. But since you and Steve wear the same size, you could trade if you wanted to."

Ethan clutches his to his chest. "Not a chance, old man."

Steve laughs. "Mine are already acclimating to my foot sweat, kid. You can keep your boring ones."

"Mine really are just shoes." Gabe looks monumentally unimpressed. "Did you get the baby boring old boots too?"

"Gabriel Lucas Brooks," I say.

"Oh, no," Whitney says. "You're going to get it now."

I clearly haven't spent enough time explaining the importance of being grateful and polite. "Apologize to your aunt right now, and then go right to your room."

"Are you sure you want to send him to his room?" Helen asks.

"Huh?" I'm confused.

"I left your other gift in there," Helen mock-whispers.

"What?" Gabe's mouth drops open and his eyes widen.

"Tell me you're kidding," I say.

"I'm not so old that I didn't know an eight-year-old wouldn't want boots." Helen smirks. "Now scoot, crumb-snatcher, before your mother blows a gasket."

Gabe's practically giggling as he shoots around the corner, leaving his boots haphazardly strewn behind him. Since their box also says Lucchese, I'm mortified he just chucked a very expensive pair of shoes on the ground in his haste.

"I didn't love my boots either," Ethan says. "In fact—"

"Nice try," Helen says.

He sighs. "I mean, it was worth a shot."

"I might have left something for you in the barn."

"Helen," I say.

"What?" She shrugs. "I'm not above buying their love, and this isn't a new concept for me, you know."

"Oh, let her get them something if she wants," Steve says. "She's been living at my place, rent free."

"What about me?" Whitney asks. "I don't get anything else?" She's already wearing her bright purple boots. They're so ugly, in spite of being beautifully made, that they almost hurt my brain.

"I don't even want anything else," Izzy says. "I love these." She's also put hers on—an exact match of mine, but brown all over, with purple and grey flowers.

"You didn't think I might like the more understated boots?" I look pointedly at Izzy's.

"Do you?" Helen raises one eyebrow.

"No." I grin. "I love the robin's egg blue."

"I thought so."

Ethan comes flying by half a second later on a bright yellow four wheeler, his head thrown back by the very unsafe and very loud speed.

"Slow down!" I shout. "You'll spook the animals."

My teenage son totally ignores me. "This is awesome!" He flies back and forth a few more times, but Steve seems to think it's all wonderful, so I let it go.

"Okay, now I really want to know what else I got," Whitney says.

"Your and Izzy's other gifts are also in the barn, and I think you'll like them. Or, I hope you will. I had to pay some guy to come measure your horses."

Izzy blinks. "What is it?"

"It's called a Pozzi Pro Barrel saddle. I was told that's what you're doing these days?"

The two girls are gone as quickly as Gabe was.

"But what did Gabe get?" I ask.

"It's called an Align T-Rex," Helen says. "It's a remote-controlled helicopter."

I groan.

"It's fine," Steve says. "I'll help him."

"If that thing gets stuck in one of the girls' hair," I say. "I'll cut your hair off too." I arch one eyebrow and glare at Helen.

"We'll make sure he plays with it outside," Steve says. "Well Helen, you've outdone yourself yet again. I think this may be more memorable than the baby shower, at least for those four."

"Aren't you going to open the last two?" Helen points at the two unwrapped boxes, one larger, one tiny.

"I'll take the baby's box," I say. But when I open them, I'm surprised. "This box says Ariat. Did the great Helen run out of money?"

Helen scowls. "I even had my assistant call those jerks —Lucchese doesn't make children's sizes, much less babies. They wouldn't even make an exception for me."

The fact that she's incensed that a boot company wouldn't make an *exception* for her shows just how out of touch she is. Even so, when I lift the lid on the baby boot box, I can't help gasping. They're so cute, and so *small*. It reminds me what a miracle it is to have a new baby, and it brings tears to my eyes.

"Thank you," I say. And I mean it. In all the drama we've been dealing with lately, it's easy to forget what a special blessing is coming into our lives. For the first time, my sister's going to be around to appreciate it as well.

Who knows? Maybe it'll alter her perspective a bit on motherhood and family. That would be a bigger miracle than Lucchese making baby boots.

Steve picks up the other one. "This one says it's to Helen." He's grinning broadly. "What's this about?"

"I knew you couldn't get me anything, since you had no idea I was doing this, but I didn't want to be left out." She leans in closer. "Your gift to me will be not making fun of me for wearing cowboy boots."

"As long as you wear them ironically," I say.

Helen laughs. "We don't lie in our family, even when the truth is brutal." Then she opens her box and pulls out a pair of boots that exactly match mine. "How do you think I knew you wanted robin's egg blue?"

"Because that's what you preferred," I say.

"You're like Helen-lite," she says. "Always have been."

"Never say that again." Steve looks disturbed.

"I'm not going to say that I'm delighted you're living here," I say. "But I'm also not going to tell you I'm sad you've stuck around. It's nice to have more family around."

Judging by Helen's smile, hearing that was just the gift she wanted.

## ✣ 25 ✣

# DONNA

I was in college the first time I met someone who was colorblind. He told me that he had the 'typical, red-green variety,' and while it was frustrating at times, it was workable.'

It blew my mind.

Although I'd heard of it, never having personally known someone who suffered from it, I hadn't given it much thought. He told me that he couldn't tell whether a banana was ripe or green. He had to pay careful attention to stop-lights—he had to notice which one was lit up and know the proper position for go and stop. In school, and presumably later in work settings, pie charts were often a big old blur.

Sitting here, listening to Abigail and Steve talk about their advice for marriage, is almost as revelatory for me.

Sure, I *knew* people theoretically could have happy marriages, and that kids might have a happy home life, but that's not the same thing as watching it in action. I suppose I kind of assumed that everyone, once they passed the initial honeymoon stage, would fight more than they'd get along. That they'd get defensive and upset more often than they'd forgive. That they'd be in things for themselves first, and only take care of others as a secondary course of action.

Listening to Steve and Abby talk about how important it is to forgive the other person and how much family matters, I realize that my family wasn't just unsupportive and chaotic.

It was toxic.

But good families do exist out there, and I want one for myself.

It also makes me think about Will's parents in a different light.

Yes, I got over them offering to buy the ranch. Will explained what they were doing, but deep down, it still felt like manipulation. It came on the heels of his mother suggesting I work for her, and that made it all feel ickier.

Just like Charlie's parents, they wanted to control me.

Only, what if they didn't? Am I really about to start running a tourist program instead of learning to run a hotel with a cafe? Because running a hotel sounds way more fun. And working with my mother-in-law, if she really is just trying to help me out, is probably a much healthier long-term career plan as well.

In fact, the more time I spend thinking about going to work every day. . .to usher tourists through my old family home. . .the stranger that concept feels. I don't want to walk them through my parents' old house, or help saddle up Pickles so that some little kid can rip her mouth off.

"Hey." I drop my hand onto Will's forearm. "When are we going to see your parents next?"

His face when he turns toward me is wary, like a bobcat scenting a nearby cougar. "We don't have to see them ever if you don't want to."

I roll my eyes. "I'm saying, why haven't they invited us over to dinner lately? Did I offend them?"

His brow furrows. "I thought you wanted a little space. They were getting a little too involved, right?"

Bless his little heart. I've been a total monster. "Not at all. I feel bad, actually. I think I overreacted."

His mouth drops open a bit, and his eyes glance around as if he's looking for a hidden camera.

"Stop." I shift my body toward him and bump the side of his arm with my shoulder. "I wasn't that crazy."

Only, I think maybe I was.

"I'm sorry I overreacted so badly when your parents were just being nice."

"You already apologized," he says.

"But I didn't really mean it." My lips twitch a bit.

He laughs then, and I join him.

"I'm glad you finally mean it." He's smiling broadly. "And I'm sure my parents would love to see us any time."

I glance at my watch. "When do they go to bed?"

"Wait." He looks around the dining room, where everyone's putting on jackets. "Do you mean, like, right now?"

I shrug. "Why not?"

"I mean, it's kind of late, and Aiden."

"Beth's at home with him already. She won't mind if we're a bit later."

"I knew you made the right call inviting her to live with you," Will says.

"It was a blessing in disguise," I agree. "No drama, really, and free babysitting. Plus, Aiden loves it. Though, I am starting to wonder whether she was desperate to stick around because of Ethan."

"Ethan Brooks?" Will's eyebrows rise. "Are you kidding?"

I shrug. "But back to your parents."

"Are you suggesting we stop by my parents' place, like, right now?" Will asks.

"I don't want to stress them out," I say. "But yes, that was my idea."

"You were listening too closely to all that cheerleading about families and small towns, weren't you?" His eyes sparkle.

He always sees right through me. "Maybe."

"I don't want you to do or say anything you'll regret tomorrow."

"You really think I might regret telling your parents that I appreciate them and that I'm sorry for overreacting to their kind gesture?"

Will shrugs. "The thing about my parents is this: they're very well intentioned, but dealing with them is sort of like dealing with a puppy. If you pat a puppy on the head, it gets all excited. In fact, dogs in general are a good analogy. Did you know that when you tell a dog 'good boy,' its brain has an actual chemical reaction in response to that? Depending on the dog breed and personality, it sometimes has the same effect as a hit of heroin does on a human, lighting up multiple pleasure receptors at once. That's why some dogs totally freak out with excitement when you pay them attention."

"What does that have to do with your parents?" I grab my purse and stand up.

Will walks me out the door, waving and saying goodbye as we pass people. Once we reach his truck, he opens my door and helps me in. Only once he's sitting next to me in the drivers' seat does he continue.

"Like dogs that want love, my parents want to make me happy. They would have had a dozen kids if they'd been able to, but they only had two. Their entire life is their children, and we love them for it. But now. . ." He drops his hands on the steering wheel, facing straight ahead.

He turns slowly to face me.

"Once I told my mom that I loved the lasagna she

made. I had lasagna every time I went to her house for weeks, and she also made me a few and put them in my freezer. Within a month, I was so sick of lasagna that even the thought of it made me sick."

Oh.

"It was important that I explain that their kind gesture was too much, and that it wasn't appreciated, not because I wanted to hurt their feelings, but because they'll keep doing things to try and make sure you like them. You have to set boundaries with my parents, or they'll love you too much."

Too much. His family loves him so much that it can be *too* much. That it can be *annoying* how much they want to lick his proverbial face. "Maybe I wouldn't burn out on lasagna as fast as you do," I say. "You've had it your whole life, but it's new to me."

"My mom's worst nightmare, and probably my dad's too, if I'm being honest, is that I'll marry someone who doesn't like them."

I think about what he's saying, and it just deepens my resolve. "Your parents love you so much that they're practically racing to make sure I like them. But even before we were dating, your mom gave me and Aiden a free place to stay, no questions asked. She's always been kind. She's always been considerate. So even if I have to eat lasagna every night for a year, I'd like to go over there and tell them 'good boy.'"

Will smiles then, and he puts his truck in drive.

"Speaking of. . ." I learn new, cute things about Will every day. "How do you know so much about dogs?"

Will keeps his eyes fixed on the road.

I drop my hand on his arm. "Seriously. Where'd all that dog brain chemistry stuff come from?"

"I don't know," he says. "Maybe I've been thinking it would be fun to get one."

"Wait, you want a dog?"

He's still at 10 and 2. His hands are *never* at 10 and 2.

"William Earl, tell me what's going on right now."

"I like you, Donna, and I was thinking about Christmas gifts a week or two ago, when you had your meltdown about the baby shower gift, and I thought, hey. Maybe, since things are going well, we get a dog to raise together."

My heart expands.

"But I don't really know a lot about them, so I figured I should learn and I bought a few books."

"You bought *a few* books?" My lips are twitching with suppressed mirth. "How many is a few?"

"Three." He rolls his eyes and glances sideways. "So what? I just read them in my free time, okay?"

Now my heart is definitely fluttering. What kind of sweet guy thinks about getting a dog—together—and then buys books so he can be an expert at taking care of it? My boyfriend, that's who.

"You should never cheat on me," I say.

His head whips toward me so fast I'm worried he'll get whiplash. "What? I would never."

I laugh. "That's good, because if you ever did?" I bite my lip. "You're terrible at keeping secrets, Will. I'd catch you immediately."

He scowls, but he doesn't argue. When we reach his parents' house a moment later, the porch light isn't on.

"Maybe we should come back another night," I say. "I don't want to wake them up."

"Trust me," he says. "It's fine. They'll be watching television in the back room."

"If you're sure."

He cuts the engine and hops out. "I am."

By the time we reach the front door, my palms are clammy and my mouth is dry. It's been way too long since we came to see them, and it's all my fault. I've already driven a tiny wedge between Will and his parents, and I didn't even mean to do it.

That might be a lie.

I don't like sharing him with anyone, and after the whole scolding they got for the putting-an-offer-down-on-the-ranch thing, they've pulled way back. Per Will, I've already started to set in motion their worst fear. I wish he'd told me that before.

The best I can do is try and fix it now that I know.

I follow Will to the front door, my anxiety ratcheting up yet another notch, and twist my hands together compulsively. Just as Mr. Earl opens the door, Will reaches back and takes my hand in his. He's smiling in such a reassuring way that it calms my nerves, just a hair.

"Oh," Mr. Earl says. "I didn't expect to see you two. We didn't forget something, did we?"

I shake my head. "Not at all." My voice came out all squeaky, so I clear my throat. "We just left a party and thought we'd drop by to say hello."

Mr. Earl swings the door wide open. "Come on in."

"Who is it?" Mrs. Earl shouts from across the house.

"It's Will and Donna."

"Oh!" Mrs. Earl must have scrambled to her feet and shot out of the room, because she practically darts through the hall and into the open entryway, a broad smile on her face. "Is everything alright?" She brushes her hands down her shirt and pants as if she's nervous they're messy.

"Totally fine," Will says. "We just came by to say hello."

"Come sit down, then." Mrs. Earl gestures toward the family room, and then starts walking there herself.

She waits for us to sit down first, as does Mr. Earl. I choose the right corner of the plaid sofa, like I always do. Will sits next to me and drops an arm over my shoulders.

"I'm so happy you came by," Mrs. Earl perches on the edge of one of their armchairs. "I guess Aiden's with Beth?"

Will nods. "It's been pretty nice having her around."

"You can always bring him here, too," Mrs. Earl says. "We'd love to play with him for the night." She looks so earnest that I could kick myself.

How could I have thought she was trying to manipulate me? Or that they offered on the ranch because they thought he wasn't good enough to inherit Will's ranch?

"That's good to know," I say. "Sometimes it's hard to find a babysitter."

"I should drive into town and buy some toys." Mrs. Earl claps her hands. "What kinds of things does he like?"

"Legos," Will says immediately.

"And Pokémon," I say.

"Transformers," Will adds.

"Really anything 'manly.'" I laugh. "He loves helping Will with cars, too."

"It sounds like that boy needs his first toolset," Mr. Earl says. "I got Will one around this age."

"Honey, some mothers worry their children might hammer a nail through their hand." Mrs. Earl widens her eyes at me as if to say, *Don't worry. I'll take care of this crazy idea.*

"Nonsense," Mr. Earl says. "That's how boys learn."

"I'm not sure—"

"I'll just put together a few boards he can hammer nails into, and some things he can screw on and off." Mr. Earl chuckles. "Will used to spend hours hammering useless nails into things."

The idea of Will as a child, hammering a board full of nails, makes me smile. "Remind me not to let your son build me any furniture."

The Earls both laugh.

Will looks annoyed, which just increases my delight-ment. Is that a word? Maybe it's just delight. . .

"Is everything alright?" Mr. Earl asks. "It's not that we aren't happy you're here."

"It's just that we want to make sure everything's okay," Mrs. Earl says. "But if there's something we're doing wrong, you can tell us."

And that breaks my heart. "I'm so sorry," I say. "That's really why we came by. You two tried to do something kind for me, and I took it all wrong. It wasn't your fault, but I haven't had a lot of kind things done for me in the past, so I misinterpreted everything."

Mrs. Earl's lower lip trembles.

"Now that I feel like I do understand your intentions, I just wanted to tell you that I'm sorry for not getting it before."

"Oh." Mrs. Earl nods.

"We'd like to see you more often, too," I say. "Like, maybe every Sunday night? And maybe we could pick a day and let Aiden come play—like a date night for us and a grandparents' night for you?" Oh, no. I did it. I took things too far.

Mrs. Earl and Mr. Earl exchange a glance I don't understand, but I don't know how to take it back. Happy families are complicated, too.

"I mean, we could also just do every other week, and I can cook once a month so it's not all on you."

"We'd love it," Mrs. Earl says. "I'm always happy to cook —and every Sunday is perfect. I know how tiring it is to work all the time and then be responsible for making dinner for two kids." She glances at her husband and he nods. "And we'd be delighted to have Aiden come over every Friday night."

Mr. Earl's beaming.

"Speaking of work." I cringe a little inside, thinking of how forward this is, but I squashed their efforts the first time, so now it falls on me. "A while back, you mentioned that you might like someone to help with the hotel?"

Mrs. Earl blinks.

Will looks like I splashed him with a bucket of cold water. Maybe I should have asked him about this first.

"The thing is, my job's ending, and I've loved it, and I've learned a lot, but the new position in the area is not really something I want to do."

"So you *do* want to come work at the hotel with me?"

"I'd love to hear more about what you have in mind," I say. "I'm not keen on just cleaning rooms and replacing toiletries as my whole job, but if there's a chance to learn about hotel management, and if I could help you out at the same time, then yes."

Mrs. Earl beams, and then she stands up. "Of course, I'd love to have you come work with me." A tear rolls down her cheek.

Her earnest countenance reminds me of my mother.

She was the only person in my family who was ever truly happy for good things that happened in my life. I miss her—more than I realized. She died, and then I really had no one. No husband who would keep me safe. No father who would have my back. And no brother to call in a pinch.

I was all alone.

When Abby and Amanda adopted me, it felt amazing to have friends. But this is different somehow. It's like, for the first time in years, not only do I have friends, I have *family*.

I stand up, too, and step toward Mrs. Earl.

She pulls me in for a hug.

I'm still pressed against her when she says, "I'm so happy you moved back and that you gave my Will a chance. He loves you so much."

I freeze then, because Will and I have been dating for a while, but so far neither of us has said the L-word. . .

Mrs. Earl releases me. "Did I say something wrong?"

It's only then I realize that I'm crying, too. I shake my head slowly. "No, you said something very, very right. I should have said it a while back, and I suspect your son hasn't said anything because I'm a little spooky, like a fractious horse." I turn slowly toward Will, and I smile. "You waited on me, and then you waited more. You've given and given and given, and it's high time for me to tell you that I love you, Will Earl. I love your smile, and your big, strong hands, and I love your generosity and acceptance."

He's standing in front of me suddenly, and he takes my hands in his. "I love you too, Donna, more than you can possibly know."

"Oh, just get a room already," Mrs. Earl says. "In fact, I know a place."

We all laugh, then.

And I suspect we'll be laughing for a long time to come.

# AMANDA

My last engagement party was much, much nicer than this one. We had a ballroom booked. The food was catered. Paul's parents paid for all of it, and his mother planned the whole thing.

I hated every second of it.

This one is much more my speed.

It's funny. After Paul died, I could have left New York City and moved somewhere much less expensive. I could have found a job that was simpler and much more consistent with pay than being an influencer. Yet, that possibility never occurred to me. It wasn't as if I would really consider moving to Gonzales, Louisiana to live near my family.

That wasn't even home when I lived there, but after living in New York for almost a decade, it *really* wasn't home. But what's the strangest of all is that somehow, the life I never wanted, a life of caring more about how my life looked than how my life *was* became my actual life. Sometimes, we wind up living in a way we don't even want to live without ever realizing it.

We just fall into it, one minute, one hour, and one complacent day at a time.

If that lawyer hadn't called, and if I hadn't essentially been strongarmed into coming out here, I'd never have broken free. It's hard to know you're stuck in a bubble when you're inside of it.

It's not until someone bursts it for you that you realize you were trapped all along.

As our friends and family slowly leave, I lean on Eddy's shoulder. "Thank you."

"For paying the tab?" He sighs. "I don't have a rich brother, so, sadly, I'm stuck footing the bill myself."

I can't help laughing. "Sure, paying the tab is good. But I meant to thank you for being patient with me."

"He's a frigging saint," Mandy says. "You really haven't thanked him for that before now?"

"You're still here?" I shake my head. "You'd think by the age of one hundred and four, you'd know how to read a room."

Mandy cackles. "I'll have you know that my mother immigrated here from Latvia in nineteen fifty-one—I was already thirteen years old."

"Wait, you weren't born here?" I have to change everything I know about her.

"That's why Jedediah and his brother were so keen on me," she says. "I was the new girl in town when I showed up." She fluffs her hair. "We Latvians are famous for our blonde hair and blue eyes, and mine were quite a sight."

"I can't believe how many things I still don't know about you."

"Well, pay attention better, girl. I'm an open book."

"An open book?" I roll my eyes. "I've combed through all your records. Nothing in there says Latvia."

"I didn't say we came through legally." She snorts. "You think Saddler is a Latvian surname?"

There's definitely some kind of story there. . . Maybe

I'll dig into it tomorrow. For now, I'm exhausted. I just want to go home and sleep.

"Ready to go?" Eddy asks.

I nod. "For sure."

"You were more fun before I left," Mandy says.

"Left?" I straighten. "Before you *died,* you mean?"

"How long are we going to be bringing that one up?" she asks.

"Oh, I'd say, about. . .forever." I nod. "Yep, that's right. Forever is the right amount of time for me to hassle you about pretending you died, making me sad and weepy and broken—we had a *funeral,* you know."

"All of that helped you get over yourself and marry your dream man." Mandy makes a tsking sound. "How long will it be before I get a thank you for that, do you think?" She's looking pointedly at Eddy.

"I wouldn't hold my breath if I were you," Eddy says. "Probably not a healthy plan for you."

"Are you mocking me for being old now?" Mandy asks.

"Wouldn't dream of it," he says. "No, to be clear, I was making fun of your heart problem."

"Here's what I want to know," I say. "Did Roscoe even go into the barn? Or did you make that up?"

"He was in a crate out back," she says. "Duh. He was never in any real danger, except that the ash I rubbed all over him would stain the white parts of his coat. Lugging that crate over and chucking it in the fire took so long I was worried you'd catch me."

"It wasn't just me whom you upset with that stunt," I say. "Lots of people were upset that you died."

"I doubt many people have been able to attend their own funeral," Mandy says, "but I highly recommend it."

"Wait, you were there?" I can hardly believe what's she's saying.

"You did not handle it well. I really was torn between

303

wanting to go hug you, and wanting to slap you for being such a baby."

Nothing she says could ever shock me more. "No way you were there. I'd have seen you."

"I was wearing a black hoodie, and no one even noticed me." She shrugs. "For the record, it's much better to have your funeral before you die. I'd never have known how many people cared about me otherwise. I actually think more people should do it."

I'm about to punch her.

Eddy takes my hand. "Alright, I better get this one home."

"You realize home is the same place for us?" Mandy's eyes are sparkling. I think she enjoys making me mad.

"Listen, you—"

"Have you thought about colors yet?" Mandy asks. "Or the venue? Now that you've got a date and it's close, you better get a move on."

"Yeah, the thing is, we have a lot of things to reconfigure with Gold Strike, especially now that you're back, so it's going to be a crazy few months."

The bells on the door jingle, which means someone has walked in—all the guests other than Mandy have left, so I'm sure it's Renita, trying to usher us out.

"Maybe Steve's place would work for the reception," Mandy says. "It has that huge enclosed arena, and you'd be sure not to get rained or snowed on, for one, but a rustic Christmas theme could really work in there."

"Who's Steve?" Whoever just came through the door has a raspy voice I haven't heard in years, but it's one that I'll never forget. It sounds like a rock polisher is speaking, like all the vowels and the consonants are rolling around, grinding against one another. Years of smoking have forged it into what it is, but it's the pronounced Southern accent that really stands out here in Manila.

I turn so slowly, it feels like I'm on the set of a movie or something, and the movie's not a romantic comedy.

It's a slasher film.

Sure enough, my mom's standing in front of the hostess station, a shiny new coat clutched tightly around herself. She smiles when I meet her eyes, and her brown teeth gleam.

"Mom?"

"So you do remember who I am," she says. "Silly old me. I thought you'd forgotten. You know, seeing as I had to watch my own kid get engaged on a YouTube video."

"What are you doing here?" I've specifically not ever given her an address.

"Well, every search I made for wedding date and time on you two famous movie stars came up with nothing, so I didn't have much choice, did I?"

I don't understand what she's saying. "You could have called."

"You never answer the phone when I do," she says.

That's true. It's my only defense mechanism. "That's what voicemail is for."

Mom rolls her eyes, and then, without warning, belts at the top of her lungs, "Dwayne, she's in here."

The only thing worse than my mom showing up for a visit is my mom and my dad both showing up. I manage to suppress my groan, but I doubt it matters. My feelings are surely written on my face.

Dad shoves through the doors, the bells indiscriminately jingling no matter who comes through. "Well if it ain't my fancy little daughter." He beams. "Come on over and give yer pa some sugar."

I don't move.

"It's so nice to meet you both," Eddy says.

"No." I can't say another word.

Eddy freezes, though, and turns back to look at me.

"It's not nice," I say. "And you should've told me you were coming."

Mandy looks as confused as Eddy. "We have an extra room—"

"At the hotel, maybe," I say.

"We're gonna need more than one room," Mom says. "Your brothers came along."

She has got to be kidding. "Why on earth would you all come?"

"It ain't every day your little girl gets married," Dad says. "Especially to a super rich rock star." He wiggles his eyebrows. "To be honest, we were all a little shocked. We'd a been here sooner, 'cept, we kinda figured it'd go belly up." He laughs. My own dad laughs at the idea that I probably wouldn't be able to stay engaged to someone like Eddy.

"Let me call my friend really quickly," Mandy says. "I bet she has a room or two free." She whips out her phone and calls Mrs. Earl, I'm sure.

I'd rather they stay in Dutch John. Then we'd have some time between when they left and when we saw them. Maybe we could pay the hotel extra to message us and let us know they were leaving, like a courtesy call telling you someone awful who's related to you is out of prison.

They should only ever come with a loud and obnoxious warning like a clarion call. *The hillbillies are coming! Look out! Hide your valuables!*

Eddy and I have survived murder charges, a forbidden relationship, a cougar attack, a national rock tour, and the death of a loved one. It was a nice run, but I'm not at all sure we can survive my family.

Maybe it was naive of me, but I'm frankly shocked they showed up. I've been quite clear in the past that I'm not interested in seeing them, and after the thirtieth time I didn't give them money, they finally stopped asking. They've never had another reason to come by.

Mandy hangs up her phone. "I've secured you two rooms with two queen beds each, and it's right around the corner from here."

"I don't understand," Mom says. "Who are you and why are you finding us a motel?"

"My name's Amanda Saddler," she says. "And your daughter and her two children live with me."

"Oh," Mom says. "I didn't realize she was that short on cash." She turns to face me. "Wouldn't you have been better off finding more products to push on your little website, instead of caring for elderly people?"

Mandy's face turns bright red. "She's not caring for me."

"Mom, it's none of your business how I earn my money."

"We're business partners and friends," Mandy says. "I'm not in need of a caretaker." She leans forward a little, raising one eyebrow along with her voice. "I wipe my own butt, thanks."

Dad's laugh is so loud it practically raises the roof. "I like her. What a nutty old bird."

"She's like the mother I never had," I say.

Mom just rolls her eyes. Like I'm kidding.

"What do you guys need?" I ask. "I think I've been pretty clear that I'm not giving you any more money."

"We didn't come for that, sweetheart," Mom says. "We just came to meet your Mr. Special and be a part of things."

Is that even possible? Could they have come. . .just to say hello? I think about them either buying tickets and flying or driving all the way out here. . .just to say hi?

Not in a million years.

"Nice try," I say. "What do you need the money for, and how much? You should just tell me so I can tell you no and you can be along your way."

"I'm hurt," Dad says. "I can't believe you think we'd only come out here to ask for money."

"But you do need me to pay for the hotel," I say.

"Well, since you don't have a room to put us up in, that seems fair." Mom leans against the door frame. "And we haven't eaten in hours. Feels like we could eat a whole cow. I hear you've got lots of those, now."

"No cows," I say. "In fact, I'm in the process of starting up a resort."

Mom whistles.

Dad catcalls. "Ain't that something special. I knew you'd do amazing things, little princess."

I know they're just buttering me up, but I can't help preening a little bit. It's more than any of them have ever done.

"We're happy to order you some food to go," Eddy says.

Renita doesn't look very pleased, but she shrugs and nods.

"Three or four burgers with fries," Eddy says, "and your famous mac and cheese, and maybe a salad with blackened chicken?"

"Your man really is something," Mom says.

"He is," I say. "And now you've met him."

"We sure have," Dad says. "We can't wait to get to know him better."

My parents don't even know me. "Uh huh. How long are you thinking you'll stay?" I can't help thinking of Steve's story about how his grandmother came to visit and he got to know her. Except if this were my story, their departure would be the one and only highlight.

Mom and Dad just take, take, take, and my brothers have been in training with them for a long time.

"Well, we don't rightly know," Mom says.

One thing I've never seen them do for very long is leave their doublewide. I start to think about why they might be here. No good ideas come to mind.

"Mom."

"Yes?" She meets my eyes and quickly looks away.

"Did one of you break a law or something?"

Her laugh is a little too high and a little too shrill. "Don't be ridiculous."

Only, I have a terrible feeling that I might have guessed correctly.

"We can talk about it tomorrow," Eddy says.

"More like, I'll call the sheriff tomorrow," I say.

"You're such a joker," Dad says. "Always have been."

I'm not at all funny, but I don't bother arguing with them about it. "Well, the hotel is across the street. You can easily walk there." I lean closer and whisper to Eddy, "Maybe send Mrs. Earl a message and tell her to glue everything down."

"They can't really be that bad," Eddy says.

I snort.

"Gosh." Mandy yawns. "I sure am tired. I'm not sure if I'm safe to toddle home on my own." She reaches her hand out, flailing around.

I grab it, partially annoyed, partially amused.

"Oh thank you, darling. I don't know what I'd do without your care." She pins me with a stare, but her eyes are sparkling. "Did you remember to pick up that extra box of diapers? Mine are almost out."

Eddy laughs at that one.

Mom and Dad exchange a look and a few whispered phrases. "We'd best get going to that hotel."

"Right," I say. "Well, I'm going to take Mandy home, but we can ask Renita to bring your food to your room for you when she's done."

Eddy leaves her way more than the cost of the burgers, and we finally head out.

Once we're inside Eddy's truck with the doors closed, I drop my face in my hands. "That was the worst thing that could possibly have happened."

"You told us they were a mess," Mandy says. "No one's shocked here."

"They're worse than I said," I say. "No matter what, we have to get them to leave."

"And about the wedding venue," Eddy says. "How about Hawaii?"

Abby can't travel when she's eight months pregnant, but otherwise it would have major appeal. There's no way my parents or brothers would be able to afford to fly out there. Of course, I wouldn't put it past them to steal my credit card and charge the tickets.

Is that why they're here? Did one of them steal a bunch of credit card numbers and get caught? Roy did that once, right after he dropped out of high school. Unfortunately, they don't usually learn from their mistakes.

"You know, meeting your parents helped me gain a new appreciation for you," Eddy says. "You really turned out well."

I want to laugh. I want to cry. It's painful how right he is. "By comparison, anyway."

"You have to invite them to the wedding," Mandy says.

"Over my dead body," I say. "And I don't mean my faked-dead-body."

Mandy laughs. "You really aren't going to let that go."

"Not a chance," I say. "Not ever."

"But you should think about it," Mandy says. "You might regret it if you get married and they aren't there."

"I regret them being there the first time," I say. "If that helps you understand."

"But you didn't love Paul," Mandy says.

"Ouch," I say.

"True though, right?" she asks.

"True enough," I say. "I loved the idea of Paul, but not the man himself, not really."

Eddy must be regretting his proposal right about now.

"I'm with Mandy on this one. Having them around might not be comfortable, but they are your family."

"You should be able to choose your family," I say.

"But you can't," Mandy says. "Believe me. I know."

"If we can't get rid of them quickly, you two will understand why I'm saying I don't want them around."

But I really, really hope, for my sake and for theirs, that they never understand. Because when they truly get how awful my family is?

I worry that's when they won't be able to handle me anymore.

# EPILOGUE: HELEN

I realized at an early age that I'm not like most girls.

Never in my life did I want to wear pink. I didn't gush over boys. I didn't pine over ponies, or puppies, or kittens.

The only thing I ever really cared about was winning. Any game, any competition, any measurement of worth, and I was all in. I would lie, cheat, steal, stay up all night, and throw someone else under the bus, as long as it meant that I won.

People said it wasn't feminine.

They said I was cruel. They called me names that rhymed with the word pitch.

I didn't care.

Because that's what people do to winners. They make them seem smaller so their own loss won't be as painful. Winners don't have to worry about any of that.

Why?

Because they won.

I won ice-skating competitions and piano recitals. I won chess matches, and debate tournaments. I won in my Taekwondo class, and at violin. I beat every other student in grades and academic rank, no matter the school, no matter the class, always.

My parents trotted me out like a show pony. They bragged about me to their friends. They fixated on success, maybe even more than I did, and I didn't mind. Because they also always did everything they could to support me, which helped me win more.

I got stronger and better and smarter every single day. By high school, my new goal was to be accepted by every single Ivy League school, and then turn them all down to go to Stanford.

It was far easier than I expected.

Stanford was a whole new level. Keeping up with the other students was a challenge for nearly a year, but once I'd taken the hardest classes they offered, by the end of my second year there, I grew bored of that as well. My parents encouraged me to double down and start doctorate level coursework, where I could set my own internal goals. They thought I should follow them into the world of academia, but I quickly realized it was too small. Too insular. A competition inside a defined bubble isn't a real challenge. It's too limited.

I wanted bigger.

No, it was more than mere want. I thirsted for it.

And by then I had realized that the only truly equal measure in this world, the only actual comparison point of value, was money. There's no more important and universally recognized metric of success than accumulated wealth.

I wanted to amass more of it than any other woman. That took me nearly seventeen years. And once I finally did that, I wanted to have more than any other person. I had a plan in place and was beginning my opening steps, when Mom called me, frantic.

She told me that, while I was out in the world obsessing about money, my confused little sister, who was exceptional in a theoretical way, but who had resigned herself to medi-ocrity, was drowning. "She's dating a farmer or something," she said. "She's gone insane with grief, and those poor kids are suffering from it."

Mom and Dad were never shy about it. We all knew the truth: poor Abigail had gotten lost somewhere. We all knew where it started. That pretty-boy loser got her preg-nant her first year of law school, and she had allowed soci-etal norms to convince her to have the child. . .and marry the father.

It was a nosedive none of us could figure out how to pull her out of, so we just watched as she crashed and burned, and burned, and burned. And then that loser went and died, making a bad situation even worse.

"His stupid uncle died too, now, and he's convinced them with some stupid term in his will to move to the middle of *nowhere*, and raise *cows*. Poor Ethan's not even planning on going to college anymore."

That's the problem with mediocrity. Once it gets a toehold, it's highly contagious. "Luckily, I just wrapped up a deal," I said. "I have another one in the works of course, but I can delay it a bit."

"Don't do anything stupid," Mom said. "But you're the only one who ever got through to her at all, so you're really our only hope."

She was right about that.

I'd flown in immediately to try and salvage whatever I could of the lives of my sister and her children.

In the process, somehow, I'd fallen head first into the vortex. Or was it more like I was infected with the plague? I made a little progress with Abigail, but it was one step forward and then three steps back. In the end, she still married the bumpkis doc who loved to waste time on horses, of all things, the animal that the invention of the combustion engine rendered obsolete. For all intents and purposes, there's no difference between them and cows, and yet some people spend all their time and money just so they can sit on their backs.

Worse than my failure to save Abigail was what happened to me while I was out here trying.

After her wedding, I went back to New York, and the deal I had lined up was ripe for the plucking. The acquisition was nearly complete when I got word that another party had also made an offer.

The Park family.

David freaking Park's sister.

Turns out, that do-gooder idiot's family is just as bad as he is.

I'm absolutely positive he discovered something about my plans while I was in the middle of nowhere, and then he used it against me. I was ready to beat them—I had my ace in the hole—right before the Fourth of July. Of course, stupid holidays always put business deals on hold.

I had nothing to do that day as I sat around, waiting for banks to reopen, waiting to beat the Park family in their feeble attempt to best me. Only, I wasn't as excited as I'd usually be about the prospect of defeating them.

They'd overextended. If I pressed, they'd buckle, and I'd win.

I should've been delighted. I should've been dancing on my penthouse balcony, watching fireworks and drinking until I was completely sloshed. I had people I could have called for company. People like me—lesser, yes, but enough like me that they understood how much above them I was. That's all I really needed.

But I didn't want to call any of them. I didn't want to drink, either. And I definitely didn't want to dance. I kept thinking about what Abby's face would look like, if she heard from David Park what I was about to do. I kept thinking about the things he said to my date at Abby's wedding, and the way she reacted.

She defended me.

My own sister thought the things David Park was saying were *bad* and that someone like me would *never* do them. Defunding programs that provided pensions for employees who hadn't saved for themselves. Eliminating groups of employees who were not providing value. Repurposing natural resources to be utilized to the fullest, even if it meant nature preserves were destroyed. These are the kinds of things the media loves to pounce on, but they're what keeps the economy at large running. They're the reason the world keeps turning—because people like me are smart enough to eliminate the fat and keep things running lean.

But Abby would be ashamed of me if she really understood.

For the first time in my life, I didn't want someone to know how well I was doing. I was ashamed of my triumphs. I should be proud of what I am. I should revel in it. But something about Abby and the person she is. . .it made me feel lousy.

On that Fourth of July, on the eve of my next epic win, I lamented. . .something. I wasn't sure what. I longed for someone like Steve to sit by my side. I wanted little minions, like her kids, to snuggle up next to me on the couch.

That's when it hit me.

In my efforts to help Abby, I failed. She won.

*She broke me.*

I'd never amass more money than any man on earth with this kind of sad-sack attitude. That's when I resolved to head back to Manila, Utah to show myself just how unhappy they all are. Once I could see that Abby's lifestyle ultimately brought her misery, once I could see how sad and lonely David Park really was, then I'd be able to get over that stupid longing and move on.

So the next morning, I don't play my ace. I let the Park family have my huge win, and I call my team and tell them to queue up a new deal. . .for January of the next year. For the first time in my entire life, I'm taking a six-month break on acquisitions.

Sometimes, in order to win, you have to do the ground-work first. Six months should be more than enough time for me to rid myself of this terminal mediocrity, to get my desire to snuggle out of my system, and to come back ready to conquer.

I'm well on my way to that after spending a few weeks here. I'm planning to buy a piece of property so I have something to do while I'm here and I don't completely lose my mind, but it's proving harder and more obnoxious than I expected. I would just drop the whole thing, but now that David freaking Park beat me on that other stupid farm, I can't just walk away.

It would be too embarrassing.

I have a question about the sale contract, so I head over to Abby's office. Luckily, she's still there. The woman cuts out early more often than high school kids who are plan-ning to drop out.

And she's on the phone, so I quietly wait for her to finish.

"Have you set up the procedure elsewhere? Or do we need to call someone to encourage them to share the results?" the woman on the phone line asks.

"Um, not exactly," Abby says.

"Have you had the procedure or not?" the bossy woman asks.

"Not," Abby says.

But what procedure are they talking about?

"Mrs. Brooks, I hope I don't have to remind you that

this is a procedure meant to rule out the risk of cancer. It's not something you should delay."

Why is she calling her Mrs. Brooks? Didn't she change it to Archer? Something about that name stuck in my brain, so it takes me a beat to process what else the woman said. *Cancer? Did she just say it's to rule out cancer?*

"I don't have cancer," she says. "And even if I do, it's *me* who has cancer, and not you. So you don't need to chastise me about it."

Abby *knew* she might have cancer? Does Steve know? Or has she been hiding it from him, too?

"I'm just trying—"

"You're trying to do your job," Abby says. "I do understand that, but let me assure you. I'm a career woman, a bright lady, and I have my reasons for waiting. When I'm ready, I'll schedule the biopsy. I'd appreciate if you wouldn't call me back again."

She hangs up the phone, and finally notices I'm here.

Her laugh sounds forced. "These people keep calling me over and over, insisting I need to go in for an annual exam. Ridiculous."

"You said you don't have cancer," I say slowly. "And then you said, 'even if I do.'"

"You know doctors," she says. "Always jumping to ridiculous conclusions."

"You wouldn't say that if there wasn't a reason you *might* have it."

"Helen," she says, "trust me—"

"But I don't. Not about this." People always say things like 'believe me' or 'trust me' when they're not trustworthy in the slightest. Why else would they need to tell you they are? "You're exactly the kind of moron who would try to be all noble and not make us sad after Nate and Mandy. You'd stick your stupid flamingo-like head in the sand—"

"Steve will make me abort the baby." She looks as determined as I've ever seen her. "If I do have cancer, if this dumb test comes back positive, he'll make me abort him." She rests her hand over her stomach, as if she can keep him safe from me, from Steve, and from the cancer that may be eating her from the inside out.

I wish the world worked like that. If people were kept safe by sheer determination, she would be fine forever. But it doesn't.

"So will I." And it's just her bad luck that I happened to walk in during the middle of her secret phone call. "And I'm a lot more terrifying than Steve."

And now she makes this face that shows me she means business. It might intimidate me, if she wasn't such a creampuff. "I'm an adult, Helen, and I can make my own decisions."

"But you're making bad ones," I say. "Monumentally stupid ones." I walk closer. "Your kids have already lost one parent." An idiot, but he loved them. And Abby thought he was amazing. I should play to that. "Nate may have irritated me, but he was a great father. Do you really want them to lose their mother, too?"

"It's not—"

I cover her mouth with my hand. "Stop talking. I'm not one of your imbecile clients. I'm smarter than you, and I'm perfectly capable of impersonating you if it comes down to that, and then I'll see all your ridiculous records for myself. If that fails, I have a team of investigators who will discover anything else I want through any method necessary. Now, tell me what is going on, and don't leave a single, solitary thing out."

It takes a bit of pressing and digging and cajoling, but eventually she caves, and when she starts to cry, I understand what's happened.

I've won.

She's going to let me get the test and treat her and do whatever else needs to be done to keep her safe.

I love to win. I circle her desk, pull her to her feet, and hug her as tightly as I can. "It's going to be alright, Abs, I swear. Helen's here."

Because I may have been in a bit of a slump, but I've regained my sense of purpose. I'm going to save my little sister, and then I'm going to get back on track. I'll enjoy what's left of my little hiatus, and I'll rededicate myself to conquering the world.

This has all just been a little setback.

You can't make a comeback until you've dealt with the setback. That's Econ 101. And I intend to make the best comeback anyone has ever seen.

**Are you ready for very last book in the Birch Creek Ranch series, titled *The Setback*? I'm planning to release it early, but I have to safeguard my sanity, so it's set for this fall. Here's the preorder: The Setback

ALSO, if you're not too happy about WAITING for The Setback, don't worry. You can grab Finding Faith FOR FREE right now. It's a full length romance with a very similar feel to the Birch Creek Ranch series, and there are SEVEN more books that follow it, with one more coming out April 1.

Also, I'd love to have you join my newsletter at www. BridgetEBakerWrites.com, or join me on my Facebook Page at https://www.facebook.com/BridgetBakerWrites for updates and news. You get a free ebook when you join my newsletter, and I think we have a lot of fun on my facebook page. <3

# ACKNOWLEDGMENTS

Huge thank you to my readers for their excitement and support. AND PATIENCE!

Also, I can't NOT thank my husband. His love for me and constant support makes my job possible, and it makes my romances inspired.

My kids are my biggest fans after hubby and mom... and I am always excited to talk to them about it. Thank you for being patient with me writing at night, in the morning, all night long, whenever. You guys are the best.

And to my cover artist Shaela and my editor Carrie, THANK YOU. To my typo hunters, YOU ARE THE BEST. All my love for helping this be as polished as it can be. <3

# ABOUT THE AUTHOR

B. E. Baker is the romance and women's fiction pen name of Bridget E. Baker.

She's a lawyer, but does as little legal work as possible. She has five kids and soooo many animals that she loses count.

Horses, dogs, cats, rabbits, and so many chickens. Animals are her great love, after the hubby, the kids, and the books.

She makes cookies waaaaay too often and believes they should be their own food group. In a (possibly misguided) attempt at balancing the scales, she kickboxes daily. So if you don't like her books, maybe don't tell her in person.

Bridget's active on social media, and has a facebook

group she comments in often. (Her husband even gets on there sometimes.) Please feel free to join her there: https://www.facebook.com/groups/750807222376182

My High Horse Czar

**The Magical Misfits Series:**

Mates: Minerva (1)

Mates: Xander (2)

**The Birthright Series:**

Displaced (1)

unForgiven (2)

Disillusioned (3)

misUnderstood (4)

Disavowed (5)

unRepentant (6)

Destroyed (7)

The Birthright Series Collection, Books 1-3

**The Anchored Series:**

Anchored (1)

Adrift (2)

Awoken (3)

Capsized (4)

**The Sins of Our Ancestors Series:**

Marked (1)

Suppressed (2)

Redeemed (3)

Renounced (4)

Reclaimed (5) a novella!

**A stand alone YA romantic suspense:**

Already Gone

Made in the USA
Monee, IL
03 January 2024

51121222R00194